The Code of the Totleighs

A Sci-fi Comedy

Pelham and Blandings Book 3

Gary Blaine Randolph

This is a work of fiction. Names, characters, businesses, events, and incidents are the products of the author's imagination. Any resemblance to actual persons, living or dead, or actual events is purely coincidental.

ISBN: 979-8-9892320-2-4 (paperback)
ISBN: 979-8-9892320-3-1 (ebook)

In honor of the matchless P.G. Wodehouse (the original Pelham G.). Thank you for your wit and mastery of the language and for the many hours of entertainment, laughs, and now even inspiration that you have given me.

Contents

Chapter 1

An Evening Out with the Lads

Pelham G. Totleigh raised his glass of Amurru fizz toward the smiling faces around the table. "To a night out on the town with friends."

Bunko Tiddlesley took a sip of his drink and chuckled. "That is if *town* is the proper word to use for the sparse collection of saloons and music halls we have here under the dome of our little colony."

"Oh I don't know," Finky Weddelmeyer said. "I think it's not too bad what we have here on Sonus."

"Not bad at all," Pelham put in. "The show was entertaining, especially those comedians."

Finky hooted. "Yes, they were a bit of all right, what?"

Earlier in the evening, the trio had attended a rowdy musical-comedy review. It was the kind of show to which audiences on other worlds have been known to bring fruit and vegetables to hurl at disappointing acts.

Of course, people in a terraforming colony such as Sonus didn't have spare produce to toss around at skits that failed to elicit laughs or tenors who recklessly strayed beyond their vocal range. Fortunately, pieces of spare junk metal and electronics were always plentiful for raining down on a stage. It was said that some of the theaters on Sonus made more money at the recycling center than they did at the ticket booth.

"It was fun," Bunko said.

"I have to agree," Pelham said with a grin. "While the selection on our little moon is neither as extensive nor as cultured as what can be found on the home world or, for that matter, on any number of planets around the galaxy, it can be fun. And who doesn't enjoy a bit of fun, eh?"

"To a bit of fun," Finky said, raising his glass again.

The Sonus colony had been planted two generations earlier. Terraforming a previously dead moon into a world that hopefully, at some future date, would abound with life was a daunting task. But Haplors, as a species, were nothing if not industrious. Most of them were anyway. Some wondered if the gene might have somehow skipped Pelham and his circle of friends, who valued leisure and merriment over work and toil.

"And what about that band?" Finky asked.

Pelham stared at his friend. "You're kidding, right?"

The ensemble in question had consisted entirely of tubaphones who had blasted out an ear-splitting march. Finky broke into a sarcastic smirk, and they all laughed.

Pelham said, "I much prefer the band here." He nodded toward the corner of the pub where a quite good quartet was giving a lively performance of traditional Haplor music.

Across the galaxy, one can find intelligent species with fins, feathers, and fur; species that walk, slide on their bellies, and fly through the air. And yet amid all the amazing variety of planets and life in the galaxy, it isn't unusual to see patterns repeat.

There is a flying lizard on Sratha that is nearly identical to a hopping lizard found on Cunedda, the main difference being the effect of gravity on the two worlds. The flitterbird of Dierre could be a twin to the green hyperfinch found on Rheged Minor, and according to the Grays who monitor the quarantined planet Earth, both those birds strongly resemble the hummingbird found there.

The Grays also report that Haplors are not all that dissimilar from Earthlings. Shorter yes. And certainly, furrier. Haplors are covered by spotted fur all over their bodies except for their faces. The fur grows longer on the tops of their heads, which they comb and style the way the Earthlings do theirs.

Pelham and his friends were in the middle of discussing whose round it was this time when Pongo Kissy-Wentworth strolled in, a cheeseball tucked under one arm. Spotting the trio at their table, Pongo called to them and made a quick overhead pass. Finky snagged the wheel-shaped ball from the air, hopped from his seat, and sped toward Pongo. Pelham and Bunko grinned at each other and dashed to join in. The four collided in an informal scrum in the open area between the lines of tables.

Or somewhat open. Pelham's extended foot tripped a server walking past with a trayful of drinks, which flew into the air and came down in a loud, wet crash, splattering ale over patrons. Finky knocked the cheeseball from Pongo's grasp. It rolled across the floor into a pair of customers playing jarts, resulting in an errant toss, in which the jart impaled itself into the wall just above the fiddle player's head.

Most of the assembled crowd roared with laughter with the notable exceptions of those now wearing their drinks, the alarmed fiddle player, and the landlord, who promptly threw Pelham and friends out.

Out on the street, Pelham G. Totleigh ran a hand through his head fur before slipping his favorite straw boater hat back onto his head and adjusting it to a rakish angle. It was quieter outside the pub, though no cooler as the atmosphere everywhere under the Sonus dome was climate controlled.

Above the dome, the planet Nuggies, which Sonus orbited, dominated the night sky. The thick atmosphere of the gas giant with its alternating bands of orange and gold and huge iridescent blue rings glowed in the sunlight reflected from their faraway red sun.

"Well, gentlemen," Pelham said, "what next?"

"More hijinks," Pongo said.

Bunko said, "I hear good things about the new place down by the hydroponic facility. It has a band with a fantastic Javidian singer."

"Oh right," said Finky, "the Governor's Head."

"No thank you," Pelham said. "The last thing I want is to be reminded of my Aunt Agutha. I get enough of her during the day in the course of my duties."

"It's only named after the governor … and only her head at that. She won't be there."

"I'm sure she wouldn't be caught dead in the place," Pelham said, "but it's a matter of principle. Besides, I have an early morning tomorrow."

"You can't leave us now," Pongo said. "I just got here."

"What do you have to do tomorrow?" Bunko asked.

Pelham said, "I have to meet with a supply ship captain, one of the Grays."

"The Grays, huh." Bunko shook his head.

"What about them?"

"Have you ever met a Gray before?"

"Can't say that I have. Why?"

"How about The Bottle and Quokel?" Pongo said.

Finky made a face. "I was banned from there for a week. What day is it?"

"Gortsday."

"Then that's no good."

3

"Wait," Pelham said. "What about the Grays, Bunko?"

"How about The Haplor Arms?" Finky suggested.

"A bit stodgy there, don't you think?" Pongo said.

"It's not as if we have an unlimited list from which to choose."

"Bunko," Pelham said. "Tell me about the Grays."

"You'll see," Bunko said. "All right. The Haplor Arms it is."

"Wait," said Pongo. "Where's my cheeseball?"

They turned to gaze back at the warm light emanating from the pub they had just unwillingly exited. Pelham wrapped an arm around Pongo's shoulder. "I'm afraid it's lost, old chum. By now, it's probably hung on the wall as a jart target."

They hailed an automated carriage and moved on to The Haplor Arms where a pub quiz was going on. They amused themselves by shouting out humorous answers to the questions, which nearly got them thrown out of that place as well.

It was several hours later when Pelham finally wandered home through empty streets and underground corridors to his apartment building. Taking the lift to his floor, he walked down the hall to his flat, blinked at the retinal scanner to open the door, and stumbled in.

Blandings had left a light on in Pelham's bedroom allowing his employer to negotiate his way past the sitting room furniture and into his room. Good old Blandings, Pelham thought. Best valet in the known galaxy. Pelham closed the door behind him and dropped his hat on a chair. He was in the process of peeling off his jacket and had gotten it down around his elbows when he collapsed face-first onto the bed.

Chapter 2

Keezo's Unexpected Journey

While Pelham snoozed through what remained of the Sonus night, in the late afternoon sun on a planet several star systems away, two small furry creatures loped across the grassy turf, the tentacles on their cheeks twitching in the warm air to try and catch a scent of food.

The fruit was nearly done for the season. They had wandered far today in search of it, far from their small community of mounds. There was almost no breeze, making it harder to pick up scents, making the scorching sun seem even hotter. As they walked, they periodically shook their black fur to cool off.

Reaching a clump of trees, the one in front scanned up the trunks and spotted yellow fruit hanging from one branch. One-two fruits. Two was not nearly enough, but it was better than nothing.

"Is fruit, Keezo?" The one behind asked.

Keezo nodded. "Is fruit. I is climb."

Keezo wrapped two long tentacles around the trunk and leaned back to pull them tight. Microscopic hairs along the length of the tentacles clutched at the bark. Keezo placed one well-padded foot against the tree, all three toes gripping at the indentations in the trunk, followed by the other foot. Then Keezo climbed. Reaching the branch where the fruit hung, Keezo stretched out a tentacle and plucked off both pieces.

"Tunna, I is drop," Keezo called.

One of the yellow fruits fell to the ground. Tunna took a bite and then gave most of the rest of it to the little one who clung to Tunna's tentacles. The little one gobbled it down.

Keezo sat on the branch to eat the other fruit. The breeze blew stronger up amid the leaves. An aroma floated on the wind, a new scent — not yellow fruit, not berries, not nuts — but something that smelled sweet and tasty. It came from over the next hill where the Bigs lived.

Wrapping a tentacle around the branch, Keezo swung down and dropped to the ground. "Bigs has fruit out, Tunna."

Tunna nodded. "Bigs is maybe give us food."

Keezo said, "We is look."

They walked on toward the intriguing scent. Topping the hill, they looked down onto a cluster of flat-walled structures that always made Keezo think of huge cooking pots arranged in rows. This is where the Bigs lived, in these odd pot-like things sticking up from the ground instead of in cozy mounds underneath the soil. The Bigs called the place their sittee. It was a funny word, but Keezo supposed they called it that because it was where the Bigs sit.

Keezo had stood on this hilltop and seen the Big's sittee before. But never before was there the round thing that today stood at the sittee edge. It was a large silver thing, like a flat stone with a bump on top. It stood up from the ground on — Keezo counted the legs — one-two-three legs. Keezo and Tunna ducked behind a rock and gawked at the silver thing.

"It is animal?" Keezo asked.

Tunna said, "I never hear of animal with one-two-three legs."

"I never hear of round, silver animal. And is no move."

A gust of wind blew from the sittee, bringing the tasty scent with it. Keezo spotted the source, a low open container — like the hollowed bowl they kept in the mound but huge and with hard, straight sides. It sat at the base of one of the silver legs and was filled with many round blue fruits.

Keezo shared a glance with Tunna. Should they? Keezo preferred to stay away from the Bigs. But Keezo was hungry and knew that Tunna and the little were hungry too. And the Bigs had food and sometimes shared their food with the Danánn. The Bigs' food mostly tasted good.

"Bigs not is mind we has some," Keezo said.

"We is ask," Tunna said, nodding in agreement.

They slipped away from the rock and headed toward the silver thing, watching for Bigs as they approached. They didn't see any.

They moved into the cool shade under the silver thing and slipped to the side of the container. They peered around. No sounds or smells of Bigs came to them.

Keezo looked at Tunna and made a shrugging motion with tentacles. "Is no one to ask."

Tunna said, "We is take now. Ask later."

Keezo stretched tentacles up to the top of the container and pulled. Keezo's body swung up and into the hopper. Picking up one of the blue fruits, Keezo took a bite. It did not taste as sweet as yellow fruit, but it was cool and juicy. "Is good fruit, Tunna. I is throw." Using tentacles, Keezo tossed two of the fruits over the side, then two more. Keezo paused to take another bite and then pitched over another three.

Keezo jumped back to the turf and sat with Tunna to eat. They tore into it, pausing only to give bites to the little. They were halfway through their feast when a mechanical *whir* sounded overhead. They looked up and saw a section of the silver thing lowering at an angle toward the ground.

Keezo and Tunna dropped their fruit and dashed to the nearest leg of the silver thing to hide. Keezo's fur rippled and transformed to a matching silver color. Tunna did the same, wrapping tentacles around the little, who had not yet learned to change.

The dropping part of the silver thing came to a rest as its end touched the ground. The whirring stopped, and two creatures walked out of the silver thing down the slope.

Keezo had never seen creatures like this. They were as big as the Bigs. And like the Bigs, they had one-two-three-four limbs, two at the bottom like Keezo and Tunna for walking and two more up under their heads instead of tentacles. But unlike the Bigs, they were gray and smooth all over without any fur.

The two gray creatures walked over to the fruit container. One of them kicked at Keezo's half-eaten fruit with a long foot.

Inside Keezo's head came a voice that had no sound. It was like a thought, except it was not Keezo's thought. It was like someone else was using Keezo's mind. "Some fell out," the thought said. "Something's been eating on them."

Then a different not-voice came into Keezo's head. "We better get this into the settlement."

One of the gray creatures pressed something hanging around its neck. The container rose off the ground to about Keezo's height. The creatures pushed the container through the air into the Bigs' sittee.

After they left, Keezo and Tunna stepped away from the silver leg, letting their fur return to its natural black.

Inside Tunna's tentacles, the little squeaked. Fully awake now from eating, the little was hungry for more. Tunna's eyes followed the sloping thing up to a dark opening in the silver round thing. "Is more fruit up there."

Keezo had sniffed it too but was hesitant. To visit the Bigs' sittee was one thing, but to enter a strange silver place full of odd creatures was something else. But Tunna had already started climbing the sloping thing, so Keezo followed.

They climbed to a large inside place filled with many containers of every shape and size. Some smelled of fruit and other kinds of food. Others had strange, non-food smells. The space was dark like the inside of a mound, the only light coming from the opening where the sloping thing led to the ground.

Keezo tried to count the containers. One. Two. Three. Four. Four and one. Four and two. Four and three. Four and four. That was as high as Keezo had ever counted, and there were still many more uncounted.

They split up to explore. Keezo found a stack of little containers with soft sides and a faint scent of something sweet coming from inside. Keezo used a tentacle to pick up one of them. It was covered by a thin, clear skin — like the clear petals of a fog flower in the rain, except strong and hard. Keezo sat down and fiddled with it to try to open it, pulling and poking with three tentacles.

Finally, Keezo bit at it and heard a *pop* from the clear skin. The rest of the skin peeled back as easily as a yellow fruit. Inside was a second skin made of something else. It peeled without problem, and a pile of dark, wrinkly fruit spilled out. Keezo picked one up with a tentacle and tasted it. It had a deep sweetness and a soft, chewy texture.

Directly opposite on a low platform stood one-two rows of red things as big as Keezo. They were pointed at the top like tree stumps that had been chewed by water rats. Keezo sat down against one of the red things to eat the wrinkly fruit.

At that moment, footfalls thumped on the sloping thing. The two gray creatures stepped inside. One of them pressed the thing around its neck, and the *whir* started up again. The sloping thing closed, plunging the space into darkness. Two small lights came on where the gray creatures stood and began bobbing up and down as they walked through the containers.

In a panic, Keezo jumped into the middle of the rows of tree-stump-shaped red things and hunkered down. The gray creatures moved past Keezo and disappeared somewhere, leaving the space completely dark.

"Tunna," Keezo said in a whisper.

No answer came. Then a rumble clattered all around Keezo. It was like one of the huge metal tools the Bigs used, the things Bigs called makeens. Keezo didn't like the noisy makeens. Everything around Keezo began to shake. The rumbling erupted into a loud blast, and it felt like something was pushing Keezo down. The weight was stifling, and the noise of the blast hurt Keezo's ears.

Then the noise and the shaking stopped, and with it, the heavy weight disappeared. But this was worse because now Keezo began floating in the blackness like a feather. Frantically, Keezo flailed with tentacles and caught hold of a nub on one of the red stumps, which seemed not to be floating.

Around the fire at night, Keezo's people often told stories. They told of how the Danánn came to the land. They told of the coming of the Bigs. Some of the stories told what happened when a person died. They said it was like sleeping and floating off into a land of endless fruit.

But no one had ever told a story about darkness and being pressed to the ground and then floating. Was this death? Should Keezo let go of the red stump and float away into the land of endless fruit? Keezo decided to hold on. Keezo was not ready for endless fruit. Looking for fruit every day was not a bad thing.

Then came a buzzing sound, and after that a low rumble, and then more buzzing. It was all noisy and confusing. And all the while, Keezo clung to the red stump thing to try and not float away to the land of endless fruit.

At last, Keezo's feet once more settled down to the floor and it became quiet again. Keezo let go and sat on the low platform in the darkness, breathing heavily and shaking all over.

"Tunna?"

Tunna did not answer.

Chapter 3

Waking Up is Hard to Do

Pelham was still face down in his bed and snoring when his dreams were invaded by the sound of an *ahem* coming from somewhere above him. He opened one eye and, with some effort, focused on a pair of flawlessly pressed trousers standing beside his bed.

"Sir," came a voice from on high.

Pelham opened his other eye and slowly twisted his head to look up into the face of his valet. He had no idea what time it was, but his body told him it must be much earlier than his normal time to rise. "What ... what is it, Blandings? And why are you ... waking me at this ... blighted hour?"

"Forgive me, sir. I thought it best to remind you of your meeting this morning with the captain of the Gray ship."

"Is that ... today, Blandings?" As conscious thought flowed slowly back into his mind, Pelham recalled the appointment. "I mean, is today today ... already?"

"It is, sir. Indeed, I fear the scheduled time is nearly upon us."

"What?" Panic gripped Pelham. His eyes widened. He rolled over and sat up. Then he grabbed his head and dropped back to the mattress. "Ow! I can't."

"You cannot make the meeting, sir?"

"I can't ... anything."

"Allow me to assist you, sir."

Blandings extended an arm. Pelham clutched at it and managed to achieve a sitting position. He swung his legs around to the floor and braced himself with a hand on one knee.

A cup of tea found its way into his other hand. He inhaled the aroma and brought it to his lips. Taking a sip, he breathed out a sigh. The tea was precisely strong enough, warm enough, sweet enough, and creamy enough. It was, in short, another of Blandings' perfect cups of tea, and it very nearly helped.

Pelham blinked. "Did you say something, Blandings, about the meeting being soonish?"

"I did, sir. In truth, you should have been up some time ago."

He moaned. "Then why in the blazes didn't you rouse me sooner?"

"I did try, sir."

"Hmm. Sacked out, was I?"

"Yes, sir. If I may employ the idiom, sir, you were dead to the world. But when I received the message from the governor, I decided—"

"Aunt Agutha sent a message?" Pelham raised one eyebrow, which sent pains shooting through his head. "What did the ripened relative have to say?"

"Do you wish to hear the missive verbatim, sir?"

"I suppose so."

"You may find it somewhat distressing."

"Most things Aunt A. says to me do tend to land on the disquieting side, Blandings. Nevertheless, pull no punches."

"Yes, sir. The governor said, and I quote, 'Pelham, you thick-headed nincompoop, you had better not forget your meeting with the Grays. We need them as trading partners and do not wish to offend them.' She then went on, sir, to bid me a pleasant morning."

Pelham eyed him. "Well, that's good. It's important to keep up the social conventions, what? Do I have time for breakfast, Blandings?"

"I regret to say, sir, that you do not. However, I have configured your usual egg and toast into sandwich form to allow you to eat it while you walk. It, of course, is not the way a gentleman should eat his breakfast, but needs must."

Pelham nodded a wobbly head. "Do I have time to shower?"

"No, sir."

"Do I have time to change clothes?"

The valet's face took on a pained expression.

"I'll take that as a no, Blandings. Then I suppose it's a good thing I didn't change out of my clothes last night."

Blandings winced.

"Righto," Pelham said with a sigh. "Well, pass me that egg sandwich, and I shall sally forth to meet the day."

"If sir might be able to return here following the meeting, I would be most glad to have a change of clothes ready."

"We'll see, Blandings. We'll see. Awfully sticky place, the office. Always something to sign or initial or whatnot."

Pelham pushed on his knees and, with a groan, rose to a forty-five-degree angle. Blandings grabbed an arm and pulled him the rest of the way up. Pelham tottered backward and forward for a moment. "Oh, my head."

"I anticipated that you might feel a bit under the weather, sir, and took the liberty of preparing one of my special post-late-night restoratives. It is by the door beside your sandwich."

"You think of everything, Blandings."

"I do try, sir."

Pelham shambled to the door. While Blandings did what he could to straighten his employer's clothes, Pelham gulped down the elixir. The tonic hit him with the impact of a meteor. He coughed twice. His left eye began to twitch. Everything went black for a moment as his insides shuddered and rebooted. Then everything came back fresh and renewed. Pelham blinked, shook his head, and regarded his valet with an appreciative eye.

"Excellent, Blandings. Most invigorating. I'm a new Haplor."

"Thank you, sir. You should be on your way."

Pelham left the flat, gobbling bites of sandwich while he walked. As he emerged at street level, the Sonus sky above the dome was still shrouded in darkness. Only the artificial lights in the dome made it seem at all like daytime, and their garish glare threatened to undo the positive effects of Blandings' restorative.

Such was life on a moon whose day lasted a full forty-two days and nights as time was measured on the home world. The colony tried to keep to a Haplor standard day using timed lights and luminosity dampeners, but the effect was never completely successful.

Pelham spotted an automated carriage coming toward him. He hailed it and rode the rest of the way to the space terminal, falling asleep and having to be awakened upon arrival by the carriage incessantly saying, "You have arrived. You have arrived."

He entered the terminal with only moments to spare to find scores of Haplors moving about. He wondered what all these people were doing here. Who would want to catch a flight at this ridiculous hour? They milled about in front of shops as Pelham tried to slide past as quickly as he could.

Turning into the freight delivery corridor he dashed up to a blue-shirted security guard sitting at a small desk.

The guard looked up from a cup of tea. "May I help you?"

"Pelham G. Totleigh, Inspector of Inputs … I mean, imports. Inspector of Imports. I always get that mixed up. I'm supposed to meet a Gray ship."

The guard twisted his head and squinted. "Well, that hardly narrows it down, now does it?"

"Pardon?"

"Most ships are painted gray."

"What?"

"You said you wanted to meet a gray ship."

"No. I don't mean the color of the ship. I mean a ship piloted by the Grays, the people, the species."

"Oh. Right. Is there something wrong with your eyes, sir?"

"My eyes?" Pelham blinked.

"They seem to protrude quite a bit."

"Protrude?"

"You know. Bulge. Bug out. Distend."

"I do know what the word means," Pelham said irritably. "What I don't know is where the Gray ship is landing … at any moment now, I might add. Believe me, your eyes would protrude too if you got as little shut-eye as I did last night."

The guard flashed him a doubtful look and consulted a device. "Landing pad three. Come on through."

Pelham rushed down the hall and passed through the revolving airlock door into thin, frigid air. He gasped. Despite their progress in terraforming, this moon was still an uncomfortable place for doing simple tasks, such as standing outside while breathing.

Thankfully, the landing pad was devoid of spacecraft. The Gray ship had not yet arrived. A lone figure stood among the floodlights.

"What ho, Munson," Pelham called.

The figure bobbed his head. "You made it. Good morning, Mr. Totleigh."

Pelham grimaced at his assistant. "Is it — a good morning, I mean? It's dashed cold, is what it is. And if you ask me, it started far too early."

A morning that began this early, Pelham thought, had to have something up its sleeve. As it turned out, he was not wrong.

Chapter 4

Gray Anatomy

The rumble of a spaceship engine roared overhead. Pelham peered up to see a silver flying saucer swoop into view, hover high above the landing pad, and slowly begin to lower. It touched down, and the engine cut off.

Pelham glanced at Munson. "This is my first time to meet a Gray."

"Is it, Mr. Totleigh?" Munson asked with a touch of acerbity in his tone.

"I've heard of them, of course."

"But up to now, you've always passed off the assignment of meeting ships to me."

"Quite right, Munson. Perfect job for you. I don't particularly enjoy getting out in the chill. This time, however, my Aunt Agutha insisted I come myself. Something the Grays want to discuss apparently. What do you suppose they want to talk about?"

"Probably a new item they hope to sell us. And as for talking, well ..." Munson fell silent as a ramp lowered from the ship.

The Grays liked to think of themselves as scientists and explorers, voyagers who roamed space investigating mysterious worlds and odd species. Everyone else thought of them as the snoops of the galaxy, interstellar peeping toms, who stalked and observed unsuspecting people and often tried to turn a profit from it.

The galactic alliance contracted with the Grays to keep an eye on Earth and the handful of other quarantined planets so the galaxy could be ready should these primitive people ever venture beyond their solar system. Which, on the surface, was all well and good. There were rumors, though, that the Grays sometimes took their scientific investigations a trifle too far, and in an up close and personal direction. They also sometimes raided Earth of various items they thought they could sell in other parts of the galaxy. It was all a bit creepy. But the galactic alliance tended to turn a blind eye to it because ... well, no one else wanted the job.

A Gray emerged from the ship and began walking down the ramp. Pelham looked up in greeting … and then immediately dropped his gaze to the ground, a hand to his forehead. One glance had been enough. More than enough.

Grays were about the same height as Haplors with large heads, huge eyes that were entirely black, and smooth gray skin. And they were completely furless, a fact that was readily evident since the one currently striding down the ramp wore nothing other than a lanyard around its neck with various devices hanging from it.

At least, Pelham thought, there were no visible naughty bits in his line of sight. Though that, in itself, raised a host of questions, none of which he would dare ask. He forced himself to make eye contact and deployed a tight-lipped smile.

He whispered to Munson, "Why don't they wear clothes?"

His assistant raised a fist to cough and said behind it, "They say it's because they possess an unusually high body temperature. Clothing makes them hot and uncomfortable."

"Yes, but I mean … would it hurt to throw on a lightweight cotton robe … or some linen shorts?"

"Shhh, sir. And try to clear your mind of thoughts."

"What?"

"Shhh."

The Gray reached the ground, putting Pelham at last eye-to-eye with the visitor rather than eye-to-anything-else, for which Pelham was relieved and grateful. The Gray nodded to him, and Pelham seemed to have a thought that said, "Greetings. I am Captain Polex Ke'rop of the Gray Confederation ship the *Space Princess*."

It came to him like any other thought in his internal monologue, except this wasn't anything he would think, not the least because Pelham was not Captain Polex Ke'rop. Besides, it wasn't in his voice. How could it be? It wasn't a voice at all.

Pelham blinked and looked around, unsure of what had just happened. The Gray was staring at him. Had he missed something? Was he still feeling the effects of the night before?

After a pause, the thought came to him a second time. "Greetings."

Munson nudged him and whispered, "Return the greeting, Mr. Totleigh."

"What?" Pelham said.

"Return the captain's greeting."

"You mean, he actually said that?"

"Well, not said exactly, but … yes."

"It wasn't ... I don't know ... my imagination?"

"You really need to return the greeting."

Pelham gave the Gray an awkward smile. "Ah. Yes. Um. Hello. Pelham G. Totleigh. Welcome to Sonus."

"A pleasure to meet you," the captain didn't say.

It was a weird and unnerving feeling, becoming aware of a bit of dialogue without, strictly speaking, hearing the voice. It was like someone had sneaked inside Pelham's brain and switched the tracks on his train of thought, as if a voice-over narrator was commenting on the scene. A wave of dizziness swept over him.

"Please accept my apologies," the voice inside his head said.

"What?"

"That you find the telepathic experience unsettling. I assure you the feeling will pass."

"What? How do you know I consider it unsettling?"

"I can discern your thoughts."

Ke'rop's head tilted to one side as if studying him, reading him. Pelham felt like a specimen being examined in a lab.

"You ... you can? You read my mind? Blimey. Then ... do I even need to speak out loud? Or ... or do I simply think what I want to say?"

What Munson had said earlier about clearing his mind began to make sense. With a chill, Pelham realized that he needed to control what he thought. He shouldn't, for instance, think about the Gray's lack of naughty bits. Oh golly, had he just thought about their lack of naughty bits? Did Ke'rop hear that ... or read that ... or whatever?

The Gray captain held up a long-fingered hand. The voice in Pelham's head said, "Please, Mr. Totleigh, stop. Stop. Speak, please."

"Ah. Then you can hear me?"

"No. We have no ears, as you can see."

Pelham craned his head and verified the statement. "Then how do you ...?"

"We find that non-telepaths have difficulty arranging their thoughts properly without talking. Unless you speak, all we pick up is a jumble of disconnected phrases and often embarrassing images."

"Ah. Righto." Pelham felt his face flush and tried as hard as he could to focus his mind on something other than naughty bits, missing or otherwise. Especially otherwise.

"So please speak." Captain Ke'rop flipped something on the top of a black cylindrical object that was gripped in one hand. A cloud of steam rolled out along with a strong, rich aroma. The Gray sipped from it.

"Oh," Pelham said, "is that tea?"

"Kowfee," Ke'rop said in Pelham's head. "An Earth drink."

"It smells interesting. What's it like?"

The Gray took another sip and yawned. At least, Pelham hoped it was a yawn because if it wasn't, it was some kind of terrifying silent scream "It gets me going in the morning."

"Like tea then."

Ke'rop's head tilted. "Yes and no. Kowfee is like a cup of tea that punches you in the face."

"Gosh, that doesn't sound pleasant. Why in the moon would you drink it?"

The captain shrugged and took a longer sip. "You come to like it. There's nothing better for getting you ready to face a grueling day of planet hopping."

"I say, I could have used some of that kowfee earlier this morning. If you can believe that this morning had an even earlier. Though Blandings' elixir always does the trick, what?"

"What elixir is that?"

Pelham shook his head. "I couldn't tell you. The recipe is something of a secret in valet circles. So have you been to Earth recently?"

"We came from there, stopping at your Haplor colony on Danánn before coming here."

"You know, I met an Earthling once?"

The Gray's huge black eyes narrowed. "You met a human?"

"No, I said an Earthling."

"The Earthlings call themselves human."

"They do? I wonder why. They're from Earth not ... Hume."

"There is no planet named Hume."

"My point exactly." Pelham rubbed his temple. All this hearing of voices in his head was starting to give him a headache.

"What did you do with it?" Ke'rop asked.

"With what?"

"The human, the Earthling."

"What did I *do* with him?"

"Yes. How did you study it?"

"Oh, you know, made conversation and whatnot."

"That is all? You merely talked with it? No ... physical examination?"

"Oh no, I didn't see a need for that. Pleasant chap as it turns out. He helped me out of a scrape I had got myself into. Longish story, that."

"Interesting." Ke'rop took another sip of kowfee.

"The Earth chap wore a hat. I think he called it a fedora. I don't suppose you could pick up one of those for me, could you? Next time you stop by Earth. It looked awfully sharp."

Ke'rop nodded. "I will check into it."

"Size five in Haplor sizing."

"I have your cargo, a palette of power converters. Would you be interested in dates?"

Pelham swallowed. "Well ... I'm not exactly interested in a relationship at present."

"You misunderstand. A date is a kind of Earth fruit."

"Oh, sorry. I suppose I wouldn't mind trying one. Didn't get my usual breakfast, don't you know."

With a free hand, Captain Ke'rop grabbed one of the devices from the lanyard and pressed a few buttons. Two more Grays emerged from the ship pushing an anti-grav palette stacked with red cone-shaped power converters. When they reached the bottom of the ramp, one of them handed Pelham a small package. Inside his head, he heard a voice say, "Dates."

Pelham took the package, cracked the plastic wrap, and thumbed open the box. He pulled out a brown oblong fruit and took a bite. "Hmm. Not bad. You know, around here we can't yet grow much other than blue fruit, and that gets a bit tiresome sometimes. We're always looking for something new" He passed the box to his assistant. "Give one a go, Munson."

Munson tried one and bobbed his head up and down.

"How many boxes would you like?" the voice inside Pelham's head asked.

"Oh. So that's why you wanted to meet? To introduce us to dates. Open up a new market, as it were."

Ke'rop inclined his head. "The fruit has many health benefits. For instance, it is high in antioxidants."

"Well, if there's anything I'm anti, it's oxidants. Of course, I'd have to run any decision to buy some past my Aunt Agutha. She's the governor. Could I maybe slip her the rest of this box? See what she thinks?"

"Certainly. We currently have several cases on board and can give you an attractive price. Of course, they were not easy to obtain. Who knows when we will have a supply like this again?"

"Still, I can't make the call myself. You may not have seen the governor when she's angry, but I have."

Ke'rop smiled. "Keep the box and pass it on to her."

For a split second, Pelham started to consider whether he would actually give his aunt the package or keep the rest for himself. But he caught himself, hopefully before Ke'rop read his mind, and instead forced himself to think about a snappy tune he had heard fiddled the night before. "Righto. I'll definitely pass this on to her."

"It is a pleasure doing business with you," Ke'rop communicated. The Grays walked back up the ramp. It closed, and the ship took off.

"Munson," Pelham said when the spacecraft had flown away, "do you know why they are called Grays?"

"I believe, Mr. Totleigh, it is because they are, by and large, gray."

"Well, yes. I did notice that part. But what I mean … well, it isn't really a proper name, is it? Not like Haplors or Srathans or Avanians. No one calls Rhegedians the Blues. They call them Rhegedians. Surely, the Grays don't call themselves the Grays, do they?"

"Ah. I see what you mean. As I understand it, Grays is merely our name for them — us being all the species in the galactic alliance. I don't think anyone knows what they call themselves. Mysterious, the Grays are."

"That they are. Well, let's shift this palette inside."

Munson's eyes swiveled from the power converters to the revolving airlock door. "I don't think the palette will fit through the door. We'll have to carry them in one by one."

"You mean … by hand?"

"I'm afraid so." Munson picked up two of the red cones, grunting with the weight, and tottered back inside the space terminal. Pelham grabbed another one only to see something small and dark shoot out from behind it. He jumped. The power converter dropped from his hands, clanging down onto the tarmac.

Whatever had darted out, ran to the outside wall of the building and pressed its body against the blue siding. What happened next amazed Pelham. The small dark body turned the exact same shade of cobalt as the building.

Pelham goggled, eyes wide and bulging. "What? I say, what?"

Chapter 5

When Pelham Met Keezo

If Pelham focused carefully, he could detect a shimmer where the little creature stood. And the eyes — he could just make out the eyes — they were staring straight at him. Pelham stood still, and after several moments, the creature slowly transformed back to black.

If Pelham had been standing close to the whatever this was, which he wasn't because it had scooted so far away, it would probably come up barely to his knee. It had two thin legs that ended in long, narrow three-toed feet. It had a compact torso and a large heart-shaped head with huge eyes. What it didn't have were arms. Instead, ten or twelve tentacles hung down from the sides of its face like a shaggy beard. The tentacles were currently waving back and forth in front of the creature like a shield.

From that and from the tremors rolling across its fur, Pelham guessed that the little critter must be terrified here alone in a strange place. Either that or it was freezing in this dashed cold air, which was equally possible.

Pelham crouched down. "Hello there." He didn't know if the lifeform was intelligent or not, but he figured it wouldn't hurt to say something in soothing tones.

The creature blinked at him. "Hello." Its voice came out like a squeak.

"Ah," said Pelham, "you speak. Excellent. Don't be afraid. No one is going to hurt you."

"Hello." The creature's tentacles relaxed.

"Yes, you said that already."

"You is Big."

"Well, I'm average sized, I suppose … for a Haplor."

The creature shook its head, the fur and tentacles swishing with the movement. "No. You is *A* Big."

"A big ... what?"

"A Big ... Big."

Pelham scratched at his cheek. "I didn't quite follow you there. But never mind. I am Pelham G. Totleigh."

"Pelie," the creature said.

"Pelham," Pelham said. He pointed at himself. "Me Pelham. Pelham G. Totleigh"

"Pelie."

"No, it's Pelham. Pel-ham."

"I is say that. Pelie."

"Hmm. Perhaps we should move on for now." Pelham pointed at the little creature. "What's your name?"

Its huge eyes clicked left and right a few times. "I is Keezo."

"Keezo? Are you Keezo?"

"I is Keezo."

"Hello, Keezo."

"Hello, Pelie."

"Pelham, actually. Hello, Pelham."

"No. I is Keezo. You is Pelie."

"Yes, I know. Except ... well ... we'll come back to that later."

Munson emerged from the revolving door. With a sharp intake of breath, Keezo's fur changed back to blue.

Pelham held up a hand to his assistant. "Easy, Munson."

"What are you doing, Mr. Totleigh?"

Pelham waved an arm toward the wall as if it should be obvious that he was dealing with the small nearly invisible creature. "The Grays seem to have had a stowaway."

"Where?"

"There."

"Where? I don't see anything."

Pelham looked at Munson. He looked at the shimmer that was Keezo. He looked at Munson again. He turned back to Keezo. "It's all right, Keezo," he said, trying to sound calming.

Keezo blinked a few times then changed back to black.

"Goodness gracious," Munson said.

Pelham stood. "This is Keezo, Munson."

"Hello," Munson said.

"Keezo, this is my assistant, Munson."

"Hello, Mudson," Keezo said.

Pelham laughed. "Mudson. That's a good one. Keezo seems to have a spot of trouble with names."

"What is it?" Munson asked.

"I'm not sure," Pelham said. "Ever seen one of him before?"

"No."

"I is Keezo," Keezo said.

"It's obviously not from around here," Pelham said. "The only things alive on Sonus are Haplors and the little creepy-crawlies we brought with us to work the soil."

"And bacteria," Munson said.

"Well, yes."

"And, of course, the plants are alive."

"Don't be pedantic, Munson. Keezo here is neither bacterium nor vegetable."

"I is Keezo."

"Yes, yes. We've established that, Keezo. And did you notice, Munson, how it is decidedly lacking in the arm department? Unless one counts that ruffle of tendrils hanging down."

"I did note that," Munson said. "Do you suppose it's a pet of the Grays?"

"The Grays don't strike me as keepers of pets. Difficult to picture them pulling a little furry animal onto their laps for a cuddle of an evening."

"They wouldn't have to worry about pet fur getting on their clothes."

"Fair point, Munson. However, Keezo here talks and understands us when we talk … to some extent anyway. Which means it has translator bots, right? Pets don't have the nanobots implanted in them, do they?"

"I've heard that some do. That way the people they live with can understand what the pet is trying to communicate. Though I'm told that mainly what the pets say is, 'I'm hungry,' and, 'Hey, hey, hey, hey,' and the like."

Pelham turned to his assistant. "I'm not sure I see how that would be better than barks and such."

Munson shrugged. "But are you sure this creature really understands us?"

"It repeated my name. And yours."

"Pelie," Keezo said.

"Or something close to it," Pelham said.

"Some birds repeat sounds."

"Yes, but there are also some that truly talk. I've met a few Avanians in my time."

"Maybe you should ask it a question and see if it understands."

"Okey dokey," Pelham said.

Keezo said, "What is … okey dokey?"

Pelham smirked. "Not much is okey dokey at present, in point of fact."

"I no is understand. What is okey dokey?"

Pelham gave an exasperated sigh. "It means to agree, Keezo. Or that things are all right."

"Okey dokey," Keezo repeated.

"So may I ask you a question, Keezo?"

"Okey dokey."

"Excellent. Now what to ask? Hmm. Keezo, on which planet does the galactic council meet?"

Keezo blinked twice and faded back to blue.

"Wait," Pelham said. "It's all right, Keezo. It's not a problem if you don't know. Come to think of it, I forget where it is myself. Which planet is it, Munson?"

Munson ignored the question. "I highly doubt, Mr. Totleigh, that this little creature stays up on interstellar affairs."

"You may be right. I'll try an easier one. Keezo, how many fingers am I holding up?"

Fading back to black, Keezo's head tilted to the side. "What is … finners?"

"Fingers," said Pelham. He wiggled the fingers of both hands in Keezo's direction.

Keezo wiggled tentacles in response.

Munson said, "Perhaps it doesn't know what fingers are because it doesn't have any … or hands … or arms, for that matter."

Pelham crossed his arms. "Well, this is all a dashed bit more difficult than I imagined. I wonder how the space explorer blokes work this out with new species."

"Perhaps you should ask it to do something."

"Good idea. Keezo, please lift your leg."

Keezo lifted a leg.

"There you go, Munson, he … or she … or it has intelligence. Now, if you and I had any intelligence, we'd move inside out of this freezing air. If you ask me, those terraforming chappies really need to work a bit faster. Come along, Keezo."

"Okey dokey," Keezo said.

"The little critter picks things up fast, what?"

Pelham took a step toward the airlock. Keezo, one leg still in the air, began hopping along behind.

Then Keezo stopped and said in a plaintive squeak, "Tunna?"

Pelham turned around. He and Munson looked at Keezo, then at each other.

"What's a tunna?" Pelham asked.

"Tunna," Keezo said. "Where is Tunna?"

Munson said, "Tunna appears to be something the alien has lost."

Pelham ran a hand over his mouth and chin. "But what in the blazes is it? Keezo, what is tunna? By the by, you can put your leg down now."

Keezo complied. "Tunna is … Tunna."

Pelham rolled his eyes. "Tunna is tunna. Well, that was helpful."

"Yes," Keezo said with bobbing head. "Tunna is helpful. Where is Tunna and little?"

"Did you say little?"

"Little." Keezo nodded with excitement. "Little is with Tunna."

"A little what?"

"A little one."

"Mr. Totleigh," Munson said, "I believe Tunna is its mate, and they have a youngling."

"Egad," said Pelham. "Keezo, is Tunna your mate?"

The head again tilted to one side. "What is … mate?"

"Well, a mate is … I mean, to mate is to … well. Help me out here, Munson."

"No, thank you."

Pelham gave his assistant a scowl and continued. "I mean to say … blast it all. I wish Blandings were here. He knows all the definitions. Well, is Tunna your companion, your friend, your partner?"

The creature nodded. "Yes, yes. Tunna. Tunna is climb into silver round thing with Keezo. Is rumble and buzz and Keezo is almost float away to land of endless fruit. But now where is Tunna?"

"Did you get all that, Munson?"

"No, sir. But I take it Tunna and the youngling also boarded the Gray ship."

"Hmm. Keezo, you wonder where they are, Tunna and your youngling?"

"Yes. Yes. Where? Where is Tunna? Where is little?"

"Munson, have a peek around and between the power converters to see if you can find another one like Keezo … or another two, as it were."

The assistant circled the palette, eyeballing it carefully. "I don't see anything, Mr. Totleigh."

"Bear in mind, Munson, they can blend in with the surroundings. Tunna might be but a red shimmer."

Munson pulled a few of the devices from the palette and looked more deeply into the spaces around the remaining ones. "Sorry. Nothing."

"Blast," Pelham said.

"Blast." Keezo sniffed, which was the first indication to Pelham that the creature even had a nose under all that fur. Peering up at Pelham with huge eyes, Keezo asked, "Pelie is help find Tunna?"

"Help? Me? As in … me?"

"You is help?"

"Me?"

Keezo nodded and kept nodding. "Pelie is help?"

"Not much," Munson muttered.

Pelham shot him a look before focusing again on Keezo. "Well, the thing is, Keezo, as you can see Tunna is not here. I don't know …" Pelham's voice trailed off.

"Help?" Keezo's voice came out in a whimper.

Pelham swallowed and gazed down at the poor little creature, alone and lost. He remembered feeling much the same when, as a youngling, he had been sent off to school on the Haplor home world. Well, until he made friends, of course. But who would be this tiny creature's friend?

And how many times had Pelham found himself in scrapes on foreign worlds and in need of a helping hand? More than he cared to recollect, that was for sure. Fortunately, he had always had Blandings there for advice and comfort. Who did this pint-sized alien have?

The Totleigh heart was not made of stone. Pelham G. Totleigh would not abandon a fellow creature in need. What was that old adage? No one is an asteroid? Something like that. Blandings would know. In fact, it was Blandings who explained, to Pelham's surprise, that the saying wasn't primarily about planetoids and celestial bodies but rather about people and how we all are dependent on each other. And right now, this little Keezo fellow was counting on him.

Pelham turned to Munson. "Where did the Gray captain say ... well, not say per se but telepath ... ized ... communicated ... Anyway, where had they come from?"

"Earth and then Danánn."

"Earth. Could this be an Earth creature, Munson?"

"Who knows? Earth is quarantined."

"Right. Right. Wait, Munson. Since Earth is quarantined, critters from there wouldn't have translator bots, would they?"

"Again, I wouldn't know ... because of the quarantine."

"So most likely, this wee fellow came from Danánn."

"Or the Gray home world. Or anyplace else where they stopped that the captain didn't happen to mention."

"Come with me, Keezo. We'll go to my office and research this." Pelham moved toward the revolving airlock door, Keezo following behind.

Munson, still standing by the pallet, asked, "What are you going to do, Mr. Totleigh?"

Pelham paused in his stride and looked back over his shoulder with his head held high. "Do? Do? I am going to help this poor creature, that's what I'm going to do. I will help it find its mate and youngling and return them all back to their home. It's the code of the Totleighs, don't you know, to help people in need. Keezo asked for my help, and I will not turn away from him ... or it ... or whatever. Yes, Keezo, I will help you find your Tunna and youngling and get you all home."

Keezo bounced up and down. "Pelie is help."

"But what about all these power converters?" Munson asked.

Pelham waved a dismissive hand. "I'm sure you can handle such a minor thing as hauling them in, Munson. I'm off to more important matters. I need to contact the Gray ship, the Danánn colony, and anybody else who might be of assistance."

"But Mr. Totleigh—"

"Now, now, Munson, this is no time to be thinking of yourself. We all must do our bit for little Keezo here. Your bit is to haul in these converters. Oh, and don't forget to give them a thorough inspection. Make sure each one is in working order. Have the form on my desk and ready for me to sign as soon as poss. Come along, Keezo."

Chapter 6

The View from Below

Keezo rushed after Pelie. They left the cold open-air place and entered a tiny space that moved around in a circle as they walked. Keezo did not remember seeing this circle space when Keezo had entered the round silver thing with Tunna. Could the Bigs have built it while they were inside the silver thing? The Bigs were always building something.

The tiny circle space opened into a huge, bright inside place. Keezo stopped, stunned for a moment by the sights and sounds and scents. Many Bigs were here, many more than Keezo could count. They dashed in every direction, carrying around huge bags. Like all Bigs, they wore things covering their fur. Keezo guessed their fur must not keep them very warm. And everywhere were makeens, some moving, some sitting still but making noises as if threatening to move at any moment.

This inside place stretched as far as Keezo could see. This must be one of the flat-walled pot things the Bigs live in. Though in all the times when Keezo had gazed at the Bigs' sittee from the hill, Keezo had never seen one of them this large. And who could live in a place like this with so many Bigs rushing everywhere and no mats to lie down on?

But for now, that was not important. What was important was to follow Pelie through the crowd. Pelie promised to find Tunna. Keezo must not get lost from Pelie the way Tunna was lost.

Keezo followed Pelie up long slopes, past big walls of flashing lights, across busy spaces, past so many Bigs and other creatures unlike anyone Keezo had ever seen before — blue people, green people, people with scales like lizards.

Once, as they passed a place filled with food smells and crowded with people, Keezo got distracted by the scents and lost track of Pelie among all the other Bigs.

"Pelie! Pelie!" Keezo called.

A moment later Pelie appeared, shouldering through the mass of Bigs. "Try to keep up, Keezo."

Pelie turned and strode off again. Keezo raced to follow.

It was a relief when they finally left the inside place and stepped out into a quieter and less crowded outside. Except this outside did not feel like outside. No breeze blew. The ground did not have dirt or sand or tufts of grass. It was as hard as rock and completely smooth and flat in every direction. No wonder the Bigs lived in pots built above the ground. Who could tunnel into this rock to make a cozy mound to live in?

Rushing after Pelie, Keezo kept gazing around, trying to tie anything Keezo now saw with memories of things previously seen from the hill. Nothing seemed to fit. But Keezo knew it had to.

The round silver thing with the gray creatures had been sitting at the edge of the sittee. Keezo had entered it and then left it again through the same opening after all the buzzing and rumbling and nearly flying away to the land of endless fruit. Which meant this had to still be the Big's sittee.

There were so many strange sights.

"What is that, Pelie?" Keezo pointed a tentacle at a big box on wheels moving past them.

"That's an automated carriage, Keezo."

"What's that, Pelie?" Keezo pointed in awe at a gargantuan green person.

"That's Princess Ralph of Diere, who is visiting our colony. But try not to point, Keezo. It's impolite."

They hurried along the hard, flat ground, passing one flat-walled pot after another. One they passed was so tall that Keezo's eyes instinctively ran up the side. The walls went up and up and up like one mound built on top of another mound on top of another. And above it all …

Keezo froze in place and gasped. "Pelie!"

Pelie walked on.

"Pelie! Pelie! Pelie!"

"What?" Pelie spun around, a hand on one hip. "Don't dillydally, Keezo. We need to hurry. And for the last time, it's Pelham. Pel-ham. Pelham G. Totleigh."

"Pelie!" Keezo's tentacles pointed up. "What is …?"

"What is what, Keezo?"

Keezo had no words to answer. The sky was not right. Nothing about it was what the sky should be.

Outside Keezo's mound, the sky grew light every morning when the sun rose. Here the sky was light but with many lights, not with the warm, yellow sun. And these lights were not high in the sky like the sun. These lights hung not far above the ground.

And then Keezo saw that the lights were hanging from something stretched overhead between the ground and the sky, something clear like the ice that formed on ponds in the cold times. Except the cold times weren't supposed to come for many days. And ice didn't form up above in the air.

And beyond the clear thing that held the lights, stars were shining. It was nighttime above the clear thing. How could it be both day and night at the same time?

The stars were all wrong too. Keezo knew the stars. Everyone did. They watched them every night. The stars told them when different kinds of food could be found and when the cold times would come and when the warm times would come again. But these stars were all different, not just different because of rotating around like stars did every night, but all mixed up like when someone kicked marking rocks out of place.

But the biggest and most troubling thing in the sky was what Keezo's tentacles pointed at — that huge orange and gold round thing with blue circles stretching across the sky. That did not belong in the sky. How did it get up there? Did this blue-ringed monster eat Keezo's warm yellow sun?

Pelie peered up. "What is it, Keezo?"

"What is big, big … sun with blue circles?"

Pelie chuckled. "No, no. That's not the sun, Keezo. The sun is that smallish red ball over there. What you're seeing there is Nuggies."

"Nuggies," Keezo said. "What is … Nuggies?"

Pelham pointed. "That is Nuggies. It's a planet."

"Plan-it?" Did the Bigs plan and build this Nuggies thing? Did they build the clear thing between the ground and the sky to protect them from Nuggies and its circles? Did they build all this while Keezo was inside the round silver thing? Is that what caused all the noise and bumping?

Some of Keezo's people said the Bigs possessed magic, that it was by using magic that the Bigs first appeared in their land and built their flat-walled pots. Keezo had never believed them or believed in magic. But the tall pots and the changes in the sky were all starting to make Keezo wonder if the stories might be true.

Pelie crouched down beside Keezo. "Sonus is a moon, and it orbits Nuggies."

Keezo had no idea what any of those words meant. What had the Bigs done to the world? Keezo looked down again at the flat, hard rock below them. "Where is grass?" Keezo's chest heaved. Everything Keezo ever knew was gone.

"Grass? We can't yet grow grass."

Keezo blinked. What did Pelie mean? No one had to grow grass. Grass just grew. It grew in the sun ... if you had the right sun. Maybe with Nuggies, all that would grow was this flat rock. Keezo worried what would happen to the world. Where would the Danánn find fruit and nuts in a world like this?

Pelie said, "Come along now, Keezo. No time to gaze at the sky right now. We need to go to my office."

Pelie turned and walked on. Keezo followed, wondering what an offiz was. Pelie walked, turned again, and walked some more. Always on the flat hard ground. Always under the weird clear thing that hung between them and the sky. Always with the Nuggies that shouldn't be floating overhead.

Bigs were walking every which way. Some noticed Keezo and smiled. Some didn't look and came close to stepping on the small Danánn. Keezo hurried to stay near Pelie's leg. Keezo's feet were beginning to hurt from all the walking on the hard ground.

This sittee of the Bigs was strange and confusing. Keezo wanted to be back home in the mound, sitting with Tunna, playing with their little, with grass growing in the ground and the right sun shining in the sky.

Then Pelie entered one of the flat-walled pots. The inside was wide and tall like a huge mound. Pelie walked across it to a wall and used one of the little tentacles on Pelie's top limb — what Pelie had called finners — to touch something. A *ding* sounded, and an opening appeared in the wall to reveal a much smaller space.

Pelie stepped inside the small space. Keezo hesitated, not trusting the little space and the sliding opening.

"Come along, Keezo. Hurry before the door closes."

Knowing only that Keezo must not lose Pelie, Keezo followed. The opening closed and trapped them inside the tiny space. Keezo clutched at the covering over Pelie's leg like a little one clasping its mother.

The small space rumbled, which made Keezo dislike it even more. It jerked, and Keezo felt almost the same as when the round silver thing had rumbled and then pressed Keezo to the ground.

Fortunately, this time Keezo was not pressed down nearly as much, and there was no floating. The door opened again, and they stepped out into a completely different place, a place like a tunnel. How did the Bigs do that? How could they change a huge place while Keezo was inside the little space? The Bigs must have more magic than any of the Danánn ever imagined.

Pelie led Keezo along the tunnel to a wall. Part of the wall swung back, and they entered a different space. Inside were the things the Bigs called furnsure where the Bigs sat. Keezo had never understood why the Bigs had to have furnsure to sit on when the ground was already there. But that's the way the Bigs were.

Pelie said, "Welcome to my office, Keezo."

Keezo gawked around. What was this place? What was an offiz? Was this Pelie's mound? This was no place to live. There was no mat for sleeping, no place for a fire. This place was large and cold and not at all cozy like Keezo's mound.

But Pelie seemed pleased to be there, and Pelie had promised to help. That was more important than Keezo understanding this place and this strange sittee. Pelie was going to help. Pelie was smart. Pelie knew words like Nuggies and offiz and finners. And if Pelie could find this offiz amid all the flat-walled pots of the huge sittee, then Keezo thought Pelie could find Tunna and the little.

Chapter 7

WoTComs Next

Pelham rubbed his hands together and eyed the communications equipment in the corner. "Now, Keezo, let's fire up the old WoTCom and see if we can dig up some answers, eh?" He looked over the device, trying to remember if it had an on switch. "Dash it all. Munson usually does the bit about establishing a connection. Or Blandings if I'm at the flat." He peered down at the little creature looking up at him with expectant eyes. "I don't suppose you know anything about WoTCom units, do you?"

"What is ... waukum?" Keezo asked with a puzzled expression.

"I didn't think so. Well, how hard can it be? I think the interface is all verbal." He sat down at the device. "WoTCom, I'd like to talk with the Gray ship that just left. There, that ought to do it."

In Pelham's experience, after a command such as that was given, a circle would start spinning around the screen while the device did whatever it did to connect to the other party. And then a face would shortly appear.

But this time none of that happened. No face. Not even the spinning circle, which Pelham always called the circle of impatience. Instead, a synthesized voice sounded from the device. "More detailed connection information is needed."

Keezo shrieked and backed up against Pelham's desk, fur fading to mahogany to blend in.

Pelham said, "It's all right, Keezo."

"Who is say that?" Keezo asked, wide-eyed.

"The WoTCom did."

"Waukum." Keezo's eyes shifted left and right. "I no is see wakum.

Pelham patted the screen. "It's right here, Keezo. This device is the WoTCom." Pelham swung back to it. "Now what more blasted information do you need? I told you I want to talk to the Gray ship, the one that landed here this morning. It couldn't have been more than an hour ago. I mean, how many ships with a Gray registration could have visited here recently?"

The WoTCom said, "Please supply the name of the ship or its captain."

"Ah. Well, you see I'm not frightfully good with names. I hear them, you know, but somehow, they don't always stick. Let me think. The ship was the something prince or princess. I remember that because I wondered if the Grays had a royal house and all that. And the captain was … I want to say K-pop. Something like that."

"Do you mean Captain Polex Ke'rop of the *Space Princess*?"

Pelham waved an agreeing finger. "Yes. Now you have it. Good show. This isn't so hard after all. If Blandings could see me now. Put me through forthwith."

A rumble came from across the room. Pelham swiveled around to see Keezo pushing his desk chair around the office. "I say, Keezo, would you mind stopping that? I'm trying to get this blighted WoTCom to do what I want."

"Furnsure move!"

"Yes, it moves. That's the point of the bally thing. If you would be kind enough to park it at that desk, I would be much obliged."

Pelham turned back to the WoTCom, relieved to find the circle of impatience now spinning merrily. After a few moments, it was replaced by the face and shoulders of Captain Ke'rop, still shirtless. Pelham was equally relieved the camera didn't employ a wider … or rather, longer … shot. The captain stared out at him.

Behind him, Keezo shrieked again. "Magic."

Pelham said over his shoulder, "Not magic. It's the WoTCom."

"Waukum."

"Righto. It works by … um … what did Blandings say? Something about creating a teeny artificial wormhole in the fabric of space-time … or some such. Now that I hear it, it does sound a smidgen like magic, what?"

Meanwhile, Ke'rop was still staring.

"Sorry about that, Captain," Pelham said. "And sorry for bothering you. We seemed to have stumbled into a bit of a scaly situation here. You see, among the power converters, we found a … well, we're not sure what he is … or she is … or whatever. But the important bit is—"

"Where is Tunna?" Keezo asked.

"Yes, that's the thing. Captain, do you happen to have a little critter on board? One that looks like the one behind me? Can you see Keezo there? Do I need to adjust the screen or anything?"

The Gray captain blinked twice, then picked up a square device from the lanyard around its neck and held it up to the camera.

"Um … perhaps I wasn't clear. We're not looking for one of those." Pelham pointed behind him toward Keezo. "But … but one of these."

Ke'rop's head shook left and right. The captain tapped on the device several times. A mechanical voice sounded. "Telepathy does not work over WoTCom. You need to use a Telepathy Relay Interface like this."

"A what now?"

The captain blinked again.

Pelham said, "Oh. You didn't hear me. Now what do I do?"

Ke'rop tapped some more. A voice said, "Do you have a Telepathy Relay Interface?"

Pelham shook his head. "Sorry. I don't know what that is. Perhaps if Munson were here—"

The line went dead.

"Well," Pelham said. "Not a particularly helpful chap. See if I recommend buying dates after that. But never mind, Keezo. We will press on. The Gray said they had come from Danánn. We'll check there. WoTCom, please connect me to the Haplor colony on Danánn."

A great clattering sounded from behind him. Pelham whirled around to see a cascade of tablet devices pouring off his desk from where Keezo stood. "Don't touch those! I haven't signed them yet."

Keezo gazed back with an apologetic look.

"Danánn station here." The voice was coming from the WoTCom. "Hello? Hello?"

Pelham spun back to see a middle-aged Haplor with an intense, square face. "Sorry. Something of a disruption here just now. Keezo, perhaps you should come over here with me."

Keezo jumped from Pelham's desk, knocking one more tablet to the floor in the process. Then hopping into Pelham's lap, Keezo climbed up to take a seat on his shoulder.

The Haplor from Danánn leaned toward the screen and twisted his head. "What are you doing with a Danánn?"

"What?" Pelham said. "No, I'm *calling* Danánn. I don't have one. I don't have a whole planet. Well, I suppose I have Danánn in the sense of being connected to you, what?"

34

"On your shoulder, I mean. That's a Danánn, one of the native inhabitants of this planet."

"What?"

"Who are you?"

"Ah," Pelham said, pleased to at last find some solid footing in the conversation. "Pelham G. Totleigh, Director of … I mean, Inspector of Imports on Sonus. And to whom do I have the pleasure of speaking?"

"Theodore Fernsby, Communications Officer. Now where did you get that?"

"Now really, Theodore. Teddy. May I call you Teddy? Should you really be referring to a sentient being using the word *that*? Wouldn't using he or she be more respectful?"

Fernsby rolled his eyes. "It would be if the Danánn had gender. As best as anyone can tell, they don't."

"They don't have … then how do they … I mean to say, what do they …? Well, this one has a youngling after all."

"We don't know any of that. We didn't even know for sure they existed until a few years ago."

"You don't say."

"There were rumors, sure. Odd sightings, mostly by people after they'd had too much to drink. It always sounded more like the ancient stories about fairies, the little people. Of course, we came across the mounds they live in, but we never saw anyone in them. Our scientists believed the mounds were remnants of an ancient lost civilization. That or moles."

"Astonishing."

"See, they can make themselves nearly invisible."

"Righto. I've seen that bit."

"Then one day, one of them wandered into the colony. Somebody fed it, and it kept coming back." Fernsby shook his head. "We had to bring in a galactic alliance team to evaluate them for sentience and intelligence. They finally gave that first one translator bots embedded in a blue fruit, and then we could communicate … more or less. I think most of them have the bots now — another alliance project."

"This one does," Pelham said.

"Which brings me back to my question. How did a Danánn end up on Sonus?"

"Came in on a Gray ship."

"For what purpose? This isn't a slave trade thing, is it?"

"Oh no. I rather presume it was all an accident. Keezo probably wandered on board or something."

"Keezo? Who's Keezo?"

Pelham pointed a thumb toward his shoulder. "This is Keezo. He told me himself. I mean, Keezo told me ... um ... Keezo's self. I say, this pronoun business gets tricky, what?"

Listen, Mr. Totleigh, you need to send the Danánn back right away."

"It's Keezo. And it's a tad more complicated than that. You see, there was a mate ... or maybe not a mate as such, given what you said earlier about ... you know ... but a companion named Tunna, and a youngling."

"Tunna and little," Keezo said, excitedly. Keezo stood on Pelham's shoulder and climbed to his head.

"Were they on the ship also, Mr. Totleigh?"

"Call me Pelham, please." Pelham moved Keezo from his head to his lap. "And it isn't entirely clear. I mean to say, have you ever tried talking to somebody like Keezo?"

Fernsby chuckled. "Not personally, but I've heard. They're not very bright."

Pelham winced. "Well, I don't know if I would say that." He had on occasion been similarly described, mainly by Aunt Agutha. It grated on him to hear it said of anyone.

"Where is Tunna?" Keezo asked. "Where is Tunna?" Keezo jumped up and down on Pelham's lap.

Pelham set Keezo on the floor. "That's the purpose of my call. This Tunna person. Can you check to see if Tunna is still on Danánn?"

Fernsby made a face. "How am I supposed to do that?"

"Oh, I don't know. Ask around. Next of kin. Check at Tunna's home and place of employment. I wouldn't want to tell you how to do your job."

"You don't understand how the Danánn live. They don't have employment. They have a hunter-gatherer culture. Not even the hunter part. We believe they're vegetarian."

Behind him, Pelham heard Keezo say, "Hello," followed by a worrying *beep*, but he didn't feel he could interrupt Fernsby mid-discourse.

"And we can't exactly give them jobs," Fernsby continued, "because they don't understand technology. We might be able to give them menial work, but if we did that, then what would that make us? Exploiters of a simpler species? No, thank you."

Another *beep* sounded behind Pelham, followed by an, "I is Keezo," and yet another *beep*. Pelham tried to turn his head without looking away from the screen but couldn't make it work.

"Anyway, they don't want jobs. They're happy living like they've always lived. And why not? They work only enough to provide for themselves and their elders and younglings. It's an easy life if you don't mind living in a hole in the ground and scrounging every day for food. Some of our own people have gone native to live with them, which hasn't exactly been good for our colony."

Pelham said, "Perhaps you could ask the Haplors who joined the Danánn. They might know this Tunna. All I want to know is whether Tunna is on the planet or not."

"You're missing the point here, Mr. Totleigh. The Danánn are listed as a protected limited-contact indigenous species. Which means that by law, you need to return that one to Danánn as quickly as possible."

"Call me Pelham, Teddy."

"I'd rather not, and I prefer Mr. Fernsby."

"Ah. All right. Well, but what about Tunna and the youngling?"

"There's nothing I can do, and frankly, they are not my concern."

"I is Keezo." *Beep.*

"Well … well, how about this, Teddy … I mean, Mr. Fernsby, has anyone been asking about Keezo? Conceivably someone filed a missing person whatchamacallit."

Fernsby sneered. "The Danánn don't file reports. They don't do forms."

"In which case, I begin to see the attraction of the lifestyle, what? Can you at least tell me this? Keezo came on a ship called the *Space Princess*. Do you have its flight plan?"

"I can get it. You can probably learn it from your people as easily."

"But since we're already talking and all."

Fernsby made a face, then disappeared from the screen.

Behind Pelham, something went *beep*, and Keezo said, "Hello."

Pelham spun around to see Keezo sitting on the floor with one of the tablet devices. He snatched it away and gawped at the screen where it said: *Ten messages sent.*

Fernsby was talking again. "The ship appears to be on a tour of Haplor colonies. It left Danánn for Sonus, then on to Unara and Tucana Three. After that, it is scheduled to return to the Gray home world."

Pelham hurriedly jotted down the information. "Thank you."

"But, Mr. Totleigh," Fernsby said, "unless you want to end up with legal problems, I suggest you catch a flight here right away and return this Keezo. Danánn station out."

The screen went black.

"Where is Tunna?" Keezo asked, looking up from another tablet.

Pelham jumped from the chair and confiscated the device from Keezo's tentacles. "I don't know. On some Haplor colony … I think. Or on the Gray ship. Possibly the Gray home world. And so far, my lines of inquiry haven't exactly paid off."

He looked down at Keezo, who was staring back at him with hopeful eyes. He took a breath. "But we're not beaten yet, Keezo. It is often said of Pelham G. Totleigh by those who know him best that in the face of adversity, he displays a certain single-mindedness, a resolute determination. We Totleighs are nothing if not resourceful, and you and I have yet to employ my most formidable resource. Let's go ask Blandings for his advice. You know, upon reflection, I probably should have done that in the first place."

Chapter 8

A Case of Mistaken Identity

"All right then, Keezo," Pelham said, "we'll just totter around to my flat."

"Flat what?" Keezo asked.

"What?"

"What is flat thing you is talk about?"

"What? Oh. No, the flat is where I live. It's ... well a flat is a sort of compact house ... all on one level, you see ... with a bunch of them built side-by-side and in a stack with other ones like it inside a building."

Keezo blinked, leaned to one side, and blinked some more. "Pelie is live in flat something?"

"That's right. Well, it's not a flat something. It's simply a flat. That's what it's called. What sort of place do you live in, Keezo?"

"Keezo is live in mound."

"Yes, that Fernsby fellow said something about mounds. And by mound, you don't mean a mound mound, do you? Dug into the dirt and all?"

Keezo nodded and waved a tentacle around in a hump shape. "Dirt is warm in cold time, cool in hot time. Mound is protects from wind and rain. Nice cozy mound."

"Sounds ... um ... lovely ... if you like that sort of thing. But aren't there bugs and grubs and such crawling around in it?"

"Yes, they is." Keezo nodded enthusiastically and stretched a tentacle down to rub somewhere in the belly region. "Bugs is good."

"Hmm. Then I take it you aren't entirely vegetarian. Doesn't sound as if those chappies on Danánn have conducted much in the way of a scientific study, what? Well, my flat serves much the same purpose as your mound. Only we have a teapot and a food replicator to provide us with something to eat. Speaking of which, it's getting on toward lunchtime. Are you hungry, Keezo?"

"I is hungry. Okey dokey."

"Then let us embark."

"Keezo is not like bark. Yucky."

"Never mind, Keezo, but do try to keep up."

Pelham ushered the little alien out the office door and into the lift, where they rode to the ground floor. Once more they set off through the city. The trek to Pelham's flat passed by many of his favorite haunts — theaters, nightclubs, restaurants. All the nightspots were closed at this time of day. But many would soon be opening for matinee performances, catering to night-shift workers. Pelham checked the posters out front for new acts and shows he might want to catch.

They were nearing the entrance to the central underground tunnels when Pelham spotted Bunko Tiddlesley emerging from an eating establishment with the pep of a laser beam shooting out from a blaster. Pelham reached him as he was straightening his clothes a few doors down from the place.

"What ho, Bunko! I see you've recovered from last night."

Bunko looked up and flinched. "Oh, it's you, Pelham. What ho. Yes, I'm steaming along … ish." Bunko gazed over Pelham's shoulder in the direction of the restaurant and heaved two heavy breaths.

"Did something happen, old scout?"

"What do you mean?"

"In the restaurant."

"What restaurant?"

"The one from which you just now made a dramatic exit. Was there an altercation of some sort?"

"More of a misunderstanding."

"Tell me all, Bunko."

"I'd rather not. You'll tell everyone, and they'll all laugh at me."

"Now I'm even more intrigued."

Bunko grimaced. "Oh all right. But you should know something is lurking behind you."

Pelham spun around, scanning the vicinity for a Haplor or an alien of some kind looming over him. He saw no one. "Where?"

"You're looking too high, Pelham. It's down there."

He dropped his gaze. "Oh, that. That's Keezo. Keezo, this is my pal Bunko."

Keezo stared up at them with huge eyes. "Hello, Bunko. I is Keezo."

40

Pelham shook his head. "So his name you can say? How hard can Pelham be to enunciate?"

"Pelie," Keezo said.

Bunko's face lit up. "Hello, Keezo. Delightful little chap, Pelie. Where did you find him?"

"Keezo came in with some cargo."

"You mean like a free prize in the box?"

"As a stowaway. An accidental passenger. I'm trying to help the poor thing out."

"Good luck. If I were you, I would seek Blandings' guidance on the matter."

"We are at this moment on our way to consult with him."

"Excellent. I should be popping off myself."

"Not before you tell me your story. What happened in the eatery?"

"Hmm?"

Pelham shot him an admonishing look. "Bunko."

"What happened? Just now, you mean?"

"I do."

Bunko's face flushed. "Well ... it's a tad embarrassing."

"Even better. I'm all ears."

Bunko stared at his shoes for a moment or two. "All right. If you insist."

"I do."

"Pelie?" Keezo said, tugging at Pelham's trouser leg. "Pelie?"

Pelham ignored the interruption.

"Pelie, what is that?"

"Not now, Keezo," Pelham said. "Bunko has an exciting tale to spin."

"It's not that exciting," Bunko said.

"I bet it is."

Another tug. "Pelie?"

"Well, first off ... Pelie," Bunko said, "did I tell you that I've been stepping out with Holly Birdwhistle?"

"I highly doubt it. I would have remembered a name like that."

"Pelie, what is that?"

"One moment, Keezo."

"What's wrong with her name?" asked Bunko, raising his chin.

"Birdwhistle? I mean, Birdwhistle?"

41

"They come from a prominent family back on Haplor."

Pelham chuckled. "Oh, I'm sure they were prominent with a name like Birdwhistle. Folks couldn't stop raven about them. People could hear of them in every meadow. I bet everyone was all atwitter."

Bunko frowned. "You can drop those tired old Birdwhistle jokes right now, Pelham, or I won't tell you the story at all."

Pelham held up a hand. "Sorry, old son. Consider the matter closed. Wait, wait. I think I need just a couple more. I hear her father is a hoot. Ha! But I'm sure Holly herself is poultry in motion." Pelham laughed alone. "All right, I'm done. Please continue."

"I don't think I want to," Bunko said.

"Pelie!" Keezo yanked so hard on the trouser leg that Pelham felt his trousers slide down his hip.

He shot a hand to the side of his trousers to halt the slippage and answered. "Yes, Keezo. What is it?"

Two tentacles pointed toward a shop window across the street. "What is that smell good place?"

"Ah. That's a bakery, Keezo. They make breads and cakes and muffins and suchlike."

Keezo's voice came out with a tone of awe. "Bakie."

"Bake-er-y," Pelham said slowly.

"Bakie. I is hungry."

"We will be trundling off to the flat soon. We can eat there." Pelham shook his head. "Sorry, Bunko. Please continue."

Bunko shrugged. "Well, you see, Holly has a distinctive coat, a sharp number in red with a black collar. Extremely elegant. And when I walked into the restaurant, I saw her. Or I should say, I saw the coat. She was sitting in a booth with her back to me."

Pelham knew Bunko well, and he had a hunch about where this was going. "Oh no. Don't tell me …"

Bunko looked down and kicked at the pavement with his foot. "I was awfully excited to see her."

"Don't you mean egg-sighted?"

"What?"

"Sorry."

"I thought what a fun surprise it would be for her too. So I dropped onto the bench beside her and kissed her on the cheek."

"And it wasn't her."

Wide-eyed, Bunko shook his head slowly. "No, it wasn't."

"On the plus side, I bet you were right about her being surprised."

"Oh, she was surprised all right, though not nearly as much as her fiancé who was at that moment coming back from talking to a server."

"Uh-oh. What sort of person was that?"

"Large-ish. Resembled one of those pipe fitter fellows who work out in the terraforming projects. You see them around. What exactly do pipe fitters do anyway, Pelham?"

"I have it on good authority, old pal, that they fit pipes together."

"That makes sense … which is more than the fiancé thought of my story."

"What did he say?"

"It's all a bit of a blur. And some of it I wouldn't want to repeat."

"Did he punch you?"

"I managed to keep a table or two between us while I tried to explain. The female — the one who wasn't Holly — told him it must have been a mix-up because, when it happened, I looked about as stunned as she was. That helped a little. The owner was getting ready to call the guards when I legged it."

"You were lucky to make your escape in one piece, my lad."

"Don't I know it?" Bunko glanced again toward the restaurant. "Which is why I really shouldn't loiter around here. What if they come out? What if she waves or something? I think I'll shove off, Pelham."

"Good idea."

"Give my best to Blandings. I'll never forget the way he extricated me from that difficulty with my father."

"As I recall, it was a nifty piece of sleight of hand."

"Absolutely. Not to mention the shrewd psychology. Blandings knew the exact right buttons to push with the old codger. Well, toodle-pip."

With one more hurried peep toward the door of the café, Bunko set off down the street. Pelham strolled in the other direction toward the tunnel that led to his apartment building, still chewing over Bunko's hilarious story.

He strode in his front door, tossed his hat onto a table, and slumped into a chair.

Blandings appeared and said, "Sir, you made it home early. I have fresh clothes laid out for you."

"I've had quite the morning, Blandings."

"Tea? I have some freshly brewed."

"Please."

Moments later, Blandings appeared beside the chair with the drink on a tray. "I take it the meeting with the Gray proved to be trying?"

"It was exhausting, Blandings. In the first place, I didn't know where to look. Did you know they don't wear clothes?" Pelham took a sip.

"I did, sir."

"You might have warned me."

"My apologies, sir."

"What about this, Blandings? Did you know that their … um … well …" Pelham waved a hand in the direction of his nether regions.

"Do you mean to indicate … private parts, sir?"

"I do. Or lack thereof."

"Yes, sir, I was aware."

"You might have prepared me for that too, Blandings."

"I did think to mention it, sir, but it proved to be a problematic topic to bring up."

"I'm sure it was. What about the way they talk inside your head? Did you know about that?"

"Yes, sir."

"Nearly gave me a headache."

"I am sorry to hear of it, sir."

"Then to top it all off, I had to deal with Keezo here."

Blandings was silent for a beat. "Who, sir?"

"Keezo. The little person who came in with me. We found him … or it, I suppose … hiding among the power converters." Pelham twisted in his chair. "Now where did he … or whatever … run off to?"

"I saw no one enter with you, sir."

"Well, Keezo can be tricky to see, Blandings. Has this strange ability to camouflage himself … or itself. Dash it all, it's tricky to even talk about the little critter. You see, Keezo is Danánn."

"I see, sir. Yes, then Keezo is not any of the common galactic genders … at least as far as scientists on Danánn have been able to determine. Though I rather wonder if they have given the matter sufficient study."

"Ah, you know about Danánns too, eh, Blandings?"

"A bit, sir."

Pelham called out. "Keezo, you can appear. It's all right. This is Blandings. He's a friend. He's going to help you. There's no need to hide. Do you see anything yet, Blandings?"

"No, sir."

Pelham heaved a sigh and hauled himself from the chair. He squinted and swept his eyes around the room. "Keezo?"

He trudged through the kitchen and both bedrooms, calling out, "Keezo." Pelham re-entered the sitting room, scratching his cheek.

"May I ask, sir, when you last saw Keezo?"

"Let's see. I introduced him … and by him, I mean … well …"

"Yes, sir. I understand. You could try saying *them*."

"Them? I introduced them?" Pelham shrugged. "It might work. Anyway, I introduced Keezo to Bunko."

"I see. How is Mr. Tiddlesley, sir?"

"That question, Blandings, is open to debate. By the by, he sends his regards. He remains grateful for your past endeavors. Keezo? Where are you, Keezo?"

"Sir, I wonder. Did you happen to speak with Mr. Tiddlesley for some time?"

"A few minutes, I suppose. He had an interesting story to tell. You see, he was in this eatery—"

"Pardon the interruption, sir, but did you note Keezo's presence with you at any time after you and Mr. Tiddlesley parted company?"

Pelham felt a shiver run down his spine. He looked up and gazed into his valet's face. "Blandings, you don't think I lost the little guy … and by guy, I mean—"

"No need to explain, sir. And yes, I regret to say there appears to be a lost Danánn running about Sonus."

Chapter 9

The Search for Keezo

Pelham staggered back a step. His hand reached behind him for the arm of the couch, and gripping it, he sat. "Keezo is running around Sonus unchaperoned? What have I done, Blandings? Are Danánn dangerous? Do they bite?"

"I assure you, sir, they do not bite," Blandings said in a reassuring tone. "It is my understanding that they are herbivorous."

"Ha!"

"Sir?"

"I'll say it again, Blandings. Ha! For once, you are sorely misinformed. Keezo told me, and I quote, 'Bugs is good.' What do you have to say about that?"

"Fascinating. However, I still believe the risk of Keezo biting a Haplor to be low given our size compared to insects."

"Ah, but how large are the insects on Danánn?"

"On that point, sir, I would need to refresh my memory. Would you like me to research it?"

"Not at the moment." He thought about Keezo wandering the streets of Sonus alone. The little alien had looked so frightened and lost when it had first scampered out from the power converters, so hopeful and trusting when Pelham had said he would help. He couldn't leave the little critter out there. "Blandings, we have to find Keezo."

"Yes, sir. I am certain that can be accomplished. Sonus is, after all, a small colony. Someone will have seen something. We can call the guard service if we need to."

"Oh, I'd rather not do that. I spoke to a bloke on Danánn who said the species had some special status or other. The upshot was that I was supposed to return Keezo back there forthwith or else run afoul of the law. I do not wish to be arrested ... again."

"Then we shall return Keezo as soon as they can be found."

"No, scratch that. I promised Keezo I … well, it's a longish story, Blandings."

"Then I suggest, sir, you tell it to me on the way." Blandings snatched a bowler hat from a peg on the wall and slipped it on.

Pelham nodded. With some effort, he pulled himself from the couch. Together they headed out the door.

As they strode through the tunnels. Pelham filled Blandings in on the details of Tunna and the little and how Keezo had seemingly wandered onto the Gray ship. Periodically in his storytelling, Pelham paused to call out, "Keezo," his voice echoing through the underground space. But he received no response other than a few annoyed side-eye glances from passersby.

When they ascended to street level, Pelham said, "It was near here that I spoke with Bunko.

"Where specifically?" Blandings asked.

Pelham looked around. "It was … It was … ah, over there, a few doors down from yon diner, from which Bunko had beat a hasty retreat. I'll need to tell you that story too, Blandings. Sometime when we find ourselves with a bit of leisure."

"Yes, sir. And what was Keezo doing while you and Mr. Tiddlesley chatted?"

"Oh, Keezo was around. I recall the little critter yanking on my trouser leg a few times."

"To what end?"

"The cuffed end, of course. Keezo can't reach very high. But let me tell you, Blandings, such was the vigor of said tugs that they were starting to have an adverse effect on the end up around my waist. I thought I was about to lose my bally britches."

"Most disturbing. However, what I was seeking, sir, was an explanation of Keezo's intent. Why tug on your trousers?"

"Ah. He … or they wanted to know what something was. This Keezo is an inquisitive little chappie, anxious to learn all about our culture it would appear."

"Do you remember, sir, what was the subject of the inquiry?"

Pelham again looked around at the neighborhood. "There it is. That bakery."

"Oh dear." Blandings started across the street toward the shop.

"What do you mean, Blandings?" Pelham asked, following.

"The Danánn are known, sir, for their prodigious appetites."

"Now that you mention it, Keezo did say something about being hungry. You don't think ..." Pelham didn't finish the thought. The sight in front of them finished it for him.

The sign over the bakery door said: *Rolling in the Dough*. The shop window displayed an assortment of baked delights, though truth be told, they were not at present being exhibited to their best advantage.

A tray of cookies was tipped on its side. A loaf of bread had a hole bored through it. Muffin papers were scattered everywhere. Doughnuts that were not designed to have holes in them did have holes or corners eaten off. A three-layer cake, with a tunnel of huge bites undermining its foundation, listed to one side. A smear of meringue ran down the front glass in a snail-like trail.

Pelham and Blandings stopped in front of the window and surveyed the damage.

"Sir."

"Blandings, you don't suppose ..."

"I think it a reasonable supposition, sir."

They rushed through the shop door, skirting around overturned display tables, stepping over bits of baguette, chunks of cupcakes, scraps of strudel. The price board on the wall hung askew and leaned several degrees forward as if threatening to belly flop onto the floor at any moment. Behind the counter, the baker sat on a stool in apparent shell shock, staring mutely at the mess.

She looked up with an unfocused expression and said in a monotone, "May I help you? Oh, hello, Mr. Blandings."

"Good day, ma'am," Blandings said.

"No," she said distractedly, peering around the shop as if she didn't recognize the place. "No, I don't believe it is. This hasn't been a good day at all. Sorry about the mess, gentlemen. Everything is half off today."

Pelham picked up a glazed twist donut with most of the twist nibbled away. "Literally half off in some cases, what?"

The baker stared at him blankly. "Hmm?"

Pelham's chest tightened with guilt. "Still, that's quite the bargain, eh? I was thinking, Blandings, we might stock up ...um ... under the circs."

"Very good, sir. We will take two dozen of the broken gingersnaps."

"Pre-snapped." Pelham tried on a chuckle, but it didn't fit. "Or even three dozen, Blandings."

"Yes, sir. Three dozen. Could you have them delivered? We are on something of a mission at present."

The baker nodded mutely.

"Tell me, what caused the damage?" Blandings asked innocently.

The baker gazed up wild-eyed. "It ... it came in when a customer opened the door to leave."

"What did?" Pelham asked. "What was it?"

"I ... I don't know. Black. Hairy. Small, though its appetite was large enough. It swallowed macarons whole. It tore through cakes and pies like a buzz saw. It burrowed a channel through my scones. At one point, I swear a small tornado of powdered sugar formed above a doughnut tray."

"Golly." Pelham plucked a beignet from the top of a smashed pie and popped it in his mouth. "Mmm. Good. Put it on our tab. And add a dozen of these or as many as you can locate."

"When I yelled at it, it disappeared. But incredibly, items kept being devoured. Tarts, cinnamon rolls, muffins. Finally, another customer came in, and whatever it was rolled out the door like ... like a hurricane moving on up the coast."

"Did you happen to catch in which direction it went?"

The baker's face scrunched into a question. "Why? Are you looking to track down discounts at other shops?"

Blandings said, "We were hoping to capture the creature."

"Good luck. It'll be on a sweetcane high now." The baker waived a weary hand. "It may have gone that way. I caught sight of people staggering as if pushed by something."

"Thank you. I believe you have our address for the delivery. And again, so sorry for what happened."

Blandings and Pelham rushed from the shop and down the street, stopping only to question passersby.

"Have you seen a small creature without arms running around?" Pelham asked a male in business attire with a bushy white mustache.

"What in the moon are you talking about?" the male asked.

"A little one. He ... or it, rather, might be a bit hard to spot. More like a shimmer."

The businessperson shook his head dismissively and walked on.

"No?" Pelham asked. "Well, have a nice day."

A female holding the hand of a youngling hurried past.

Pelham asked, "Excuse me, ma'am. Have you by chance seen a little furry creature with big feet and long thingies hanging down?" Using his fingers, he pantomimed tentacles hanging from his jaw.

"Is something like that running loose?" the female asked, eyes wide and unblinking.

"Nothing so threatening, I assure you," Blandings said.

Pelham said, "But seriously. Have you seen it … or anything odd?"

The female sneered. "Do you think I would be out and about with my child if I had noticed something like that?"

"I saw it, Mummy," the youngling said.

"Not now, Oliver. I'm speaking with these gentlemen."

"But I saw it. A little creature with things hanging down."

"Oliver, it isn't nice to make up stories."

"But I did, Mummy. It ran past us when we were beside the Broadstone store."

"Oliver."

"It was black and came up to my waist and had big, big eyes."

Pelham said, "That does sound like it."

The female started pulling the youngling away. "Sorry."

"Which way, Olie?" Pelham called. "Which way did it go?"

The youngling pointed down the street in the opposite direction.

"Let's go, Blandings."

They set off, questioning anyone who would talk with them but getting little to no information.

At a street corner, they came upon an old female selling bundles of cut flowers. Pelham rushed up to her and tipped his hat.

She nodded back. "Looking for some flowers to bring home to the missus?"

"What? Um … no, I'm not married."

"The lovely lass you're seeing then."

"Well, actually, I'm not seeing anyone."

Blandings stepped forward. "We would like to buy a bundle of rosanthemums, red, if you please."

The flower seller smiled. "Here you go, sir. Thank you very much." She handed Blandings the flowers as he passed her a payment stick.

"And some information if you have it," Blandings said. "A small creature has escaped, and we are trying to recapture it."

"Goodness me. It is dangerous?"

Pelham said, "Only to pastries. It's about yay high, black fur with tendrils—"

"I believe, sir, the proper term is tentacles," Blandings said. "Tendrils grow on plants."

"You don't say, Blandings. All very interesting but not germane at present. By the by, is *germane* the word I want?"

"It is, sir."

"Good. But to return to the matter at hand, this creature has …" He glanced at Blandings. "… tentacles hanging down from its jawline. If it has a jawline. Difficult to say with all that fur."

By this time, the flower seller's eyes had grown as wide as tea saucers. "Blimey. You know, I did see it. It shot past here a few minutes ago."

"Did you see where it went?" Pelham asked.

She pointed a finger. "It ran into the music hall there. Didn't even buy a ticket."

Blandings said, "Thank you," and hurried to catch up with Pelham, who was already heading for the ticket window.

As they entered, Blandings tipped his hat to a female usher and handed her the flowers. The theater was immense with hundreds of seats on the floor, a full balcony, and rows of boxes along the side. On stage, a Haplor female was singing a bawdy song about a female from Antares Five who danced the can-can and the jive.

As she finished and the audience burst into rowdy applause, Pelham whispered, "Do you see Keezo?"

"No, sir. And I fear Keezo may be difficult to spot in such a huge crowd."

Then a high-pitched voice floated over the clapping and cheers. "Funny! Funny!" It came from somewhere toward the front of the auditorium.

"But perhaps not so difficult to hear, eh, Blandings? This way."

They edged down the aisle as another act took the stage. This one featured a small Haplor male with a long, sad face, who was being threatened by a much larger Haplor while the two of them sat at a table.

Pelham stopped and nudged his valet. "I've seen this one, Blandings. Watch what happens."

"Down in the front," someone yelled.

They slid into a pair of empty seats.

The big Haplor on stage rose from his chair and leaned across the table, shaking a fist at the little one. The small Haplor jumped up on his chair and bounded across the table onto the big Haplor's back and then up onto a bookshelf. He slid down a curtain to the floor and bounded to an armchair and over the wall out of the scene.

The audience exploded with laughter. A few rows ahead of where Pelham and Blandings sat, the silhouette of a small figure jumped up and down, tentacles flapping in the air. Blandings bobbed his head in that direction.

Pelham rushed to the row, knelt beside it, and called in a stage whisper, "Keezo."

"Pelie! You is see funny Big? Big is go up and out."

"I did, Keezo. Fantastic show, what? Let's get you to the flat."

"Keezo is want to see show."

"I think you've seen plenty."

"Show is funny. I is want to stay."

"If you come along, I'll get you something to eat."

"Okey dokey." Keezo began climbing across people toward the aisle.

They objected with groans and howls.

"Ow!"

"Hey!"

"Oi! What's all this?"

Keezo said, "I is like Big on stage. I go over people."

"Sorry," Pelham said. "Sorry. Keezo's not from around here."

Chapter 10

Blandings has a Suggestion

Keezo hopped up and down in the theater aisle with excitement. "Pelie, is you see? Is you see? Big is come out and is throw many fruitses in air and is catch and throw and catch and throw. Is you see, Pelie?"

Pelham glanced around at the crowd. Disapproving scowls were being thrown in his direction.

"Hush that thing," somebody hissed from a few rows back.

"Shhh," Pelham whispered to Keezo, patting the little Danánn on the head. He hoped the gesture would have a calming effect. But after a bakery full of goodies and the thrills of the music hall, how could it?

"Yes, Keezo, I've seen this show myself a time or two ... or three."

This production was, in truth, one of Pelham's favorites, and he was pleased Keezo had enjoyed the stage show. But the little creature was exhibiting far too much exuberance even for the rowdy crowd of a Sonus theater.

Keezo's eyes danced. "Then lots of Bigs is come. They is jump and swing and walk on rope up high. So scary."

"Shut your gob!" someone shouted. "We're trying to enjoy the show."

Someone else yelled, "Which ain't so easy given these acts."

The crowd laughed at the comment, easing some of the tension.

Pelham reached down to bundle Keezo up in his arms, but the Danánn slipped out and twirled around in the aisle.

"And much singing of songs I not is understand. Pelie, what is ... floozy?"

Pelham yanked the alien toward him. "Hold your voice down."

"Quit your yapping," someone else hollered. A red and black servo unit sailed down from the balcony and bounced at Pelham's feet.

Pelham ducked nearer the line of seats. "I believe, Keezo, it is time we make our exit. Come along. Hold my hand."

Keezo waved a couple of tentacles in his direction.

Pelham's fingers recoiled. "On second thought ..." He leaned over and picked Keezo up in his arms.

"Sit down," someone yelled.

"Just leaving," Pelham called.

The comedian on the stage glared after them. "There they go, folks ... finally. But they'll be performing later — a special ventriloquist act where both of them play the dummy."

The audience burst into laughter and applause. Pelham waved without looking back and hustled up the aisle to where Blandings was waiting.

In the lobby, Pelham set Keezo on the floor and wiped a hand across his forehead. "What an unnerving experience. By the by, Blandings, the little critter is surprisingly heavy. Must be all the pastries, what?"

"Perhaps, sir," Blandings said. "However, I do think we should carry Keezo home rather than risk losing them again."

"You're probably right." Pelham rubbed his arm. "You can take your turn first."

"As you wish, sir, though I should point out that before I take such a liberty, Keezo and I should be formally introduced."

"Ah, yes. I quite see your point. Keezo does seem a bit standoffish with new people. Performs a disappearing act. Keezo, this is Blandings."

"Hello, Bandy," Keezo said. "I is Keezo."

Pelham shot his valet a smile. "You'll find, Blandings, that Keezo is not always accurate on pronunciations. Blandings, this is Keezo. Say hello to my little friend."

"A pleasure to make your acquaintance," Blandings said, inclining his head. "Would it be acceptable, Keezo, if I carried you? We have a long walk ahead of us."

Keezo leaped into the valet's arms. "Bandy, in show I is see a Big in tall, black hat. Is make bird appear from nothing."

"Yes. Quite entertaining, I'm sure. Sir, I advise we set out at once. With luck, Keezo may run down by the time we reach our door."

Unfortunately, this proved to be a rare instance when Blandings was wrong. Keezo was still going on about the dancers and singers and other acts in the show when they walked through the door of the flat.

Keezo hopped to the carpet and gawked around at the place with wide eyes. "Pelie and Bandy live here? This is Pelie's mound? This is flat place?"

"That is correct, Keezo," Blandings said, "roughly speaking."

Keezo stared at the carpet. "Ground is flat ... and woolly. Wallses is flat. The alien's eyes tilted toward the ceiling. "Top is flat. Lots of flat is here."

"Yes, yes, Keezo." Pelham dropped into a chair as Keezo streaked off into Pelham's bedroom. "Blandings, how can such a small creature spout this many words? My ears ache from all the listening. Is it bedtime yet? I'm exhausted."

"It is yet late afternoon, sir."

"Astounding."

Keezo dashed back into the sitting room. "Pelie's mound is big."

The alien bounced across the furniture, sending pillows flying through the room. Keezo climbed the bookshelves, books and other items getting shoved off onto the carpets. Blandings managed to catch the more breakable ones. Using tentacles to pull, Keezo climbed straight up the wall, knocking pictures askew. Soon the normally impeccably tidy flat looked like a scene from a news vid of a dreadful storm.

"What is this, Pelie?"

"That's a vase that belonged to my mother, Keezo," Pelham said wearily. "Please don't touch it."

"What that?"

"What? Oh, that's a trophy I won back in my school days for the five-dashlength race."

"What that?"

Pelham dropped his head to his hand "And all that energy, Blandings. Good luck getting Keezo to sleep after all the sweets and the excitement of the ..." Pelham looked up to find the valet gone from the room. "Blandings?"

"Sir?" Blandings glided in from the kitchen carrying a glass on a tray.

"Ah, thank you, Blandings? Amurru fizz? You read my mind."

"No, sir. This is for Keezo."

"An Amurru fizz for Keezo? I shouldn't think that would be a good idea, Blandings."

"You misapprehend, sir. This is not alcoholic."

"Surely, it's not your hangover cure. As you can plainly see, the little creature already has sufficient vim. A fair bit too much, in my estimation. Keezo most definitely does not need a pick-me-up."

"No, sir. The drink should, in fact, have the opposite effect."

"You don't say. That's all right then."

Keezo ran a circuit around Pelham's chair, leaping over the Haplor's knees without breaking stride. Blandings snatched Keezo from the air and presented the beverage. "Keezo, drink this, please."

"Okey dokey." Keezo wrapped several tentacles around it and took a tentative sip followed by a large gulp to drain the glass. Blandings set Keezo on the couch. The Danánn blinked twice and leaned back against the cushion with a sigh.

"Blandings, you're a miracle worker," Pelham said.

"Thank you for saying so, sir. It is much appreciated."

"Not at all, Blandings. Not at all."

Pelham shut his eyes and relaxed back against the chair. What a day, he thought. The ridiculously early morning, the unclad Gray talking inside his head, finding and losing and then finding Keezo once more. Not to mention trying to get a lead on what happened to Tunna and the little one. Pelham's eyes clicked open again. "Blandings."

"Sir?"

"What are we going to do about Keezo's missing partner and their youngling?"

"Am I correct, sir, in assuming that you wish to help Keezo find them?"

"I do, Blandings. I gave my word."

The valet turned to the small alien, who was now sitting peacefully on the couch, tentacles gently waving like so many flags in a light breeze. "Keezo, did Tunna get on the ship with you?"

Keezo blinked. "What is ... ship?"

Pelham and Blandings shared a look.

Pelham said, "The place with the power converters."

"What is ... pow verters?"

"The place with the Grays and the ramp."

"Ramp? You mean sloping thing?"

"Yes, Keezo. That's it."

Keezo nodded slowly. "Tunna go up ramp with Keezo."

Blandings said, "Then Tunna is not back on Danánn. The logical course, sir, would be to follow the Gray ship, searching along the way. I believe you said it had stops on Unara and Tucana Three."

"Yes, and then they were returning to the Gray home world."

Blandings' brows furrowed. "Hopefully, we can find Tunna on one of the Haplor colonies without having to visit the Gray world."

"Why? What's the matter with the Gray world?"

Blandings' head tilted to one side. "Nothing, sir. Though I doubt you would enjoy encountering thousands of Grays, shall we say, dressed in the same manner as the one you met today."

Pelham shuddered. "Undressed, you mean. Indeed, I would not. But there is a flaw in your plan, Blandings."

"Is there, sir? What is it?"

"I can't miss work. Aunt Agutha would have my head on a platter. Or were you thinking, Blandings, that you would make the rounds without me?" Pelham rather liked the sound of that, getting Keezo out of his head fur sooner rather than later. True, he might struggle to fix his own breakfast of a morning without Blandings around. On the other hand, it would be decidedly more peaceful.

"No, sir. I believe we should both go."

"Ah. Too bad ... I mean, what then? What about my work responsibilities?"

"It occurred to me, sir, that your aunt, the governor, might be amenable to a proposal of you taking a tour of the other Haplor colonies for the purpose of expanding trade and mutual support. Indeed, she might find it a commendable display of initiative on your part."

"Aunt Agutha find something praiseworthy about yours truly? That'll be the day. But I think you're onto something there, Blandings. Let me make sure I grasp the salient points. You propose I approach Aunt Agutha — and may I say, Blandings, that right there I find something I don't much care for — but I approach her and suggest I tour some of the other Haplor colonies."

"Yes, sir."

"To talk to them about how we could mutually assist each other."

"Precisely, sir."

"Trade and such, which is, of course, my job, if I'm not mistaken."

"It is, sir."

"And while we're there on those other worlds, we try to locate Tunna and the youngling."

"Yes, sir."

"You know, Blandings, that might work. Yes, I'll ask her first thing tomorrow."

"As you wish, sir," Blandings said.

Pelham caught a hint of disappointment in Blandings' tone.

"What is it, Blandings?"

"Well, sir, although Keezo is currently in a tranquil state, I am not at all certain how long we can maintain that disposition."

"Can't you pour more of that miracle concoction of yours down his throat ... its throat, I mean?"

"I fear such a practice would not be advisable from either a medical or an ethical standpoint."

"We shouldn't be going about drugging aliens overly much, you mean."

"Precisely, sir."

"Then, I take it, you think I should ask Aunt Agutha about the trip sooner?"

"I do, sir."

"But surely not tonight. I'm knackered."

"I am afraid so, sir."

"You want me to disturb her at home?" This scheme was sounding more and more doubtful. "Wouldn't that be akin to waking a hibernating roonaceros?"

"I do not believe that to be the case, sir. I happened to run into Benton at the market yesterday morning."

"Aunt Agutha's butler?"

"Yes, sir. And he informed me that your aunt recently expressed a certain eagerness for some dinner company."

"That's odd."

"It seems she has been having some trouble of late with your uncle."

"Uncle Spence? Well, he always was a bit of an odd egg, and of course, now that he's getting up there in years ..." Pelham waggled his head and let the sentence finish itself.

"Indeed. I judge, sir, that if you sent the governor a message asking if you could dine with her to discuss an idea, she would readily agree."

Pelham thought it over. "You may be right, Blandings. Then again. To willingly subject myself to an evening with Aunt Agutha. I go all dizzy inside just thinking about it."

"I understand, sir. I might point out that the alternative would be to spend the evening with Keezo. I expect our guest to recover relatively soon and resume previous activities."

"Egad. You're right, Blandings. Send off the message to my aunt."

"Yes, sir. I took the liberty of doing so while I was in the kitchen. You are expected there within the hour."

Chapter 11

Uncle Spence's New Hobby

Given the limited space under the Sonus dome, few housing units were designed for single families. Like Pelham, most people lived in apartment buildings. One exception was the governor's residence, which was set at the end of the central street against the side of the dome. While it would be an exaggeration to call it a mansion, the house was by far the most elegant and spacious dwelling in the colony.

Pelham came up from the tunnels and strolled the short distance to the imposing entryway. Leaning over to the speaker set into the wall, he said, "Pelham G. Totleigh."

While he waited, he admired the tall double wooden doors made with lumber brought from Haplor and the surrounding stone arch that was shaped from rock mined in the initial digging on the moon back in his grandfather's time.

As he continued to wait, he noted the graceful light above the door, the imposing pavers at his feet, the ever-present planet Nuggies above the dome.

He was running out of things to notice and about to press the speaker button again when the door finally creaked open to reveal the well-lined visage and impeccable appearance of Benton, who had been Aunt Agutha's butler for as long as Pelham could remember.

"Good evening, Mr. Totleigh," Benton said with a shaky voice. "Please, come in."

Pelham stepped into the entry hall while the aged butler shuffle-stepped to close the door behind him. "Good evening, Benton. How are you doing?"

"I am fine, sir. Thank you for asking. Mr. Rainsby is in the parlor."

Pelham lowered his voice. "How is the old turnip? I heard something about Aunt Agutha having a bit of a time with him."

A look of suppressed shock filled Benton's face. "Oh no, sir. Rest assured, Mr. Rainsby is in fine health as always."

With embarrassment, Pelham realized he should not have said anything. What the hired help share with each other might be one thing, but of course, someone of Benton's propriety — not to mention vintage — would never let anything slip to the general public.

"Thank you, Benton. You may go. I'm sure I can find my way to the parlor." Pelham didn't want to make the geriatric butler traipse all over the house.

Having nothing of it, Benton said in an aggrieved tone, "I will be happy to announce you, sir."

He turned and began doddering down the hall. Pelham followed, forced to employ a step-stop, step-stop footwork pattern to keep from striding past the oldster.

They eventually entered the parlor where Uncle Spence sat in a chair scowling through a magnifying glass at a tablet device. His head fur stuck out in every direction in wild, white tuffs. An elbow peeked out from a hole in his sweater, and he wore threadbare slippers on his feet.

"Mr. Pelham G. Totleigh, your nephew, sir," Benton announced before shambling off.

"What ho, Uncle Spence," Pelham said cheerily.

The old geezer looked up. "What?"

"It's me, Pelham, nephew at large. I'm here visiting the relatives, as it were, by which I mean you."

"What? Oh, hello, Pelham."

"How have you been, Uncle?" Without waiting for a formal invitation, which Pelham thought might or might not come if Spence was, in truth, growing a touch potty, he took a seat in a chair that shared a side table with his uncle's chair.

Pelham gazed around at the room. The same wallpaper as always. An abundance of throw pillows and crocheted blankets. Knick-knacks here and there ... and there and there too. Doilies pinned to the chair arms. It all worked to give the room a sense of fussiness.

"Oh, you know how it is," Uncle Spence said. "My hearing isn't what it used to be. My neck is stiff all the time. I wake up at least five times in the night. I rose from bed this morning with a pain in one knee for no discernable reason. I tell you, Pelham, aging is not for the faint of heart."

"I'm sorry to hear all that, Uncle Spence," Pelham said. And he *was* sorry, both that the old bird felt so poorly and also that he, Pelham, had been subjected to the detailed account. He started to add something to the effect that at least Uncle Spence had life, but he remembered how the aged relative had to spend said life with Aunt Agutha and decided to let it pass.

"Of course, there are compensations to retirement," Spence said. "I have more time and wealth to devote to hobbies."

"Such as?"

"I've started collecting Earth artifacts."

"Do tell."

"Yes, yes. Here's one of them I just picked up." Spence reached for a clear globe attached to a base. Inside stood a tiny alien-looking house with a steeply pitched roof. Beside it rose a miniature tree, the branches green but tipped with white. "Now watch this." He flipped the thing upside down and then right side up again. A flurry of white particles floated through the globe.

Pelham laughed. "That's marvelous. Is that supposed to represent snow?" He had seen snow as a youngling when he attended school on the Haplor home world, where they had enough atmosphere to make weather.

"According to the Grays, yes."

"I take it then it snows on Earth."

"It must. Since they're quarantined, they wouldn't know about snow unless they had it."

"Why are you interested in Earth objects, Uncle?"

Spence chuckled. "I don't know. Why does anybody collect anything? I suppose it's the mystery of a forbidden planet. I never understood why Earth was quarantined anyway."

"I thought it was because they were, you know, a bit of a mess … fighting among themselves and all that. Though I don't think they're all like that. Did I ever tell you, Uncle, I met an Earthling once?"

Spence seemed not to hear him. "They didn't quarantine the Thomians, and they're a bunch of thugs and criminals."

"That's true. You know, the Earthling I met was a likable enough chap."

"I tell you, Pelham, I've become rather pro-Earth of late … as I've looked into their culture. Did you know they have a food called not-chose? It has crispy, salty chips covered in a cheese sauce. I got a little of it from the Grays. So good. Any society that can produce something like not-chose is all right in my book."

"I've had Earth waffles. They're scrumptious. That Earth fellow I met gave—
"

Spence talked on. "There's another of my pieces hanging on the wall over there."

Pelham gawked at the framed print. "What is it?"

"That, my lad, is a famous piece of Earth art. It shows a group of Earthlings playing a game called Poke Her."

"Those aren't Earthlings, Uncle Spence."

"Of course, they are."

"Earthlings don't have floppy ears and long noses. And I'm relatively sure they don't have tails. They also wear more clothes than just those collars."

"Piffle, Pelham."

"Whatever you say, Uncle."

Spence picked up the magnifying glass from the side table and the tablet from his lap. "Now, do you see this? This is the next piece I'd like to acquire."

Pelham stared at the screen, unsure of what he was seeing. Judging by the shape of it, it might be a leg of some species. It stood in a shoe that had a tall, thin heel and a sloping sole. The leg was essentially bare except for the merest bit of netting stretched tightly around it. A glowing, fringy cone covered the top.

"What is it?" Pelham asked.

"It's a lamp, a leg lamp. It's an Earth relic."

"And you'd like to add this to your collection? Has Aunt Agutha seen it? I only ask because … well, it seems to have a rather stirring effect on a fellow."

"That's because it's a religious artifact, Pelham."

"It doesn't strike me as particularly spiritual."

"Well, it is. Reputedly, it's tied to an Earth religious holiday. The Grays say the Earthlings put them in their windows. Something about it symbolizing light shining through the darkness to guide people along on pilgrimages."

"If this is supposed to be someone out in the cold," Pelham said, "you'd think they'd wear trousers. And I doubt this shoe with the pointy heel would be overly comfortable for walking long distances."

"Well, that's Earthlings for you. Strange people, the Earthlings."

"Did I ever tell you I once met one, Uncle?"

"This particular leg lamp is in a group of pieces recently picked up by the Grays."

"Ah, righto. I've heard that they take merchandise from the Earthlings. Can't say I much approve of that sort of thing."

Spence shrugged. "The Grays say the galactic alliance doesn't pay them enough to cover the expense of monitoring Earth, leaving them in need of supplemental income."

"One tried to sell me some dates today."

"What are dates?"

"Some variety of fruit. Do you suppose it likewise was stolen?"

"Difficult to say. I prefer to think they leave some kind of remuneration behind on Earth when they take things." He turned back to the listing for the leg lamp with a wistful smile.

Pelham said, "Well, if that's what you want, Uncle, and assuming Aunt Agutha will allow it through the door of her home, I say go for it. It might be exactly what this room needs."

"I would, but ..." He shook his head.

"But what?"

"It's part of a consignment of Earth bits and bobs that were delivered to Unara, which means Sallow will probably end up with it."

"Who?" Pelham asked.

"Sallow. Oswald Sallow. Surely, you've heard of him."

"I don't think I have."

Uncle Spence looked at Pelham as if his nephew had said he'd never heard of air.

"Don't you keep up on current events?"

"Not particularly. I keep up on the latest shows."

"Sallow is a vidcaster," Uncle Spence said the word with a face like he was sucking on the terminal of a power converter. "Has a huge following by all accounts, mostly spouting rubbish, anti-alien tirades. He thinks Haplors are the best species in the galaxy."

"Well, we have done pretty well for ourselves, what? Colonies and automated carriages and all that."

"Sure, but that doesn't mean Rhegedians and Bononians and the others aren't more or less just as good. We've all accomplished plenty to reach the stars and meet each other. But Sallow has some crazy theory that some of the other species are full of replicants who have infiltrated in from a parallel universe and are bent on destroying us."

"What?"

"Exactly."

"But if this Sallow character dislikes aliens, why would he want to buy an Earthling leg light?"

"It's a leg lamp. And the reason is that he's completely obsessed with Earth. I think it started from fear. The galactic alliance reevaluated Earth's status a few years back, and Sallow was one of the leading voices against lifting the quarantine."

"What was his reason?"

"He gave hundreds of reasons. Most of them didn't make much sense. I think the real reason was that stirring people up against something was a good way to draw more viewers to his vidcast, which meant more advertising money for him."

Pelham scratched at a cheek while he tried to think that through. He had never really got the hang of money and the myriad ways people accumulated it. He had inherited a sizeable pile of it when his parents passed, and since he always had enough, he rarely gave it a second thought.

Spence said, "Of course, to come up with his lamebrain excuses for not lifting the quarantine, Sallow had to do some actual research into Earth. I think he came to admire some aspects of their culture."

"Well, they aren't all bad, you know. I met an Earthling one time, Uncle."

"And then he started collecting Earth artifacts. He keeps the Grays busy picking up knickknacks and baubles. That's probably why the current shipment went there."

"Where?"

"To Unara. It's where Sallow lives."

"Unara, the Haplor colony? Funny, Blandings and I were recently discussing the place."

The sound of shuffling feet came from the hall. Benton appeared in the doorway, somewhat out of breath from the trek. "Dinner is served."

Pelham followed Spence into the dining room. The large room sparkled with wall sconces and a huge chandelier. Around the walls, images of ancient ancestors stared back at him with stern faces.

At one end of a long ornate table sat Aunt Agutha, as stiff as steel and as unyielding as a boulder, each and every hair of her head fur hammered into place.

Uncle Spence moved to the seat at the opposite end. A place was set for Pelham in the middle. He slipped into the stiff, high-backed chair.

"Good evening, Auntie."

"Good evening, Pelham." She eyed him suspiciously. "So what have you bungled this time?"

"What? Nothing!"

She scoffed. "You haven't made a hash of something?"

"No. Of course not."

"You haven't misplaced vital imports?"

"Aunt Agutha, you wound me."

"You didn't make a hideous faux pas with the Gray captain, did you?"

"No. You might even say we had a meeting of the minds. Ha!"

"Hmm." She scowled at him "Then if it's not some ridiculous quagmire you've got yourself into, what does bring you here tonight, my idiotic nephew?"

Chapter 12

Dinner with Aunt Agutha

"What brings me here?" Pelham repeated the question, leaving out the part where Aunt Agutha called him an idiot.

His mouth went dry. He had been primed to recount Blandings' cover story of visiting other colonies with an eye toward greater trade links. Now under her steely gaze, he melted like a glob of butter in a hot pan.

He reached for his water glass and brought it two-handed to his mouth. He looked around the dining room table. Uncle Spence was fiddling with his napkin. Aunt Agutha was staring him down.

Would she really approve of him taking a few days off work? Or would the mere request open him up to more abuse?

"Oh, you know," Pelham said. "Just wanting to say hello and spend some time with the aged relatives."

Agutha scowled and cleared her throat pointedly.

He stammered, "Well, ... um ... *aged* isn't the right word I suppose, is it, Auntie? Sorry. Um ... ripened? No, that doesn't sound much better. Wizened? I mean, wise and experienced. That's it. Plus, it's been a while since I had some of Andros' excellent cooking." Pelham congratulated himself on successfully steering the conversation away from the purpose of his visit.

"We no longer employ Andros," she said, clipping the syllables.

"What? You don't?"

"Andros insisted on cooking with entirely too many spices. It was like a nightly criminal assault. Your poor uncle's digestion couldn't take it."

"I liked it fine," Spence said, smiling at a painting on the wall of a Haplorian landscape.

"You liked eating it. But then you'd be up half the night." Aunt Agutha shook her head and said conspiratorially to Pelham, "At Spencer's age he needs a simpler diet."

Pelham said, "Well, I admit I'm a tad disappointed. I was hoping for some of Andros' famous bactaren bourguignon."

Agutha dismissed the notion with a tsk.

"Or her flitterbird confit."

She waved it off.

"What?" Spence asked, looking up with a dazed expression. "Is that what we're having? That does sound good."

"No, dear." Aunt Agutha shot a glare in Pelham's direction, and he decided it might be best to stop listing delicious dishes of old.

Benton entered with slow, unsteady steps, clearly struggling to hold aloft a tray containing three bowls. Pelham resisted an urge to hustle around the table and give the old gaffer a hand, fearing both censure from his aunt and the embarrassment it would cause the butler. Benton slid the tray onto the table, then wheeled around with his back to the family to suck in several breaths. When he turned again, he straightened his vest and served the bowls.

Pelham ran his spork through the reddish liquid. It appeared to be soup, though it mainly consisted of broth with a few shriveled vegetables floating around like lonely fish in a pond. He waited until Aunt Agutha had sporked in a mouthful and then followed suit. To Pelham's astonishment, it had almost no taste.

"Ah," Agutha said, "isn't that better than all those pungent spices?"

"Righto," Pelham lied. "I always hate it when flavor gets in the way."

"I thought we were having flitterbird confit," Spence said.

Aunt Agutha shot Pelham another steely glare. "Now what shall we talk about?"

Swallowing, Pelham decided it was time to venture out on a limb and face the music. Which confused him for a moment. What kind of music would be located out on a tree limb? "Must be a bird," he said under his breath.

"Flitterbird?" Uncle Spence asked.

"No, Uncle, I was thinking of something else." He cleared his throat. "But um … well, since you wondered about a dinner topic, Auntie … um …"

"Out with it, Pelham," Aunt Agutha said.

"Yes, ma'am. Well, you see, I had something of a brainstorm."

"Did you now? Fortunately, a storm couldn't do much damage up there in that empty head of yours."

"What? Oh, ha! But you see, I was thinking about how ... well, we are a Haplor colony—"

"That has only now occurred to you?"

"Yes. I mean, no. I mean ... I mean ... we — and by we, I mean Sonus — we surely share needs and concerns with other Haplor colonies, such as ... well, to mention a few ... Unara, Tucana Three, Danánn, Unara."

"You said Unara twice."

"Did I? Well, I didn't want to overlook it. Anyway, I thought in my capacity as Director of Inputs—"

"Inspector of Imports, you ninny."

"Yes. That's it. It was on the tip of my tongue. In any event, I reckoned it might be beneficial for me to visit some of the other colonies to find out what they produce or have extra of that we might need and vice versa. Determine if we might help each other, as it were, what? High-level discussions and all that. Just a short visit. I wouldn't be gone long."

Aunt Agutha froze, spork in midair.

"Aunt Agutha?" Pelham asked. "Are you all right?"

"Aggie?" Uncle Spence called from the other end of the table.

She shook it off and made eye contact with Pelham. "Well, Nephew, I am flabbergasted."

"But ... but ... but, Auntie, please reconsider. I think the plan has several merits."

"As do I."

"But think of the possib ... What did you say?"

"I said, Pelham, the plan has merit."

"You did?"

"Yes."

"You do?"

"I do."

"You don't say."

For once, she wasn't calling him a fathead ... at least not explicitly. He was unsure of how to react. He wondered if he could find a way to exit quickly before she changed her mind.

"That is what has me puzzled, Nephew. How in the moon did someone of your limited intelligence ever come up with it? Are you sure this isn't one of Blandings' ideas?"

"Um … no. Or yes, rather. I mean, I thought of it."

"Not your assistant? What is his name?"

"Munson. No, I thought of it, Auntie." Pelham knocked knuckles against the side of his head. "These things come to me sometimes. Always thinking, what?"

"Really? I've never seen any signs of it previously."

"Ha. Ha."

"When would you want to make this trip?"

"Oh, soonish. Why not tomorrow?"

"And you have all your work caught up?"

Pelham thought about the stack of unsigned tablets on his desk. He shot her a toothy grin. "Absolutely. I'm sure Munson can take charge in my absence."

"I'm sure he can. All right, we'll speak of it more after dinner."

Pelham's heart sank. More talk? Just when he thought he was in the clear. He dreaded to think of what other points she might wish to make.

"Yes, Aunt Agutha." He went back to his soup.

Benton returned with a tray of plates, each containing an odd shaking, shimmering mass of something green. "Dessert."

The butler served the plates. Each of the green gelatinous mounds was circular, like a round tower with bits sticking up on the battlements. Chunks of something yellow hung suspended inside.

Pelham poked his with his silverspork, which set it quivering like some kind of frightened mountain. "What is it?"

"Ah," said Spence. "This, my lad, is a popular Earth dessert. It's called J Lo."

"J Lo? Why is it shaking like that? It's not alive, is it?"

"Of course, it's not alive. I found a recipe for it in an old Earth publication called the *Ladies' Home Journal*."

"A recipe? Do Earthlings have food replicators?"

"Not that kind of recipe. It isn't the molecular structure of the dish. It's a set of instructions for making it from ingredients by mixing and cooking and suchlike."

"Astounding."

Aunt Agutha said, "I can remember my mother doing all that back in the days before replicators were invented."

"Sounds like a dashed lot of work," Pelham said.

Spence said, "Thank goodness for translator bots, or else I couldn't even have read the bally thing. I had to make it once by hand following the recipe. Then I had the replicator deconstruct the whole thing and store the molecular structure. Now Benton can dial it up any time he wants."

Spence sporked a juddering bite into his mouth. He chewed, swallowed, and sighed with a satisfied expression. "It's quite tasty."

Pelham was skeptical, but not wishing to offend, he took a nibble. In no way could it compare to Andros' crème brûlée, but Pelham had to admit it wasn't bad.

As they finished, Aunt Agutha said, "Spencer, you go on into the parlor. I want to speak with Pelham alone for a moment."

Uncle Spence trudged off.

Pelham smiled at his aunt nervously and with foreboding.

"All right, Pelham, I'll make you a deal. You can go off on this tour of yours if you'll promise me two things."

He gulped. "Whatever you want, Aunt Agutha."

"First, don't be an idiot for once. Don't muck this up the way you've done nearly everything else in your short and mostly wasted life."

"Aunt Agutha, really——"

She raised a hand to silence him. "I'd like to leave our sibling colonies with a good impression of Sonus. Do you think you can manage that, Pelham?"

"Certainly, Aunt Agutha."

"You'd better take Blandings with you to advise you and keep you out of trouble."

"I wouldn't go without him, Auntie. Believe you me."

"Good. Now the second thing." She leaned in and lowered her voice. "Spencer has been obsessing over an Earth artifact."

"The light-up leg thingy?"

She cringed. "You've seen it? It's atrocious. It boggles the mind to think why he wants it."

"Well, I can see a slight appeal."

"You would. But while you're on Unara, I want you to buy it for your uncle. I want to give it to him for his birthday."

"Excellent idea. I know he'll love it."

She made a face. "I certainly won't love it. But sometimes in a marriage, one must give a little."

70

"So I've been told. One of the reasons I've been hesitant to take the plunge."

"It might do you some good, you know."

"To be married?"

"On the other hand, one should consider the sad fate of your marriage partner. How could anyone inflict on another sentient being the torment of living with you?"

"What? Oh, I think I'm fairly easy to get along with. Wait, is that right? I ended with a preposition there. Should one say easy with which along to get? That sounds worse. But in any case, Blandings manages to put up with me."

"You pay him."

"Handsomely. But don't worry a thing about the leg lamp, Auntie. Leave it all to me."

"I'd rather not."

"Pshaw. If there's one thing I can do, it's shop. I picked out this tie myself. What do you think of it?"

"I hate it. Looking at it is giving me a headache."

"Sorry." Blandings had said nearly the same thing. Pelham stuffed as much of the tie as he could into his jacket. "But fret not concerning the lamp. I'm sure I can handle it."

"You are, are you? It seems rather doubtful to me. But short of flying off to Unara myself, what choice do I have? As I understand it, the … artifact can be found in a curio shop there in the colony. There surely can't be more than one."

"Unless everyone on Unara is keen on curios. But I shouldn't think that would be the case."

"Do you even know what a curio is, Pelham?"

"It's a little doodad, a thingumabob, right?"

She shook her head. "I'll book your passage tomorrow."

"No need for that," Pelham said, remembering past trips when she had booked him into questionable accommodations. On one journey, he had even been forced to ride in the hold of a Donovian cargo ship. "I'll have Blandings take care of it."

Aunt Agutha reluctantly agreed, and that was the end of the inquisition. Pelham returned to the parlor to find Uncle Spence asleep in a chair. He left the governor's residence and made his way back through the tunnels.

When Pelham returned to the flat, he found it dark and reassuringly quiet. Something stirred on the couch as he entered.

"Sir?" A pajamaed Blandings rose to his feet.

"Is that you, Blandings?"

"Yes, sir."

"What the blazes are you doing out here?"

"Under the circumstances, I thought it wise to give Keezo my bed while I slept out here where I could keep an eye on things."

"As always, your reasoning is sound, Blandings, given what Keezo did to the place, not to mention the bakery."

"Yes, sir. Thank you, sir."

"All is quiet here then?"

"Keezo went to sleep easily. No doubt this was a trying day for our small guest."

"Righto. Losing track of this Tunna person, getting transported to a strange new world, sampling the delights of Sonus."

"Yes, sir. If I may inquire, were you able to obtain permission for our proposed journey?"

"Yes, Blandings. Aunt Agutha thought it a brainy idea. It almost left her speechless."

"Indeed?"

"I'll need to do a small favor for her in return. Run an errand of sorts. Oh, I nearly forgot. Please book us passage on something first thing in the morning."

"Yes, sir. I will be happy to do so."

"Aunt Agutha offered to handle the reservations, but … well, you know, Blandings, what she has stuck us in at times past."

"I do, sir. A wise precaution on your part. I will make the arrangements. Do you require anything else?"

"Not this evening. I'm ready to drop."

Pelham looked forward to several hours of blissful slumber, followed by a quick hop to another world. He thought they should easily be able to find Tunna, assuming this Tunna caused anywhere near the amount of kerfuffle that Keezo did. Then his life could return to normal patterns with valets sleeping in their own beds and all his keepsakes staying in their assigned places rather than getting chucked about the flat. And most of all, with Pelham not being forced to dine on weak soup and J Lo with Aunt Agutha.

Chapter 13

A Big's Life

Oswald Sallow sat in his study in his favorite armchair. It was luxurious and grand, made of the finest replicated leather. The shelves behind him held awards he had been given, images of him standing beside celebrities and leaders of industry, framed screenshots of his favorite reviews praising him as a visionary. Everything about the scene proclaimed that Oswald Sallow was a Haplor of means and influence. As he sat, he stared at a tablet device in his hands, memorizing his lines.

"Okay, boss," a deep-toned voice said. "Go."

Sallow looked up toward his hulking assistant and the camera that the assistant was pointing in his direction from across the room.

"Folks," Sallow said, "as you know, I travel a lot. I venture out from my home here on the planet Unara to speak to groups of students and fans like you on all the colony worlds. Recently, I visited our so-called Haplor home world. I say so-called because honestly …" Here he shook his head sadly for emphasis. "… I saw Javidians there and Axans and Cuneddans … on Haplor. I could barely recognize the place. They even had a Dieren restaurant right in the center of town, and I kid you not, folks, Haplors were going into it to eat Dieren food."

Sallow stood and tossed the tablet into the chair. It was an excellent gesture, he thought, a great piece of stage business that symbolized his dismissal of the growing galacticization of Haplor culture.

"Folks, what's wrong with Haplor food? What's the matter with the food we all grew up on? I asked that exact question to someone passing by, a young person. And do you know what his answer was?"

Sallow paused and took a beat to again shake his head. "This person said, 'Oh, the aliens are just like us, only different.' Can you believe it? 'The aliens are just like us, only different.' Folks, the alien species are different all right. But they aren't like us, are they? How could they be? Srathans are reptilian. The Oecanthus are more like insects than anything else. Snuuls slide along on their bellies with four arms waving in the air."

He took a step closer to the camera. "They have completely different DNA. They come from totally different worlds, weird worlds with binary and trinary stars, strange gases in the atmosphere, wildly different gravity. Their food was developed in those alien environments using ingredients growing there. And because modern food replicators build everything out of basic quarks and electrons, we don't know what those original alien ingredients — still present in the molecular recipe — even are."

Sallow paused to let that sink in. "Folks, with alien DNA utterly and thoroughly dissimilar to ours, how could aliens possibly be like us in any meaningful way? How can we expect them to think like us or share any of our values? Don't forget that long ago when the Anterons first encountered Delusians, they ate some of them."

He chuckled. "Yet everyone walks around repeating the mantra, 'They're just like us.' No, folks, that is wrong. Only we are like us. And we are in danger of losing the sense of who we are as Haplors. But it doesn't have to be that way. Come with me. I'll show you someone who makes traditional Haplor food and serves it with traditional Haplor values right here on Unara. And as it happens, they recently became a new sponsor of this vidcast. We'll drop in to find out more right after this message."

Sallow froze, a fixed expression pointed at the camera, a slight smile pasted on his face.

"Cut," said the deep-voiced Haplor behind the camera.

"Daddy." This voice came from a Haplor female standing in the doorway.

Sallow turned. "Ah, Marigold, how good to see you. What do you think of my opening?"

"It's fine, I suppose. I wasn't listening too closely. But clearly, we have to do something about that leer."

"What leer? What are you talking about?"

"That thing you were doing with your lips at the end."

"You mean smiling?"

"You call that a smile, Daddy? Honestly, it could use some work."

"Whatever do you mean, darling?"

"It looks … well, it looks like you picked up how to smile from a badly written instruction manual."

Sallow frowned and turned to the Haplor holding the camera. "What did you think of my smile, Gubbins?"

"Me, Mr. Sallow?" The imager slid from the stool where he had been sitting and rose to his full height, towering over the other two. "Oh … um … oh, I didn't really see a problem." His gaze shifted to the camera screen in his hand, which he tapped a few times. "The important thing is what you think. Here it is … where you did it." He held the screen up for the others.

"Ugh," said Marigold. "See what I mean?"

"I rather like it," Sallow said. "I think it exudes strength and confidence."

Marigold scrunched up her nose. "If you ask me, it comes across as vaguely threatening,"

Threatening wasn't all bad, Sallow thought. Threatening could be useful sometimes. "Any other comments on the shoot, Gubbins? Did you get it all?"

"I mean … well, I haven't had time to review it, but I think we got it all. The late afternoon light was good. Your voice was great. And your presence. All top-notch."

"Good."

"But …"

"But what, Gubbins?" Sallow asked in a cross tone.

"Well, I was thinking we should try a take from a different camera angle, a longer shot of the room. Then I could cut between the two to make the vidcast more visually interesting."

"Nonsense, Gubbins. We've always shot it this way."

"I know, but I think—"

"No." Sallow held up a hand. "Our followers have certain expectations, one of which is consistency."

The imager grimaced. "All right. Oh, there was one other thing. I wonder if we should cut the part about the Dieren restaurant."

"Why? Are you afraid they'll sue me? Let them. A lawsuit would simply mean more publicity and more like-minded people tuning into the vidcast."

"But have you ever tried Dieren cuisine? It's delicious."

"Were you even listening, Gubbins? The comment stays in. I'm the producer of this vidcast. And the talent. You are but the engineer. And my bodyguard when I need one."

"Yes, Mr. Sallow."

"Now, shove off and give that a thorough review and edit. If it's good, we'll go to the restaurant tomorrow morning and shoot there."

"Yes, Mr. Sallow." The big Haplor shuffled from the room.

Marigold said, "Bodyguard? Seriously, Daddy."

"You don't think Gubbins could protect me?"

"I'm sure he could fend off a small army. I just don't think you need to worry about protection. Not here on Unara."

Sallow tutted. "Marigold, you don't realize the lengths to which the shadow authorities would go to silence me."

"Sometimes I'd like to silence you, Daddy … at least a little. I wish you wouldn't be so negative in your vidcast."

"That's how vidcasts work. In every episode, we have to have something we're against."

"But those poor people on Haplor are just trying to run a restaurant. What did they ever do to you?"

Sallow stepped over to a display case hanging on a wall. Inside were small figurines of Earthlings wearing capes and masks and standing in defiant poses. "Do you see these Earthlings here? They're called superheroes. They have special powers. They can fly or shape-shift or run incredibly fast. Many of them have super strength or the ability to heal quickly."

"I think those are made-up stories, Daddy."

He shook a finger at her. "Every story has a kernel of truth, Marigold. Don't forget that. What if some Earthlings actually have those powers, and we allow them to leave their solar system? And it's not only the Earthlings who are a threat, you know. The Grays can read minds. Astridians are giants. The Tuatha can heal. We Haplors are not large people. We must be careful."

She rolled her eyes. "I don't think being able to heal someone is much of a threat."

"It would be if we ever had to fight them."

"Yes, Daddy. Whatever you say. Oh, if you're going to the town center tomorrow, the curio shop has received a new shipment of Earth artifacts."

"Interesting. Wait, where did you hear that?"

Marigold said nothing.

Sallow fixed her with a stare. "Have you been messaging with that shopkeeper again?"

"Now, Daddy, Cecil is a wonderful person."

"He's a salesclerk, Gort help us. You, my dear, with your intelligence and beauty — not to mention my renown — you could be attracting the attention of Haplors high up in the business world. You can do better than a peddler."

"He isn't a salesclerk … or a peddler. He owns the store."

"It's a tiny store."

"You like shopping there well enough. And Cecil cared enough to give us advance information on this shipment."

"What sort of things are in the consignment?"

"He didn't say, but he thought you definitely would be interested."

"I probably am. I'll check the network for the details."

"Then you'll stop by the shop tomorrow?"

"Most likely."

"In that case, I'd like to come with you."

"To see Cecil?"

"To be with you, Daddy. To enjoy a morning out with you and watch you record your vidcast. And to see Cecil also … but only briefly." She shot him the smile he never could resist.

"Of course, my dear. We can breakfast together at the Haplor restaurant. Your presence will make the vidcast even better."

"It's a date then." Marigold waved her fingers at him and slipped out of the room.

Sallow sat back down in the armchair. He picked up the tablet device and brought up the app with his latest viewership numbers, pleased to see that they had risen again. He thought he was due a reward for all his hard work — perhaps something interesting from Earth.

He switched apps and searched for this new shipment. When he saw it, his eyes lit up. Yes, now there was something that would make his collection the talk of all Haplorhood. Wouldn't this make Lucius Wentworth on Haplor jealous? And old Spencer Rainsby on Sonus too. Yes, he would definitely visit the curio shop tomorrow. He looked across his study. He even knew where he would set it.

Chapter 14

Keezo, His Eyes Open

Keezo's eyes opened with a start. For a moment Keezo didn't recognize the level white surface overhead, the colored straight walls on every side, the furnsures. Then Keezo remembered Pelie and Bandy and the flat place. That's where Keezo was. Keezo was stretched out on a huge soft thing in Pelie's flat inside the Bigs' sittee.

But where were Pelie and Bandy? Were they out looking for Tunna and the little? Keezo crawled out from under the coverings and bounced along the length of the soft thing, at the end jumping down to the woolly ground. Walking through an opening in the wall to another part of the flat place, Keezo found Pelie sitting on furnsure and Bandy placing the things the Bigs wore into large, hard-sided bags.

"Where is Tunna?" Keezo asked.

Bandy said, "Good morning, Keezo. I trust you slept well."

Pelie looked up, finners holding a cup of something hot and steamy. "What ho, Keezo."

Keezo didn't know what to say to any of that and so merely nodded. "Where is Tunna?"

Pelie said, "That's what we hope to find out today, old sport."

"Are you hungry, Keezo?" Bandy asked.

Keezo nodded again, this time with more enthusiasm. Keezo hadn't eaten anything since the bakie with all the yummy Bigs' food.

Pelie said, "I know the little critter eats grubs and bugs and such, Blandings, but I doubt we have any of that programmed into the food replicator."

"No, sir," Bandy said. "I investigated the matter last night. According to the best research, the Danánn eat fruit, nuts, and vegetables, in addition to arthropods. I suspect our friend would enjoy a blue fruit. Follow me, Keezo."

Bandy walked through an opening in the wall to yet another part of the flat. "Replicator, one blue fruit, please."

Something made a humming noise, and a round fruit appeared on a surface above Keezo's head. Reeling in amazement and confusion, Keezo took a step back, fur changing to the yellow of the wall. "Magic. Bigs is has magic."

"Not magic, Keezo," Bandy said. "This is a food replicator, and it has made a perfectly good blue fruit."

"Food repacater?"

"That's right." Bandy set the fruit on top of a furnsure in the room, a tall thing with a wide, flat top and long legs. Bandy pulled out from it a smaller furnsure and held out a top limb toward Keezo. "Hop up here."

Keezo leaped to the smaller furnsure, and Bandy pushed it closer to where the fruit sat.

"Eat," Bandy said.

Keezo dug into the fruit. It was cool and juicy like the ones Keezo and Tunna had eaten outside the round silver thing with the gray creatures. Before Tunna and the little had been lost. Keezo sighed, remembering it all. But Keezo knew Pelie would find Tunna. Pelie had said so.

After two more fruits, they all left the flat place, Bandy carrying the hard-sided bags, Keezo walking beside Pelie. They walked a long way through a tunnel and then along the hard, flat ground Keezo had taken the day before with Pelie. They returned to the large inside place where the round silver thing had been.

This time, after walking up and down the long ramps past all the Bigs moving every which way and the makeens that were moving and the makeens that were not moving and all the flashing lights and the places with food, they again stepped out into cold air and walked up a ramp into a different kind of thing.

This thing was not round and silver like the thing with the gray creatures. It was white with a point like a blade and wings like a bird. The inside was different too, not dark and full of containers, but light and full of furnsures in long rows.

A big person, taller even than Pelie and Bandy, stood inside. The person had no fur other than on the top of their head, and the person's skin was as blue as the sky. "Hello, welcome to Rhegedian Galactic. May I help you find your seats?"

Bandy said, "I believe I can find them, thank you."

"You may leave your bags here," the blue person said.

"Much obliged."

Bandy led the way to three furnsures sitting side by side.

Pelie said, "You take the window seat, Blandings. We'll put Keezo in the middle, and I'll sit on the aisle. Here you go, Keezo."

Keezo climbed to the furnsure and sat.

Bandy tapped on a clear piece of wall. "If you watch through this window, Keezo, you can see our travels through space."

"Winno. Okey dokey." Keezo looked at the winno. It let Keezo see through the wall to the outside where a Big was holding a tool up to one of the wings. More magic, Keezo thought.

Other Bigs entered. Some were very strange. One had horns and a flat nose. Another was like a lizard walking on just one-two feet. Another one was small, though still bigger than Keezo, and had a round black head. They all sat on the furnsures.

Then from somewhere came a rumbling sound just like what the round, silver thing had made. Keezo scooched closer to Pelie and wrapped a tentacle around Pelie's top limb.

"It's all right, Keezo," Pelie said. "What you are hearing is the ship taking off."

"Is taking off what?" Keezo asked. Why would part of the thing get taken off? Keezo gazed around to see what part it was.

"What?"

"Is wings coming off?"

"Ha. Hope not, eh?"

Something like snakes emerged from the furnsure and started wrapping themselves around Keezo. Keezo tried beating them away with a foot, but they kept coming. Then Keezo noticed that Pelie and Bandy also had snakes and were letting their snakes wrap them up. That's when Keezo realized they were not snakes at all but more like flat ropes. Keezo quit kicking and let the ropes wrap around Keezo's body and click in place.

The rumbling grew louder, and Keezo felt the terrible pushing down just like from the place with the gray creatures. Then came the floating. Only this time the flat ropes held Keezo in place so there wasn't any danger of floating away to the land of endless fruit.

Keezo peered at the winno thing. A gray, barren, pock-mocked surface was rolling below them like a giant rock. Keezo wondered what it was, where it came from, and what had happened to the Big with the tool and the rest of the place where they were.

"What is I see in winno?"

Bandy said, "That is a view of outside the ship."

"Winno show what is outside this place where we sit?"

"That's right, Keezo."

The surface below kept turning. Tiny mountains came into view. In one of the valleys, Keezo saw what looked like a little sittee for tiny Bigs under something shiny, something like a nutshell, except Keezo could see through it. It was like the clear thing Keezo had seen between the Bigs' sittee and the sky only very small.

Above the gray surface, the sky was black like nighttime with stars shining. Then the blue rings of the big orange and gold thing that Pelie had called Nuggies rose over the gray surface like a monstrous sun. It filled the sky and then quickly disappeared once again.

For a moment, all Keezo could manage was a kind of whine. Finally, Keezo stared up at Pelie and asked, "Where is ground?"

Pelie pointed at the gray surface. "That's the ground down there, Keezo."

That was not the ground. The ground wasn't cold and gray and rolling on a big boulder. The ground was warm and full of plants and trees with fruit. Where were Keezo's hills, Keezo's mound?

"Where is we?"

"We're in space," Pelie said.

"What is ... space?"

"Space is ... Well, space is the space between all the stars and planets."

Plan-it. There was that word again. "What is ... plan-it?"

"Well, a planet ... um ..."

"Sir," Bandy said, "would you allow me to attempt an explanation?"

"Go right ahead, Blandings. You're better at all this brainy stuff."

"Keezo," Bandy said, "do you see those stars?"

"Stars, yes," Keezo said. Keezo at least knew stars, though these stars looked different from the ones outside his mound, and they didn't twinkle.

"Good. Each one of those stars is a sun that shines down on different worlds. That's what a planet is, a world. People live on some of the planets."

Pelie said, "People also live on moons. We do."

"Perhaps, sir, we shouldn't complicate matters."

"Righto. Carry on, Blandings."

"Thank you, sir. Keezo, one of those stars shines on your world and is the sun you know."

Keezo blinked. "Sun not is little like stars. Sun is big."

"Yes, but you know that the further away something is, the smaller it looks, right?"

Keezo nodded. Everyone knew that. Trees were little from far away but grew big when you reached them.

"Now where Mr Totleigh lives — our flat — that is way down there under that dome we keep seeing. That's where we live. You remember how big it is. It only seems small because we are high above it."

"We is way up in air?" Keezo's chest began beating wildly.

"Strictly speaking, we are above the air."

"Which isn't all that hard to do," Pelie said, "since on Sonus we haven't got much of the stuff."

Keezo watched the tiny Bigs' sittee roll under them once more. Was that the place they had been? How far away must they be for it to be so small? The sittee again rolled out of sight, replaced by uninterrupted gray. Where were the green hills and trees Keezo was used to?

"Then where is Keezo's mound?"

Bandy pointed to the stars. "Your home, Keezo, is orbiting one of those stars. You traveled here in a ship like this one all the way through space."

Keezo felt dizzy. The chest pounding grew stronger. Keezo pulled every tentacle around tight and began to rock back and forth.

"Pelie not is live near Keezo?"

"Afraid not, Keezo," Pelie said. "Our homes are billions of light-years—"

"Hundreds, sir."

"Righto. Thank you, Blandings. Hundreds of light-years apart."

"What is ... light-year?" Keezo's head was starting to hurt.

"I believe it is the distance light travels in one year. That's right, isn't it, Blandings?"

"Yes, sir. Using the galactic standard year."

Still rocking, Keezo blinked and blinked again. Light did not have legs to travel. Light was light. It came from the sun. Keezo traveled. Keezo had walked across the hills to the Bigs' sittee and into the round silver thing and then out of the round silver thing to Pelie. How could Pelie's flat be separated from Keezo's mound by dark space?

But ... but the Bigs' sittee with Pelie was different from the Bigs' sittee that Keezo had seen from the hill. And the gray surface shown on the winno was not

Keezo's hills. Could they be two different places? Did the round silver thing with the gray creatures move between the places across the dark space?

It was hard to think such thoughts. There were many things Keezo understood. Keezo knew hills and mounds and trees and how to climb to find fruit. But Keezo did not know space and plan-itses and light-years and people being carried out into the black space far, far from home. Keezo's chest pounded so hard it hurt. It was becoming hard to breathe.

Pelie patted Keezo's head. "Don't worry, Keezo. Everything will be fine. We're on our way to find Tunna. And then we'll take you both home and your youngling too."

Keezo took a breath and leaned back in the seat. Yes, Pelie knew what to do. Pelie understood the black space and plan-itses. Yes, the stars did shine like the sun. They might be big suns looking small because they were far away. It was beginning to make sense.

Then a buzzing sound started up from somewhere. Keezo peeked at the winno to see what was happening and saw the gray surface below them crumble away to nothing.

Keezo shrieked, "No! No no no no." Having finally begun to settle into this new reality, it was a shock to now see it dissolving like in a bad dream.

Pelie said, "Ah, that's merely the chrono drive kicking in. You see, Keezo, to travel faster than the speed of light, we need to use a special engine. What you're seeing is space as we travel back in time."

"Sir," Bandy said, "I don't think it advisable—"

"No no no no no." Outside the winno, stars whirled around, moved closer, melted into clouds of dust. Keezo wrapped a tentacle around Pelie's arm and squeezed.

Pelie said, "Back in the early days of the universe … well, not days per se since I suppose one needs a sun rising over a planet to have a day, and neither of those existed yet. But regardless, at that time all the whatsits in the universe were much more crowded together. I'm right, aren't I, Blandings?"

"Yes, sir, but I don't believe Keezo is ready—"

"So once we get back there … or rather, then … those light-years become mere sprintspans that we can quickly traverse."

Keezo could hear Pelie's words, but like the stars outside the winno, their meaning kept dissolving into nonsense and nothingness. Keezo huffed frantic breath after frantic breath.

"Sir."

"Then we just travel forward in time to where we were ... or *when* we were, what?"

Keezo moaned out the words, hoping to somehow make sense of them. "Space, plan-itses, light-years. No ... no ... no."

The walls of the place ... the ship, as Bandy had called it, began closing in. There was not enough air. Keezo breathed harder and harder, faster and faster. Darkness crept in from the edges of Keezo's vision. Then everything went black.

Chapter 15

The Interstellar Guild of Importers

Pelham glanced from the unconscious Keezo over to Blandings, puffed his cheeks, and blew out. "Quiet at last. That was a bit of an ordeal, eh?"

Blandings meanwhile was hurriedly repositioning Keezo in the seat, tilting the little alien's head back, and propping up Keezo's legs with a pillow.

Finally, the valet nodded. "I am pleased to report, sir, that Keezo appears to be breathing normally."

"Ah. Good."

"It can be a shock when one first learns of space travel and life on other planets."

"Can it? I think I always knew. I had a picture hanging in my nursery of several species arm in arm ... or arm in wing, arm in fin, as it were."

"You were born into a society, sir, that had already made contact. I understand some primitive cultures, upon making the discovery, have erupted into wars or brought criminal charges against scientists."

"Scientists put on trial? For what, Blandings? Beakering and entering? Assault with a deadly telescope?"

One corner of Blandings' lips rose an infinitesimal amount. "Very humorous, sir."

Pelham appreciated Blandings for many reasons. Being a great audience for comedic material, however, was not among the valet's talents.

"Well, I'll be glad when we can at last deposit Keezo back at his home mound."

"Yes, sir."

"I had no idea what a strain it can be to put up with someone of limited intelligence."

Blandings coughed. "I imagine it must be trying, sir."

"Have I ever been to Unara, Blandings? I can't seem to remember."

"No, sir."

"Have you?"

"I have, sir. I was formerly in the employ of Mr. Archibald Winton, the mattress tycoon."

"There are mattress tycoons?" Pelham pictured someone wearing a top hat and a bushy white mustache, sitting atop a tall stack of bed cushions.

"Yes, sir. Perhaps you have heard of the Snoozer Mattress Company. They moved operations to Unara during the time of my employ."

"Why did you leave him, Blandings? Didn't like Unara? I assume it was you who gave him the heave-ho. Surely, no one could find fault with your work."

"Thank you for saying so, sir. No, Unara was fine. We parted company over sartorial matters."

"Say what?"

"Mr. Winton insisted on wearing a certain checked jacket."

"A checked jacket doesn't sound so bad, Blandings. I have a blue-on-blue checked suit myself."

"The jacket in question, sir, had a wide pattern in peach, blue, green, yellow, pink, and light brown."

"What in the blazes? Or what in the blazers, I might say? All those colors in a single coat?"

"I am afraid so, sir. And not in a subtle design either. It pained me merely to brush it. Being Mr. Winton's valet, I felt the garment reflected poorly on both of us. I had no choice but to hand in my notice. One must draw the line somewhere."

"One does. But Blandings?"

"Yes, sir?"

"I know you and I have at times disagreed over questions of style. Do me a favor. Should I ever express an interest in anything as objectionable as that, do let me know."

"Indeed, I will, sir."

"Wheeze out one of those muted coughs you do."

"Yes, sir."

"In the meantime, what can you tell me about Unara?"

"As you probably learned in school, sir, Unara is in the same star system as Haplor."

"Is it?"

"Yes, it is the next planet out from Haplor. It was the site of the first Haplor colony."

"What sort of place is it?"

"The air is thin but breathable for Haplors. The gravity is between that of Haplor and Sonus. Being further from the sun, it is cooler than the home world. During daylight hours — and I might add that their day is not much different in length from a Haplorian day — the temperatures are cool. At night, however, they plunge into deadly cold."

"Not much nightlife then, I would presume."

"That would be correct, sir. The planet is also known for sulfuric mud pools and noxious gas vents."

"Sounds smelly."

"It can certainly be malodorous, sir, though the warmth of the mud pools does serve to moderate the climate. The colony was not officially founded by the Haplor government. The original colonists were people who wanted to distance themselves from modern Haplorian life. Many came on co-op ships that were constructed specifically to make the journey and then be deconstructed upon arrival and used as colony components."

"How do you know all this, Blandings?"

"I read, sir."

The buzzing from the chrono drive stopped as they reached the present-day galaxy. Pelham peeked out the window and saw that they were orbiting a brown planet of mountainous continents separated by green oceans. The engines fired, and they began their descent toward the planet's surface.

After the usual atmospheric buffeting about, which to Pelham's delight did not awaken Keezo, they swooped down over jagged peaks and followed the path of a surging mountain stream. Then the ground dropped away to a level plain of sandy-colored soil dotted with clumps of vegetation. Here the stream broadened and slowed, meandering in long, lazy curves through the landscape. The plants grew thicker and greener along its banks. Then the random shrubs gave way to agriculture — orchards, vines and vegetables, grain crops planted in rows. Finally, a town came into view sitting on a broad curve of the river.

"Unara city," Blandings announced.

"Seems rather larger and more populous than the Sonus colony," Pelham said.

Blandings nodded. "It is older and does not have to fit under a dome."

They landed at an open-air space port on the edge of the city.

Pelham leaned over and put a hand on Keezo. "We're here."

The Danánn did not stir.

"Keezo seems completely knackered, Blandings. Perhaps you should carry him."

"I will be carrying the bags, sir."

"Oh, rather. Well, I suppose it's up to me then." Pelham leaned over and hoisted the little creature to his shoulder.

Stepping from the ship, Pelham gazed up at a powder blue sky. "It's great to breathe fresh air, what?" He inhaled and immediately began to gasp.

A Haplor passenger walking down the ramp behind them chuckled. "Welcome to Unara. For a place actually having a breathable atmosphere, it has one of the weakest ones anywhere in the galaxy. You'll find out tonight when it turns as cold as a crocoraptor's kiss."

A customs official nodded them through. Haplors could enter any Haplor colony without red tape, and it wasn't clear whether the official had even noticed the still-sleeping Keezo.

"Well, Blandings," Pelham said as they entered the terminal, "now that we're here, how do we go about searching for Tunna?"

On Pelham's shoulder, Keezo stirred. "Tunna? Tunna is here?"

"I hope so, Keezo," Pelham said.

Keezo dropped back off to sleep.

"Since Keezo was discovered by you," Blandings said, "it is possible your counterpart in the Unara import office came across Tunna."

"Excellent suggestion, Blandings." Pelham approached an information desk where a female Haplor faced the crowd with a jaded expression. "Pardon me. Where might I find the Inspector of Imports?"

She breathed out an exasperated sigh and frowned at Pelham for a moment before tapping on a tablet device and saying in a monotone, "Hall H."

"Thanks awfully." Pelham started to turn away, then stopped, and circled back. "And Hall H … um … where would that be? Sorry. I'm new around here. First time visiting your fair—"

She cut him off. "Terminal B."

"Much obliged. Terminal B. Um … and—"

She shot him an aggrieved look and held out a seemingly ponderous arm. "Through those doors."

"Righto. Thank you. I hope you have a …" Pelham stopped talking as she had already broken eye contact.

Blandings led the way through the doors and around the terminal to a short hallway marked as H, where a sign on a door said: *Import Office*.

Entering, they found two desks just as in Pelham's office back on Sonus. One of the desks was currently unoccupied. At the other one sat a female Haplor with gray head fur.

Pelham said, "Ah, yes. Curious as to whether I might speak with the Inspector of Imports."

The female looked at him askance. "And who are you?"

Pelham shot her a smile. "The Sonus Inspector of Imports. Pelham G. Totleigh."

"Are you now? Well, I'm Jasmine Spector, Unara Inspector of Imports. What can I do for you, Pelham G. Totleigh?"

"Pardon? Did you say your name was Jasmine Spector?"

"I did. Why? Do we know each other?"

"I don't know if you've ever noted it, but you have the word *inspector* embedded right in your name. It could almost be Jasm Inspector. Astonishing, what?"

She grimaced at him. "What do you want, Pelham G. Totleigh?"

"May we sit? We — and by we, I'm referring to myself and my valet Blandings — we are heavy laden, as it were, with bags and Keezos and all."

"You have a valet? For Zahn's sake, how much do they pay you on Sonus?"

"Oh, I'm not entirely certain. Do you know the amount, Blandings?"

"I believe, sir, the question was rhetorical," Blandings said.

"Ah. Righto. But about the sitting?"

She waved toward two chairs in front of her desk, and they sat. Blandings lined up the luggage beside his chair while Pelham kept the sleeping Keezo draped over his shoulder.

Looking from one to the other, Spector said, "Now perhaps you'll tell me what brings you here."

"Yes," Pelham said. "You see, I've come in search of information. Confidentially. One import inspector to another. As part of our brotherhood, you might say."

She scowled. "I would be a sister, not a brother, that is if we were related, which we're not."

"Sorry. Didn't mean to offend." He tapped his head. "I have a goodish bit of trouble with the old word processor sometimes. A fellowship then, a fraternity."

"Again, not a fellow. Same thing for fraternity."

"Association? Guild? Camaraderie? Um … gang?"

"Are you trying to form a trade union?"

"What? Goodness no. Not that I'm anti-union or anything. Frightfully useful organizations, so I hear. Though if Aunt Agutha ever thought … I shudder to think of the repercussions."

"Mr. Totleigh, what are you trying to say?"

"Um … well, it's about this." Pelham pulled Keezo from his shoulder and shifted the comatose alien to face forward. Keezo stretched three or four tentacles in the air and blinked.

Spector jumped from her chair. "What is that thing?"

"That's Keezo. What did you think was on my shoulder this whole time?"

"I don't know. A bag or something."

"I assure you, Keezo is no bag. Keezo is a Danánn."

"Hello," Keezo said.

"What do you mean, it's a Danánn? Danánn is settled by Haplors." Spector pointed a finger. "That is not a Haplor."

"I is Keezo," Keezo said.

Pelham shrugged. "Apparently, these people were there first."

Spector rolled her eyes. "For the love of Gort. You mean they started a colony on a planet that already had an indigenous intelligent species?"

"Hello," Keezo said.

"Hello," Spector said. "Now shush."

Pelham looked down at Keezo. "Well, intelligence is something of a … um … spec-something. What is the spec-something these things run along, Blandings? It's on the tip of my tongue."

"Could you mean a spectrum, sir?"

"I do. Spectrum. Thank you, Blandings. Intelligence runs along a spectrum. Some species are naturally a tad brainier than others, don't you know."

Spector stared at Pelham for a few moments before saying, "You don't need other species to realize that."

Pelham nodded, not exactly following her meaning.

Spector continued. "You know, that's the kind of thing that gives Haplors a bad name. Flying in and taking over planets. That's why the Snuuls hate us — when we terraformed that moon in the Muc system to the point where the Snuuls couldn't live there."

"As it happens, I don't think the colonists on Danánn were aware of their existence at the time. They're a shy species. Keezo, do that camouflage thing."

Keezo blinked.

"Do you want to show the nice inspector here how you change color?"

Keezo blinked again.

"No? Well, no matter. The point is that Keezo here wandered onto a Gray ship along with his ... or rather its ... or rather their — see, as I understand it, they don't have gender as such, which, as you can imagine, makes them a touch confusing to talk about. Anyway, Keezo got separated from a companion or mate or whatever they call it — oh, and also a youngling—"

"Little," Keezo said, nodding.

"Right. They call their younglings littles. But that's immaterial. The point is ... um ... the point is ... um ... Blandings?"

Blandings cleared his throat. "Keezo came off the Gray ship at Sonus along with some cargo. We don't know what happened to Keezo's companion and youngling."

"Righto," Pelham said. "We thought they might be here as this was the next port of call for the ship. Have you seen anyone who looks like Keezo?"

Spector shook her head slowly and said, "No. Never."

Pelham turned to the valet. "Well, that's the pip, what? Now what do we do, Blandings? Move on to Tucana Three?"

Blandings said, "Ms. Spector, might Keezo's companion have slipped past your inspectors unnoticed? As Mr. Totleigh said, they possess the ability to blend in with their surroundings."

"I doubt it. We run a pretty tight ship here." She stared at Keezo. "But I suppose it is possible. I didn't notice this one. Feel free to inquire around town. Maybe somebody saw something."

"That," said Blandings, "is an excellent idea. Thank you for your assistance."

"Yes," said Pelham, rising to leave. "So good to chat with a fellow ... um ... I mean a ..."

"I believe you mean a colleague, sir," Blandings said as he gathered up the luggage.

"In fact, I do. Thanks awfully."

"Bye-bye," Keezo said.

Chapter 16

It Costs an Arm and a Leg Lamp

After depositing the bags in a locker at the space port, Blandings and Keezo set off around the town to inquire after Tunna's whereabouts. Pelham, meanwhile, hired an automated carriage to take him to the business district in search of the shop where the leg lamp was supposed to be for sale.

He alighted from the carriage into chilly morning air in the middle of a street lined with two- and three-story buildings of a reddish-brown adobe. Spotting a Haplor male walking along the street, he called, "Excuse me. I was wondering if you could direct me toward the shop that sells ... well, what would you call it? Bits and bobs from off planet."

The other Haplor scrunched up his face. "Bits and what?"

"Bobs. Collectibles. Bric-a-brac. Curios. Items from Earth and probably other alien planets as well."

"Oh, curios. Why didn't you say so? It's called the Curio Shop, and it's just down that way a block or two."

"Ah. Excellent. Thanks terribly." Pelham strode off, gratified that for once things were running along smoothly for him.

He found the shop and opened the door to a cluttered maze of tables, shelves, and display cabinets. The store had items of brass, wood, and stone in every size and shape. Musical instruments from Muc, bowls from Bononia, pottery from Porta. A pile of brown goo was labeled as Snuulian art, though Pelham thought it stretched the definition of the word.

None of the items sported price tags. Pelham assumed that meant the prices were negotiable. Aunt A. hadn't given him a spending range, but he knew it wouldn't be a good idea to go over whatever price she had in mind.

Not wanting to appear too keen on the leg lamp, Pelham decided not to stride directly to the counter and inquire about it. Instead, he ran a finger along a shelf stuffed with old-style paper books, pulled out a volume, and flipped through the pages. It turned out to be Itani love poetry and pretty spicey love poetry at that. Cringing and feeling heat rise to his cheeks, Pelham quickly slipped the book back into its place. He found his hand now covered with dust. He wiped it on a nearby towel featuring an image of some kind of food he didn't recognize and inscribed with alien script, which his translator bots reformed to say: *Let's give them something to taco bout.*

"May I help you?"

Pelham looked up to see a young, skinny male Haplor. He was so incredibly thin that Pelham thought he could rival Keezo's ability to disappear merely by turning sideways. Hand this bloke a rake, and it would be difficult to tell the two apart.

"Ah, righto. My uncle has a birthday coming up," Pelham said, afraid to wander too far from the truth lest he lose his way. "What interesting objects do you have?"

"I don't think I've seen you before. Are you visiting Unara for the festival?"

"Festival?"

"Alliance Day."

"Oh, righto. That is coming up, isn't it."

"Tomorrow night. We always have a big celebration, a sort of village fete in the park. Does your uncle like rugs?"

"I suppose so. He has some. Though I suspect my aunt picked them out."

The skinny shopkeeper unrolled the end of a rug with weird, swirling shapes in pinks and greens. It made Pelham's head spin just looking at it. "This one came from the planet Fornax."

"They can have it," Pelham said. "No thanks."

"What about toys? I have a Thomian little larceny kit."

"Don't think so. What about … I don't know … anything from … Earth?"

A grin spread across the shopkeeper's slender face. "As it happens, we received a new supply yesterday. Follow me."

They set off deeper into the shop, twisting and turning between display areas until they reached a glass case. Pelham spotted the leg lamp against the wall and was starting to point to it when the salesperson pulled a black thing from inside the case.

"This is what the Earthlings call a clock. They use it to tell time." The shopkeeper picked up a tag hanging from the piece and read from it. "This one is styled as 'an Earth cat with the head on top, the tail as the pendulum, and the hands in the middle.'"

"What's a cat?"

The scrawny salesclerk shrugged. "I think it's some sort of animal. I hear the Earthlings are keen on them."

"Extraordinary." Pelham studied the thing. The top part did look a bit like an animal with large eyes and pointy ears. And the bottom certainly resembled a tail. But the middle? Those things on it looked more like sticks than hands. Or tentacles like Keezo's, except they were stuck on the belly of the beast. And why would an animal have numbers on its tummy? "I'll pass."

"What about this?" the shopkeeper asked, reaching for something red with white pieces across the front. "This is said to resemble an Earthling's teeth. Now watch this." He gave something on the side a couple of turns, and the teeth began clacking up and down.

"Now that's funny," Pelham said. "I don't think my uncle would care for it, and certainly not my aunt. But the lads back home would find it a corker. How much?"

"Five bills."

"I'll take it for myself. What about that leg thing there behind you?"

"Ah, yes. Step to the end of the display case, and I'll bring it around."

The shopkeeper wrapped his fingers around the upper thigh of the leg lamp in a way that made Pelham slightly uncomfortable. "I have to be careful. It's fragile. It said so on the box."

As he gently lifted it, the fringy lampshade tipped forward, exposing more thigh, and Pelham glanced away.

"What's that cable running from it?" Pelham asked.

"That's what the Earthlings call an electrical cord."

"What does it do? I met an Earthling once, and he had no such thing connected to his foot."

"As I understand it, that is how Earthlings supply power to things."

Pelham scratched at a cheek. "Astounding. They don't use wireless energy fields?"

"No. Cords. If you had the proper power source, you could make this light up. I think I have an Earth electricity transformer in stock. You might consider buying both."

"What's the price?" Pelham asked. "Just for the leg thingy."

"Ninety-five bills."

"Sold."

A creaking sound came from the door at the front of the shop. Pelham glanced up to see three Haplors entering. One was a lovely young female who beamed the most radiant smile in Pelham's general direction.

She was followed by two males. One of them bore a striking resemblance to one of the mountains the Rhegedian ship had earlier flown over. Pelham gawped at the size of the fellow. The other one, Pelham thought, could pass for a barrel with legs added to the bottom and a largish pumpkin plopped on top for a head. The specimen — a pompous fuddy-duddy if ever Pelham had seen one, and he had seen more than his share of fuddy-duddies in his time — rubbernecked at the items for sale with a haughty arrogance.

"Good morning, Cecil," the female said with warmth in her voice.

"Good morning, Marigold," the slim shopkeeper replied, rocking forward and back like an excited noodle.

Pelham watched them gaze at each other with a kind of adoration that reminded him of a stanza he had read in the Itani love poem ... before it continued on to other more fruity images. Neither of the young Haplors seemed ready to break the connection anytime soon.

Pelham said, "Oh, are you two ... eh?"

"What?" said the shopkeeper, his face flashing red.

"What?" said the female, turning away to scrutinize a statuette of a white yak.

"What?" yelped the pumpkin head. He scowled at Pelham, then bellowed out, "Cakewood!"

"Cake wood?" Pelham said. "Doesn't sound too appetizing, what?"

"That's my name," the shopkeeper said in an apologetic tone. "Cecil Cakewood."

"Oh, sorry then. Didn't mean to .... I guess we hadn't introduced ourselves. Pelham G. Totleigh. Now about this lamp—"

"And as for you," the pumpkin head said, glaring at Pelham, "I'll thank you to not discuss my daughter. She is none of your business, you feebleminded dope."

"I say now, steady on," Pelham replied.

The pumpkin head strode through the store toward the counter. "Cakewood, I want to see a piece of merchandise."

"Yes, Mr. Sallow. As soon as I finish with this customer ... um, sir."

Sallow, Pelham thought. Where had he heard that name?

"Make it snappy," Sallow barked. "We have to finish our vidcast and upload it."

"Yes. I understand," Cecil Cakewood said, nervously shifting his eyes between Sallow, Marigold, and Pelham.

Sallow turned to the mountain-shaped male and waved an arm at Pelham. "Gubbins, look at this ne'er-do-well of the type so common nowadays. Weak chin. Eyes like two fried eggs sticking out from his face. Note the blank expression, the clothes."

"Are you talking about me?" Pelham asked. "What's wrong with my clothes? They are the height of fashion."

"Exactly my point. He's a dandy. You should be imaging him for the vidcast, Gubbins."

The mountain mumbled, "I think you could be risking legal action."

"I don't care."

"And it's ... well, it's not a very nice thing to do — heaping abuse on private individuals."

"Nice? Nice? Gubbins, we're in an epic struggle for the future of all Haplorhood. We can't afford to be nice. We don't have time to be nice. Here is exactly what is wrong with young Haplors today. An idle young person with nothing better to do than browse shops full of trinkets from alien cultures."

Pelham said, "I noticed you came into the shop too."

"I would wager he doesn't even have a job, Gubbins."

"There's where you're wrong. I am Inspector of ... um ... Imports ... on Sonus."

Sallow sneered. "A government job. That's even worse. Start imaging this, Gubbins.

"Well ..." the imager said without raising the camera.

"What does government ever produce?" Sallow asked. "What does government provide that anyone can eat or wear or use to make your life better?"

Pelham raised his arm. "Ah. I know that one. On Sonus, the government is leading the terraforming effort of our moon by growing plants that not only provide food but also release carbon dioxide to build up the atmosphere. Or is that carbon monoxide? Which one has the two molly-whatevers? Molly-cules, is it?"

Sallow pounded on the counter. "All of which should be the domain of private enterprise."

Pelham scoffed. "I doubt private enterprise would take on anything like terraforming a world, accruing costs for generations before it ever paid off." Pelham remembered that bit from one of Aunt Agutha's harangues when he was trying to pay attention to anything other than the names she was calling him.

"If a project can't pay off in a reasonable amount of time, then it shouldn't be done in the first place. That is the definition of a boondoggle. That's the difference between Sonus and Unara right there. Our founders were tough individualists who came here on their own money and forged a colony for themselves."

"Well, if it's toughness you want to talk about, the founders of Sonus, which included my grandfather, Phineas R. Totleigh, lived inside a cramped spaceship for more than a year while they worked every day constructing the dome. That's a Sonus year, mind you, which is seventeen … no, not seventeen … um … five … carry the one … about five and a half years in Haplor time."

Sallow chuckled out a sour laugh. "Our founders didn't have a dome to protect us."

"You didn't need one," Pelham said with emotion. "You already had an atmosphere to breathe."

"Not much of one. I'd like to see you try to stay warm here at night out in the wilderness. You'd freeze to death."

"Well, you're a big bully."

In his excitement, Pelham took a step toward Sallow. He didn't mean it to appear threatening. It was more like nervous pacing. But the mountain responded by moving between them and holding up a meaty paw. Pelham gulped and stepped back again.

"Daddy, please," Marigold said.

"You're right, dear," Sallow said. "There's no point in arguing with idiots. Cakewood, sell me the lamp, and we'll be on our way."

"Which lamp?" Cecil asked.

"That one right there. The one shaped like an Earthling leg."

Cecil said, "But …"

"I've already purchased it," Pelham said.

"Show me the receipt," Sallow said.

"You interrupted us before we got that far."

Sallow crossed his arms. "Then the sale isn't final. Sell it to me, Cakewood."

Marigold said, "That lamp, Daddy? You don't want that lamp. It's dreadful."

"I do want it, and I'm getting it."

"Now see here," Pelham said, "I told him I'd take it for ninety-five bills."

"I'll pay one hundred for it, Cakewood."

Cecil said, "But …"

"One hundred ten," Pelham said.

"Now, listen here … What did you say your name was? Totleigh? Now, listen here, Totleigh—"

"Make it one hundred fifteen," Pelham said.

Sallow sneered. "One hundred twenty … and Cakewood, you can come visit Marigold at the house to see how I display the lamp." He slipped an arm around the young female.

Pelham said, "One hundred and—"

Cecil stretched out an arm to stop him. "Sorry. Sorry. I'm selling it to Mr. Sallow."

Pelham stared in disbelief. "What? Wait. Wait. What?"

Sallow laughed. Pelham found it the ugliest laugh he had ever seen in his life.

Chapter 17

Aunt Agutha Issues a Threat

Pelham shuffled along the street away from the shop, his chin down, his arms limp at his sides. The leg lamp had been within his grasp. And then somehow it had slipped away. No, not bally somehow. It had all been because of that blighter known as Sallow.

"Blandings," he said over the translator bot connection he maintained with his valet.

"Yes, sir?" Blandings' voice sounded in his ear.

"Any luck in finding Tunna?"

"Not as yet, sir. We have spoken with several people but have thus far failed to uncover any promising leads."

"I can't say I'm surprised. This isn't shaping up to be my lucky day."

"Sir?"

"A stinker by the name of Sallow swooped in and bought the leg lamp from under my nose."

"Do you by chance mean Oswald Sallow, sir?"

"You've heard of him, Blandings?"

"I have, sir. He is a prominent vidcaster of rather extreme views. He is also a leading citizen here on Unara and a magistrate, I believe."

Pelham huffed out a disappointed breath. "A magistrate? There goes my idea of taking him to court for coercing the sale. That is if *coercing* is the word I want in this context."

"It would depend, sir, on whether he employed threats or influence to gain the advantage in the transaction."

"He most certainly did, Blandings. He manipulated the affections of a lovesick salesclerk. He also had a ruffian standing by for any thugging needs that might arise. And that's not all, Blandings."

"Sir?"

"He laughed at me."

"Mr. Sallow, sir?"

"That's right."

"I am sorry to hear of it, sir."

"You know, Blandings how the laughter of some people is akin to music, a joy to hear?"

"I do, sir."

"Small younglings, for instance."

"Indeed, sir."

"Or Worty Worplesdon. Now there was a chappie who had a laugh."

"Yes, sir. I remember Mr. Worplesdon fondly."

"Of course, you do. It's his laugh that makes him so endearing. Worty and younglings — lovely laughers. But I advise you, Blandings, do not count one Oswald Sallow among their number."

"I will bear it in mind."

"His laugh reminds me of the cry of a dying yak. Or rather how I imagine one would sound. I've never had the misfortune to be around a yak in its final moments."

"No, sir."

"But I digress, Blandings. The point is this. What should I do now that this blot on the landscape named Sallow has misappropriated the lamp?"

"I believe, sir, you should communicate with your aunt, the governor."

The morning was warming nicely, but a shiver still ran down Pelham's spine. "Aunt Agutha?"

"I am afraid so, sir."

"Rather a drastic proposal, don't you think, Blandings? Holding a confab with Aunt A. twice in as many days?"

"She may, sir, have a suggestion for an alternative gift."

"You know, you could be right, Blandings. Do you think Uncle Spence would like a set of chattering teeth?"

"I highly doubt it, sir."

"I didn't think so either. I picked them up all the same." Over the remote connection, Pelham could somehow sense his valet wincing. "Well, I daresay I should get on with it. Where do you suppose I can find a WoTCom in this colony?"

"On that, sir, I am pleased to report that Keezo and I are currently standing outside a sort of general store with a sign in the window advertising precisely such a service."

"Excellent, Blandings. Give me the address, and I'll hail a carriage."

"No need, sir. I can see you from here. We are in the next block."

Pelham spun in a circle, spotted them, and hurried over. They entered the store, and soon thereafter, Pelham, Blandings, and Keezo found themselves crowded into a small booth separated from the rest of the store by a curtain. Pelham sat on a bench facing the screen while the others stood to the side out of frame.

Pelham said, "All right, Blandings. I am as prepared for this as I can be. Make the connection."

Blandings reached over and tapped the screen. "Place a call to Sonus, the office of the governor."

A circle began spinning on the screen. In a nearby and hopefully well-shielded containment unit, a pinprick wormhole was created in space-time, reducing the distance between Unara and Sonus to something like being in the next room.

The spinning circle was soon replaced by a view of the outer reception area to the Sonus governor's office. No one seemed to be in attendance.

"Hello?" Pelham said. "Hello?" Is anybody home?"

At that moment, the door to the inner office opened, and a young male Haplor scooted out on wobbly legs. He paused to lean against one of the visitors' couches and scoop in several deep breaths.

"Todd?" Pelham said.

The Haplor's eyes darted up with a haunted look.

"Over here, Todd."

"Oh, Mr. Totleigh."

"I take it you've just been in with her."

Todd nodded silently.

"Unfortunately, it is my turn next. Would you put me through?"

Todd moved toward the screen and began tapping. "Good luck."

The screen did a star wipe from Todd's face to the stern countenance of Pelham's aunt.

"Hello, Aunt Agutha," Pelham said as cheerily as he could manage. "How are you today?"

Her eyes narrowed. "What do you want, Pelham? Did you buy the lamp?"

"Ah. Well, we've run into a slight hiccup. A minor snag."

"You nitwit." She bit off the words. "What kind of snag?"

"This other fellow bought it out from under me."

"What you mean is you wasted time in some watering hole and arrived at the shop too late to buy it."

She shot him the kind of glare that could knock flying birds out of the sky. Pelham was glad he was light-years away.

"No. No. I was there first, Auntie. Most assuredly I was. I had the price negotiated and all. But then this other fellow, this Oswald Sallow, came in and—"

"Sallow." Aunt Agutha said it like a swear word.

"Judging from your tone of voice, I assume you've met him."

"Yes, unfortunately. He and Spencer have competed over pieces before."

That was a bit of good news, Pelham thought. If Aunt A. didn't like Sallow, then she might see him, rather than Pelham, as the real problem in this scenario.

"He used underhanded methods, Auntie. You see, the shopkeeper seems to be sweet on Sallow's daughter and—"

"Does Sallow know we're related?"

"It didn't come up."

"Good. Go to him and offer him more money for it. You can go up to one hundred bills."

"We already entered into a bit of a bidding war. I think the final price was one hundred twenty."

She made a sort of grumbling growl sound. "All right. You can offer him … up to one hundred fifty. Up to. Don't jump to that price."

Keezo, who had been leaning a bit to the side, now leaned further toward the screen, beginning to come into frame. Blandings pulled the Danánn back and produced a muffin from his pocket. Keezo took it and sat on the floor to eat.

"But Aunt Agutha," Pelham said,

"But what, you simpleton?"

"He won't sell it to me. He doesn't like me."

"At the moment, I don't much like you either. But he doesn't have to like you as long as he likes your money … or *my* money, rather."

"I doubt it. You see, we argued."

She shook her head. "Is it your practice to go about starting arguments with random people you meet?"

"He started it, Auntie. I was defending Sonus. This Sallow rotter said the Sonus settlers, Grandad included, were not as tough as Unara settlers."

Her face hardened and her eyes narrowed. "He said that?"

"He did."

"And you say he used unscrupulous means to induce the store to sell it to him?"

"Absolutely."

"Then here's what you do, Pelham. Steal it from him."

"What? I mean … what?"

"I was perfectly clear. Break into his house and steal it from him. It is a fate he richly deserves."

"I couldn't agree with you more regarding what he deserves, Auntie. He's a blight on the planet, a stain on the terrain. But I say, really. Robbery? I … I don't want to break the law."

"Poppycock, Pelham. We both remember the incident when you tried to steal a hat and were caught hanging from a drainpipe."

Pelham swallowed. "Yes, vividly. But I've matured since then."

She tsked. "I've seen no evidence of that."

"I'm especially averse to reenacting the getting caught scene of the story. Blandings says this Sallow is a magistrate. He could throw me in jail."

"You've been in jail before."

"True. And I never much cared for it." He tugged at his collar. The day certainly seemed to be warming up.

"Then all you have to do, you dunce, is not get caught. Seems to me that would be sufficient motivation for you to do something correctly for once. Unara doesn't have a great deal of crime. I doubt if Sallow has much in the way of security on his house."

"He has a bodyguard the size of a small asteroid. And he's probably a light sleeper."

"Honestly, Pelham, how hard can it be to break into someone's house? I understand robbers do it all the time."

Pelham glanced at Blandings in desperation. The valet mouthed, "Another present."

"Or," Pelham said, "how about this? Maybe I could pick up something else from Earth for Uncle Spence's birthday. The shop has loads of other items. One I particularly recall was an Earth timepiece shaped to resemble a creature they call

... I think it was a gat. Pointy ears and whiskers and all that. It looked mighty sharp."

Aunt Agutha fell silent. At first, Pelham thought the connection might have frozen up, which would at least liberate him from this trying conversation. Then he noticed her jaw slowly working from side to side. Though he doubted it, Pelham hoped that meant he had convinced her to abandon the idea of him stealing the leg lamp, and she was instead considering the gat with the odd hands on its stomach.

Finally, she spoke. "Your assistant, what is his name again?"

"My assistant? You mean at work? Munson?"

"Yes, Munson." Her eyes narrowed into intimidating slits. "How long has he worked for you?"

"Oh, I don't know. Two or three years at least." Pelham wondered why in the moon she was asking about Munson. What about the gat clock and the leg lamp?

"I thought as much. It's probably time for him to receive a promotion."

"Oh, righto. It would be well deserved." Pelham breathed out in relief. The aged relative seemed to have come around to a more benevolent mood at last. "Old Munson is a dependable worker and all. Tell me, would he be granted a new title and everything?"

"Yes, he would. I was thinking about Inspector of Imports."

"Beg pardon? Isn't that my job title? You can't have two inspectors of imports, can you?"

"No, you can't, Pelham. But that's not a problem. We can make you Assistant Inspector of Imports."

"What? Demote me? Make me work for Munson?" His mind flooded with images of him being forced to do all the things he currently made Munson do — dig through heavy, grimy piles of things and make sure they all worked and tediously count them. "You don't honestly mean that, do you, Aunt Agutha?"

"I expect loyalty from my department heads, Nephew. If you can't perform a simple task such as stealing an Earth artifact, I might have to reevaluate your position."

"But ... but ... Aunt Agutha."

"Have I made myself clear, Pelham?"

"Well, yes, Aunt Agutha. But—"

The screen went blank.

Chapter 18

Blandings Undercover

Blandings watched as Mr. Totleigh slumped down on the bench of the cramped WoTCom booth. He noted the dazed, dejected look on his employer's face, the eyes bulging, the gaze distant. Poor Mr. Totleigh, Blandings thought. He possessed the most troubling talent for stumbling into predicaments.

"Sir?"

His employer looked up with beseeching eyes. "What are we going to do, Blandings? I mean, I suppose I could attempt the robbery. I've broken into other places in times past."

"Have you ever done so successfully, sir?"

"Well, not entirely."

"Then may I suggest an alternative?"

"Please do."

"Mr. Sallow has thus far not met me. Nor is he aware of our connection. I could pose as a collector of Earth artifacts and attempt to purchase the lamp from him. It is possible he is experiencing buyer's remorse after running up the price and would be willing to sell it at a profit."

Pelham straightened. "That's a capital idea, Blandings. Do you think you can pull it off, as they say?"

"I believe so, sir. The ruse will require a small expenditure for the printing of a spurious calling card."

"That's not a problem. It's money well spent if it keeps me from being arrested for burglary."

"Yes, sir. Perhaps while I take on this assignment, you and Keezo could continue the search for Tunna and their youngling."

"Righto. We'll hit the town. Better than sitting around and stewing."

With a minimum of inquiries, Blandings obtained the address of Oswald Sallow, the fake business card, and one other item he hoped he would not need but wanted to have should it become necessary. He walked to the house, which turned out to be but a few blocks from the town center.

The residence, though built of desert adobe like most buildings on Unara, was constructed to more expansive and stately proportions than anything else in the vicinity. It stood on a large lot dotted with small, native plants and enclosed by a low stone wall. Blandings entered at a gate and followed stepping stones to a broad front door.

Locating the speaker grill, he pressed the button beside it and said, "Horace Smythe-Pucket to see Mr. Sallow."

After a short interval, the large door swung back to reveal a Haplor huge enough to fill the opening. Blandings thought this must be the bodyguard Mr. Totleigh had mentioned.

"Yes?" the Haplor asked.

Blandings presented his card. "Horace Smythe-Pucket. I would like to see Mr. Sallow if it is convenient."

"Regarding?"

"Call it a business proposal."

The bodyguard frowned. He looked Blandings over, nodding slightly. "Come inside. I'll see if he is available."

Blandings stepped into a grand entryway, and the bodyguard disappeared into the recesses of the house. While he waited, Blandings examined with appreciation the ornate chandelier, the spiral staircase, the tiled floor. All had been crafted to the finest standards.

The bodyguard re-emerged, followed by a stocky, mature Haplor holding the false calling card out in front of him like a weapon. "I'm Sallow. I see you are from Upper Waggonham on Haplor, Mr. Smythe-Pucket."

"I am," Blandings said, inclining his head. "Have you ever visited our fair city?"

"No." Sallow's eyes narrowed. "But I hear the riverwalk is beautiful."

Blandings detected the test. He had selected the town because it was only vaguely known. Most Haplors knew it existed but were unlikely to know much about it or to know anyone from there. Sallow must have realized that as well and had suspicions.

"I fear you have been misinformed, Mr. Sallow. Upper Waggonham is nestled beside a lovely lake, but no river runs near it."

Sallow nodded, presumably now satisfied. "Ah. All right. Why don't you step into my study where we can talk? Would you like tea?"

It was a rare treat for Blandings to be served tea, rather than serve it. "Thank you, yes, if it isn't a bother."

"Not at all. Gubbins, have Chef make some. You can bring it in."

Blandings followed Sallow down the hall to a spacious room decorated in warm tones. The walls were paneled with wood that surely did not come from the scrubby trees of Unara. An ornate, red carpet covered the central part of the room with hardwood flooring extending beyond.

A large wooden desk stood near glass doors opening out to a small patio of green stone slabs. To the right of the hallway door was a seating area. Sallow indicated for Blandings to sit on a couch. Sallow took a nearby armchair.

The shelves lining the walls held few books, which was not unusual, especially in the colonies. It was much easier to beam digital content across the light-years than to transport physical media, just as it was easier to replicate food rather than to deal with storage and refrigeration of ingredients.

What the shelves did hold were awards, certificates, memorabilia, and various collectibles. On one was perched a black ball with the number eight painted on the side. Beside it sat a cube covered with brightly colored squares. A nearby acrylic stand displayed a small card with a picture of a mustached Earthling wearing a red shirt and matching cap and holding a club as if ready to swing it at something.

Across the room, a table held a collection, lined up in rows, of finger-sized, four-wheeled vehicles in bright colors. On a nearby pedestal stood a figurine of what Blandings took to be a female Earthling. The doll was extremely thin, dressed in pink with a bubble-shaped helmet covering the head. A sign below the doll proclaimed it as: *Astronaut Barbie*. Blandings wondered if Earth spacefarers were required to be so emaciated. Possibly their rockets lacked sufficient thrust to launch normal-sized Earthlings into space.

Then he spotted it. Standing in the corner was what must be the leg lamp. The netted stocking and fringed lampshade matched Mr. Totleigh's description. It was nearly as tall as a Haplor and glowing a warm orange from the knee up.

Gubbins entered with a tray. Given the quick preparation time, the tea was obviously replicated. Blandings preferred tea made by hand. Not that it — or any replicated food or drink, for that matter — tasted much different from the original. How could it when the molecular structure was identical? Blandings simply found the process of brewing tea rewarding in itself, a statement of handcraft in a technological age.

"Cream? Sweetcane?" Gubbins asked.

"Please," Blandings said.

The bodyguard poured the cups, handed them off, and then retired from the room.

Sallow said, "Now what is this business proposal?"

"That," Blandings said, pointing at the leg statue.

"It's a stunning piece, isn't it? A fine example of Earth art."

"It is. May I?" Blandings leaned forward in his chair to indicate that he wished to examine it more closely.

Sallow swept out an inviting hand.

Blandings stood and approached the leg lamp. He walked around it, nodding at it appraisingly.

Across the galaxy, the form and shape of a species had always been a popular subject for art. Blandings thought of the marble sculptures of Legestra celebrating that species' six graceful limbs. Or the famous Colossus of Delusia, though that mammoth statue always struck Blandings as a way of compensating for Delusians' short stature. But the figure of a single leg, made of plastic, covered with netting? Earthlings were a peculiar people.

"I understand, Mr. Sallow, that you bought it only this morning."

"Hmph," Sallow said with a scowl. "I need to have a talk with Cakewood. He shouldn't be disclosing personal information about his customers."

Blandings did not wish to land anyone in trouble. He shook his head and waved a hand. "No, I obtained the information through, shall we say, other means."

"Oh?" Sallow's brow knitted.

"Yes." He opted to say no more. His host would most likely infer that Blandings, or rather Horace Smythe-Pucket, had connections with one of the payment stick processing companies, which would imbue him with an aura of power.

"All right, I bought it. What of it? It wasn't stolen, was it? I bought it from a reputable store. I believe they obtained it directly from the Grays. Of course, the Grays probably snatched it from Earth, but we aren't considering that a crime now, are we?"

Blandings gave a slight shrug. "Some would maintain that it is. But that is not my concern. I merely wish to purchase the piece from you. You see, I also am a collector of Earth artifacts."

Sallow stood and joined him at the lamp, enthusiasm in his eyes. "What kinds of items do you have?"

Blandings had prepared for the question. "I have a fabric statuette stuffed with plastic pellets of a pink Earth bird known as a mingo. I have a deck of Earth cards used to play games such as Jack Black and Texas Odin. And I possess a set of recordings by the famous Earth singer, Elfus."

"Interesting. But I am afraid the lamp is not for sale." An unpleasant smile spread across his face. "You see, it's something of a trophy to me. I outbid a rather objectionable young Haplor for it. You know the kind. One of those spineless blockheads our species is producing far too many of these days. It was great fun. Each time I look upon the lamp, I chuckle, remembering the encounter."

"I see."

They both returned to their seats. Blandings took a long sip of tea. "I am prepared to offer one hundred fifty bills for it."

Sallow raised his eyebrows. "That is a fair bit of money, Mr. Pucket. "

"Smythe-Pucket, if you please."

"Smythe-Pucket. But no. Sorry, the leg is not for sale."

"Would you consider a trade for the deck of cards?" Though the other items Blandings had mentioned were made up, he knew Mr. Totleigh had the cards on him and estimated his employer would be willing to part with them to obtain the leg lamp. "There are, I believe, fifty-two of them. Imagine displaying the entire set as you do that Earthling with the club."

Sallow shook his head. "I don't think so."

Blandings took another sip. Unfortunately, he had, if he might employ an idiomatic play on words, no other cards to play. If he could not persuade Sallow to sell him the lamp, then they would have to obtain it by other means. He set down the cup and stood. "Then I will thank you for the tea and your hospitality. It is always enjoyable to meet a fellow collector of Earth artifacts." Blandings stepped toward the desk. "And, of course, to see your lovely home."

Sallow stood. "You are quite welcome."

Blandings moved to the double glass doors. "This view is marvelous. I adore Unaran plant life."

"Do you? Not all from the home world do. Some call it sparse and scrubby."

Blandings inclined his head. "Whatever your vegetation lacks in lushness, it more than makes up for in artistic form." He stuck one hand in a pocket and placed the other hand on the door handle. "May I?"

"Of course," Sallow said.

"You are sure it's all right. I would not want to be presumptuous."

"Certainly."

"Pardon?"

Sallow spoke louder. "Yes, I'm sure."

Blandings swept open the door and breathed in. "Ah, the fragrance is marvelous." He pulled his hand from the pocket, using his body to shield from view the device he was holding. He pressed a button on the device and returned it to his pocket.

Blandings pulled the door closed. "Thank you again. I must go. I have taken up too much of your time."

"Not at all, Mr. Smythe-Pucket," Sallow said. "It was my pleasure. I will walk you out. By the way, have you ever watched my vidcast? I don't wish to brag, but the Welkinda Herald calls it eye-opening."

Chapter 19

A Perilous Proposal

While Blandings' offer to buy the leg lamp was being spurned by Oswald Sallow, Pelham and Keezo were having a similar lack of success walking up street after street in search of a lead on Tunna.

"Excuse me," Pelham asked a young female Haplor who was passing by. "I was wondering if you happened to see anyone like my friend here."

"What friend?" she asked.

Pelham pointed down to where Keezo was peeking out from behind his kneecap.

The female's eyes widened, and she took a step back. "What is that thing? And what is wrong with you, bringing a wild animal into the colony?"

"No, no. Keezo isn't an animal. Though I suppose he can become a bit wild in the presence of baked goods. Say hello, Keezo."

"Hello, Keezo," Keezo said.

The female inhaled sharply with a sort of *erp* sound and retreated several more steps until she backed into a bush, twirled around, and hurried off.

Pelham shook his head at his small companion. "Well, Keezo, that's the fifth failed attempt. How are we ever going to track down Tunna if no one will even talk to us?"

"Keezo not is know," the Danánn said, looking puzzled.

Continuing down the street, they passed a hotel just as the round, purple body of a Donovian emerged from inside.

Pelham raised an arm to hail him. "Pardon, old sport."

The Donovian stopped, the bulbous eyes on top of his head rolling around to focus on Pelham. "Yes?"

"Hoping you can help. Everyone in town seems unnerved by my little alien friend here. I thought you might be more amenable, seeing as how you're an alien yourself."

"I'm not an alien," the Donovian said.

"What? Of course, you are."

"All you are the aliens."

"I think not."

"You're not Donovian."

"True." Pelham wobbled his head from side to side. "I suppose it all depends on one's perspective, what? In any case, we're looking for this person's mate or comrade or however one might classify their relationship."

The Donovian blinked at Keezo. "He doesn't have any arms."

"That's correct," Pelham said.

"And what are those things hanging down from his face?"

"Blandings says they should be called tentacles."

"Like a sealsquid?"

"I'm not sure. I've never heard of sealsquids. But my question is whether you've seen anyone like Keezo here."

The Donovian shook his round head. "I have never seen a sealsquid that looked like this one. It has legs."

"Yes. That's because it isn't technically a sealsquid, you see."

"You just said it was."

"I don't believe I did."

"Well, make up your mind." The Donovian huffed and walked off.

Pelham sighed. "Keezo, I think it's time we throw in the sponge."

"What is ... sponge?"

"A sponge is ... well, a sponge isn't really the point per se, now is it? What I'm alluding to is we should concede the game, raise the white flag, lay down arms."

Keezo blinked. "What is ... arms?"

"Again, not exactly the matter at hand. Though you can't have hands without arms. Maybe we should consult with Blandings. He always has a helpful suggestion. I wonder how he's doing on buying the leg lamp. Surely, that will work, right? Sallow overpaid for the bally thing. One would think he would be anxious to unload it."

Keezo blinked again.

"Of course, the question is," Pelham said, "what if Sallow won't sell? Then where are we, eh, Keezo?"

"We is here."

"My point precisely. We is right here. Out on the street without a prospect in sight. We'd have to fall back on Aunt Agutha's plan to steal the blasted thing." Pelham mused on that for a moment or two. "You know, Keezo, since we've decided to abandon the Tunna search for the nonce, maybe we ought to check out old Sallow's house before it gets dark, get the lay of the land as they say, what? Just in case we end up having to commit larceny."

"Larsa-what?"

"Quite. First, we need to find the place."

Pelham started to contact Blandings to ask for Sallow's address but then stopped. For all he knew, his valet might, at that moment, be in the middle of delicate negotiations with the blighter. Besides, Blandings might not approve of him reconnoitering for a possible break-in. Blandings had a history of trying to dissuade Pelham from various plans and schemes. Honestly, the fellow completely lacked the Totleigh nerve and propensity toward action.

Pelham flagged down an approaching Haplor male. "I say. I'm trying to locate the home of Oswald Sallow."

The male bobbed his head. "Are you a fan of his too?"

Pelham laughed. "Well … um …"

"If you continue along this …" The male's voice trailed off and he grew still. He muttered, "Don't look now, but there's something behind you."

"What? Oh, you mean Keezo?"

"Is that thing yours? See here, mate, it's illegal to introduce off-world species into a new ecosystem."

"No, Keezo is harmless … mostly. And I'm not releasing him … or it. More of a traveling companion, you might say."

"An alien? What are you up to?"

"Nothing. And as was recently pointed out to me, we're all aliens to someone."

The male gave him a hard look and walked on.

Pelham and Keezo walked on to another street. Up ahead, an older female steered a youngling's pushcart around the corner and headed in their direction.

Pelham said. "All right, Keezo, we need a different tactic. Go stand beside that rock wall over there and do that blending-in thing you do."

Keezo stepped over to the wall but remained black.

Pelham waived a come-on gesture. "Go ahead. Camouflage yourself. Change colors."

The female was approaching. Pelham desperately needed Keezo to engage the cloaking technology. Inhaling sharply, Pelham said in his best frightened tone, "Oh no! Quick. Hide, Keezo, hide. Great danger."

With wide eyes, Keezo blended into the gray rock. The female with the pushcart approached, giving Pelham a disapproving stare worthy of Aunt Agutha.

Pelham tipped his straw boater hat. "What ho."

The female said, "Are you speaking to me?"

"I am. Yes."

"Because just now it seemed as if you were talking to yourself, shouting in a most animated fashion."

Pelham laughed carelessly. "Ha. Oh, that. I was um … I was a tad bit upset at myself for forgetting some directions. I was invited over to Oswald Sallow's house, and I seem to have lost my bearings. Do you happen to know where he lives?"

She gave him a funny look. "You're standing in front of it."

"I am?"

She pointed at the imposing home inside the rock wall.

"Ah," Pelham said. "Much obliged."

The female moved off, eyeing him as she retreated.

Pelham examined the grounds. The stone wall was easily hurdle-able. The shrubs would provide little cover, but it was only a few steps across the yard to the house. Pelham counted two doors, a grand front entryway and a double glass door opening to a patio on the side of the house. In addition, multiple windows ringed the ground floor, all easily accessible.

The more he considered the scheme, the more he believed he could deliver the goods. After all, he had participated in a successful sting operation on Haplor to catch a criminal. And on Vogus, he had infiltrated a secret group of revolutionaries. Why couldn't he engage in some simple burglary?

"Hello there."

Pelham turned toward the unexpected voice and saw the young female from the curio shop, Sallow's daughter. And here he was, as they say, casing the joint. He felt like a youngling caught with his hands rammed deep in the biscuit tin.

"Ah. Hello. Good to see you again. Magnolia, if I remember rightly?"

She pursed her lips. "Marigold."

"Ah. Righto. Sorry about that."

"And what was your name again?" she asked.

Given the planned smash-and-grab, Pelham was disinclined to use his real name. "Um … Bunko Tiddlesley … of the Shiftsbury Tiddlesleys. Shiftsbury back on old Haplor, don't you know."

Marigold's head tilted. "No, that's not right. It was Tottenham … or Tottersley … No, wait. Totleigh. That's it."

Reluctantly, Pelham smiled and bowed his head. "Pelham G. Totleigh."

"What was all that about Tiddlesley?"

"Nothing. Nothing. Sort of a game we are playing."

"We? You and who else?"

"Well …"

"By the way, I want to apologize for my father. He tends to run over people like a charging roonaceros. What brings you out here, Mr. Totleigh?"

"Oh, merely admiring the neighborhood. Lovely garden in this one. And the wall construction, of course." He ran a casual hand across the stone. "Do you happen to know who lives here?"

"We do."

Pelham dropped his jaw in feigned surprise. "You do? What a coincidence! So this is where you live? And your father too, I suppose?"

"Yes."

"And the leg lamp? Well, it doesn't *live* here, of course. But your father probably has it prominently displayed somewhere by now. Installed it in the kitchen, did he?"

"The kitchen? Of course, not. It's in his study with the rest of his ridiculous collection."

"He has a study. Impressive. I'd wager it has a great view of this magnificent yard, what?"

"What are you talking about?"

"Your father's study. And the view from the aforesaid. I was … um … I was wondering what part of the house it was in … merely out of curiosity."

She shook her head. "It's through those glass doors. If he happened to be in it, he could see you right now."

"What?" Pelham ducked down below the level of the stone wall.

"Don't worry. I saw him in the dining room having lunch."

Pelham straightened. "Ah. On another note and apropos of nothing, do you get a lot of crime around here?"

She shrugged. "There are often some pickpockets down by the space port. As magistrate, Daddy's been trying to crack down on them. I hear he's tossing out some surprisingly long sentences."

Pelham uttered a nervous chuckle. "And by long sentences, I don't suppose you mean he's been a touch loquacious in his judgments?"

She laughed. "No. He's tossed them in the nick for months and months."

Pelham swallowed. "A stickler for law and order, I see."

"You could say that. You know, you rather rubbed Daddy the wrong way."

"Believe me, the feeling is mutual."

"Well, you're entitled to your opinion. Some people become quite agitated about Daddy's political views. I think it's all silly. But … your mutual animosity does give me an idea."

"You want to bring your father and me together? Make us friends? You wish to see us holding hands around the campfire while singing songs of yore?"

"I should certainly hope not. No, I want you to ask him for my hand in marriage."

"What? I say … what? We barely know each other. I'm flattered, of course … but I rather got the impression that you were interested in that salesclerk."

Marigold's eyes flashed. "Cecil is *not* a salesclerk. He owns the shop. And I want to marry him."

"Then why … me … you want me to … what?"

"For some absurd reason, Daddy doesn't want me to marry Cecil. Daddy thinks owning one store isn't enough. But if you, a person Daddy absolutely detests — no offense—"

"None taken," Pelham said.

"If you ask for my hand, then Cecil might look much better to him … in comparison to you, I mean. What do you say, Mr. Totleigh?"

"What do I say? Are you off your nut? If I asked old Sallow for your hand, he's likely to explode."

A grin swept across Marigold's face. "I know. Isn't it delicious?"

"No, it isn't. He'd sic that mountain in trousers on me, that goon, that henchman of his."

"You mean Gubbins? He's as gentle as a quokel."

"He doesn't look it. Besides, can't you marry whomever you wish? You hardly need your father's permission, do you? I thought that went out with corsets and all that rot."

She emitted a mirthless laugh. "I need his permission if I want to inherit anything. Daddy has deep pockets, and he's willing to use them to obtain whatever he wants."

"Exhibit A," Pelham said, "the way he poached that leg lamp."

"I don't want to be cut out of the will. That's why my marriage to Cecil needs to have his blessing. Please, Mr. Totleigh."

Pelham held up a hand. "While it has often been said that Pelham G. Totleigh is never failing in sympathy for those in need, I am afraid I must decline. Your father would skin me alive."

Marigold shrugged. "That's too bad. Because if you did help me, I could see to it that you end up with that lamp."

"The leg lamp?"

She nodded.

"How?"

Marigold shrugged again. "You know where I live. Stop by when you're ready." She pulled a handkerchief from her pocket and handed it to him. "This has my monogram. You can say you found it. I'll take it from there."

Pelham stared down at the beautifully embroidered MS on the cloth. Actually, it would be a bit of fun to see the old bird go apoplectic. If the maneuver wasn't so abounding in personal danger, he might consider participating. But he couldn't risk it. He held it out to her. "Thank you, but no."

She refused to take it. "If you change your mind, drop by at your convenience." And with that, she strolled away.

"Keezo?" Pelham said.

The Danánn faded back into visibility.

"There you are, Keezo." Pelham shook his head. "Well, seems we have a choice before us. We can either break in to steal the blasted lamp at the risk of being sent to prison, or else we can propose marriage and risk sudden, violent death. My only hope is that Blandings was successful in getting old Sallow to sell."

"Bandy," Keezo said.

"Sir?" Blandings' voice sounded in Pelham's ear over the nanobot connection.

"What ho, Blandings. Keezo and I were just speaking of you. Did your scheme work? Were you able to purchase the leg?"

"Regretfully no, sir. Mr. Sallow seems unwilling to sell at any price."

"Well, dash it all. Isn't that just the pip?"

Chapter 20

Pelham Plans a Heist

Pelham watched the river roll past him and exhaled a deep breath. Outwardly, all was serene and calm as he sat on the bench in the park and waited for Blandings. Inwardly, however, his mind roiled with anxiety.

What should he do to acquire the leg lamp? What would Aunt Agutha do to him if he failed to obtain it? And when was he going to be able to move on from that assignment to the matter of reuniting Tunna and Keezo?

He gazed to his left where Keezo was climbing a weird alien-looking tree. The clump of funnel-shaped bare trunks extended like fingers from a hand, each one topped with bushy branches. Keezo reached the leafy top, plucked one of the red fruits growing there, and began to munch on it.

Beyond the tree, Pelham caught sight of Blandings gliding toward them across the sparse ground cover. He waved.

"Ah, Blandings," he said when the valet reached him. "Your directions were faultless. Two blocks off the city center, as you said."

"Thank you, sir. I happened upon this park this morning and thought you would enjoy it. Sitting out in nature is not something we can often do on Sonus."

"Not for long anyway."

"May I inquire as to Keezo's current location?"

Pelham pointed to the top of the nearby tree. "Quite the prodigious climber, eh?"

"Indeed, sir. And eater as well."

Already a half dozen of the red fruit cores littered the ground below the branch where Keezo sat.

Pelham turned back to the river. "It's a lovely sight, what?"

"Very much so, sir."

"Though I can't say much for the aroma. It smells like a wet bush jackal. If you know what I mean."

"I do, sir. An apt, if distasteful, description. However, the pungent scent does not emanate from the river but rather from sulfuric mud pools in that cluster of trees."

Pelham took a gander in the direction Blandings had indicated. A short distance away, steam rose from a small thicket. "Mud pools, you say. Over there?"

"Yes, sir. There among other places. Geothermal vents are endemic to the planet. You may remember that I mentioned them during the flight."

"I remember something stinky being discussed."

"Locally, they extend from the end of the park on out into the surrounding countryside."

"So that bubbling sound I hear, is that where it's coming from?"

"Yes, sir. The sulfur bubbles rise to the surface of the hot mud and pop. The odor is contained in the bubbles."

"I rather wish it would stay contained in them. But in any case, we aren't here to discuss the local ecosystem, Blandings, but instead how to obtain the leg lamp for Uncle Spence. You don't think Sallow will sell at any price? Under the circs, I would be willing to toss some personal funds into the purse."

"He seemed adamant, sir. He regards it as a trophy of sorts."

"A trophy of what?"

"Of his triumph over you, sir."

"The blighter. Then that leaves us but two options."

"Two, sir?"

"One is to steal the bally thing. The other is a proposition made to me by Sallow's daughter when I ran into her." Pelham outlined Marigold's scheme.

"Sir, I find both alternatives fraught with danger."

"As do I, Blandings, but we must proceed with one of them."

"I would advise caution. We should take some time to ponder the situation. A different solution may yet come to mind."

"Of the two, I'd prefer to steal it."

"But, sir—"

"Let me fall into the hands of the law if I must, but not into the ire of one Oswald Sallow and his meaty-fisted henchman, eh?"

"That much is true, sir. I met Mr. Gubbins. Nevertheless—"

"Through some shrewd questioning of the young Ms. Sallow, Blandings, I was able to learn the location of the leg lamp and the most direct means of ingress to reach it."

"You mean in Mr. Sallow's study through the glass patio doors?"

"What? Oh, so you learned it as well. But you see what this means. It will be a simple matter of slipping in, grabbing the merchandise, and then legging it. Ha! Leg it with the leg lamp, what?"

"But, sir, if I may echo the idiom, leg it to where? This is a small colony, not much larger than Sonus. Do you not think that Mr. Sallow will suspect you and come looking for you?"

Pelham tutted. "He'll still have to find us. We'll take the first spaceship out of here."

Blandings pulled a tablet device from a pocket and consulted it. "Not many flights are scheduled, sir. Assuming you wish to continue the search for Tunna—"

"I do, Blandings. I gave my word." Pelham's eyes flicked up to check on Keezo and found the little alien sitting on a branch and chomping down on yet another piece of fruit.

"There is a ship leaving for Tucana Three tomorrow at midday."

Pelham nodded thoughtfully. "Hmm. Yes. Then we'll need a room for the night and the morning. You can book us in under assumed names. And don't buy our seats for the flight until we are ready to go. As a magistrate, old Sallow might be able to track that sort of thing."

"Judicious suggestions, sir."

"Thank you, Blandings. That's what comes from reading. In *More Adventures of Bongo*, the protagonist, a young Fornaxi named Bongo, if you recall, was on the run from criminals who were trying to steal Little Wiggles, her pet tumpta. She employed similar measures."

"Most ingenious of her, sir."

"I thought so."

"And yet I am far from sanguine about our chances of success. The break-in, the robbery, getting away. There are multiple points at which the plan could fail."

"But what else can I do, Blandings? It's either steal it or march in and profess my love for the daughter of a bloke who hates me and employs a building-sized hooligan."

"As I recommended earlier, sir, time may suggest another course of action."

"What do I have in the way of dark clothing, Blandings?"

"Not much, sir. You have dark trousers. However, if you recall, you insisted on packing tunics and jackets of a more flamboyant coloring … against my advice."

"It does no good to point fingers now, Blandings."

"No, sir."

"Not at this late date."

"I am sorry, sir."

"Then I'm going to have some difficulty dressing for the part of burglar number one. Wait, Blandings, that's the answer."

"What is, sir?"

"Burglar number one."

"Sir?"

"It implies the existence of burglar number two."

"I hope you do not mean me, sir."

"You do dress in dark colors, Blandings, but no. I mean Keezo. He … or they … or Keezo is already black … and tiny, harder to see, you see. And don't forget, Keezo can switch on the camouflage when needed."

"But do you think, sir, Keezo could carry anything as heavy as the lamp?"

"How heavy do you think it is, Blandings?"

"I could not say, sir. I did not have an opportunity to lift it. Nor would I have been comfortable doing so, given its … contours."

Pelham puffed his cheeks and blew them out slowly. "I know what you mean, Blandings. The thing is highly suggestive. Let's try an experiment." He raised his voice. "Keezo, come here, please."

Keezo gulped down one more fruit, slid down the trunk of the tree, and loped over.

Pelham stood and scanned around for something weighty. He pointed at a stone nearly the size of Keezo's head. "Keezo, can you pick up that rock over there — the greenish one?"

Keezo dashed to it, stretched a tentacle around the stone, hoisted it, and gave it a lick. "It no is good."

Pelham made a face. "I shouldn't wonder. Blandings, what do you think of that feat of strength?"

"Impressive, but I believe the lamp to be heavier, sir."

122

"All right. What about that branch over there? Not as thick as the leg but longer."

"That should suffice."

"Keezo, please bring me yonder branch."

Keezo moved to the fallen limb. The little alien wrapped a tentacle around it and strained. Nothing moved. Keezo added a second and third tentacle and tried again. This time the end of the branch rose from the ground. Keezo wobbled back to Pelham, dragging the branch.

"What Pelie is want done with it?" Keezo asked in a strained voice.

"Nothing, Keezo. You can put it down now." Pelham sat back down on the bench. "Well, Blandings, that should prove Keezo's strength. I think with enough tentacles — and mind you, our friend here has plenty of them — Keezo can hoist a simple leg lamp."

"Yes, sir. But will you be able to communicate to Keezo the job requirements?"

"Oh, I think that can be accomplished. Keezo, do you know what the word *take* means?"

"Take," Keezo said.

"Yes. Take. Do you know what it means?"

"Take."

Pelham scratched at his cheek. "Blandings, we seem to have got stuck coming out of the gate. Any suggestions?"

Blandings reached into a pocket and pulled out a key. He leaned over and held it out in his hand. "Keezo, take this."

Keezo stretched out a tentacle, snatched the key from Blandings' hand, and popped it in his mouth.

"Keezo, no!" Pelham said. "Don't swallow that. We need it. We do need that, don't we, Blandings?"

"Yes, sir. It is the key to our flat."

"Spit it out. Spit it out."

Keezo's tongue shot out. The key sat on top, covered with saliva. Pelham and Blandings exchanged hesitant glances.

Pelham said, "Of course, we do have my copy of the key."

"Yes, sir. Still, I doubt Keezo should be consuming metals."

"Probably not."

They shared another glance. Blandings extracted a handkerchief and draped it across his palm before reaching for the key. He dropped it, handkerchief and all, into a pocket.

Pelham said, "Well, we know Keezo understands the word *take*. Now, Keezo, do you know what a leg is?"

Keezo lifted one leg and shook it.

"Good. Good. We're well on our way. Keezo, tonight we're going to go to a house, and I want you to enter it and take a statue of a leg."

Keezo said, "What is … houz?"

"What? Never mind. I'll show you the house when the time comes."

"What is … statue?"

"A statue is … um … hmm. What would you say, Blandings?"

"The definition of a statue, sir, is a three-dimensional representation of a person or animal. However, Keezo is unlikely to understand most of those terms."

"I barely followed you myself, Blandings. Keezo, a statue is a thing that has been made to look like a person … or in this case, the leg of a person. How was that?"

Keezo blinked.

"What you'll be looking for, Keezo, is a large leg … without the rest of the person … only the leg part. Do you understand?"

A tentacle stretched up and scratched Keezo's head.

Pelham said, "We'll go over it all again later." He began counting off items on his fingers. "Leg lamp located, check. Burglar prepared, check-ish. Getaway plan devised, check …" He stopped halfway to the fourth finger. "Wait. What about getting into the blasted place? I just realized, Blandings, that glass door will likely be locked."

"That will not present a difficulty, sir."

Pelham scoffed. "Not a difficulty? A locked door? Not likely. May I remind you, Blandings, that Keezo's ability to become nearly invisible does not make the little critter insub … whatever. Not insubordinate, but the other one."

"What other one, sir?"

"The one where a chap can pass through walls and doors and such like."

"Insubstantial?"

"Exactly. Keezo can't pass through a locked door."

"No, but Keezo can unlock the door."

"What? How?"

"I took the liberty earlier, sir, of acquiring a specialized device that resets electronic lock codes."

"They sell such things, Blandings? My word. If one can reset anyone's lock code, why then isn't crime rampanter … or … more rampant?"

"The device works solely on doors that are already unlocked and open, and then only after a vocal confirmation by the registered homeowner. When it became clear that my efforts to purchase the leg lamp would not prove efficacious, I was able to induce Mr. Sallow to say, 'Yes, I'm sure,' and to allow me to open the door, thus giving me the ability to reset the code."

Pelham blinked a few times. Then his eyebrows rose in admiration. "My man Blandings."

"Thank you, sir." Blandings pulled out a tablet device and tapped on it. He held it up. A large number one showed on the screen. "Keezo, do you see this?"

"I is see."

"Good. This is a one."

"A one."

"Yes. Tonight, Keezo, when you see a button with a one on it, press it."

"Keezo press a one."

"Excellent, Keezo."

Pelham said, "That's the code? One?"

"Yes, sir."

"One. By itself? Nothing else?"

"No, sir. I thought I should keep it simple."

"Good thinking, Blandings. For Keezo's sake, what? Wait. How did you know we would be sending Keezo in to do the deed instead of myself? I only recently had that idea."

"Hmm?" Blandings busied himself with straightening his clothes. "We should book the hotel room, sir."

"Righto. I passed one earlier. A rather odd Donovian was staying there." Pelham rose again and headed for the park entrance. "Come along, Keezo. Oh, look at that, Blandings. Do you see that sign?"

Stuck into the ground a short distance away was a placard with the words: *Alliance Day Festivities Here Tomorrow Night.*

"Yes, sir."

"Must be nice to be able to celebrate Alliance Day in the open air with a large group. Too bad we won't be here."

"Yes, sir. Assuming all goes to plan."

"Of course, it will go to plan, Blandings. You worry far too much. Mark my words, this heist is going to come off without a hitch."

Chapter 21

Legging It

Keezo didn't entirely understand all this talk about taking legs. Legs were attached. They could not be taken. What good would it do to take one anyway? Keezo didn't see how an extra leg would make anyone run faster or climb higher. It would only get in the way. But Bigs were funny like that, always talking about odd things. Danánns talked about real things — finding food, eating, sleeping.

"Where is we go?" Keezo asked, following after Pelie and Bandy. They seemed to be leaving the open area with all the trees and fruit. That was too bad. Keezo liked that place.

Pelie said, "We need to check into a hotel."

"Okey dokey. What is ... oh-tell?"

"It's a place where one can sleep, spend the night."

"Is like mound? Is like Pelie's flat place?"

"Yes, Keezo. Exactly. Well, not exactly. It's smaller. And you rent it by the night. I'll show you."

Another new Bigs' word learned — oh-tell. Keezo had learned so many new words and seen so many new things over the last two days. If they ever got home again, Keezo would have exciting stories to tell around the fire at night, stories of plan-itses out in the black space, stories that would make all the littles' eyes stare in wonder.

They returned to the place with the rows of flat-walled structures the Bigs built above ground. They walked and walked. Finally, Pelie and Bandy entered one of them. Inside was a large space with furnsures everywhere.

Pelie said, "Sit with me here on this couch, Keezo, while Blandings makes the arrangements."

Keezo climbed up beside Pelie and watched Bigs moving around the open space. Soon Bandy returned.

"Everything squared away, Blandings?" Pelie asked.

"It is, sir. I have arranged to have our bags brought over from the space port. I should mention that I checked in under the name Harlan Sable."

"Oh, I like that one, Blandings. Quite elegant. Is that you or me?"

"You, sir. Valets need not be named."

"What about mascots? Furry companions?"

"I thought it best to make no mention of Keezo, sir."

Pelie tapped the side of his nose. "Righto. Well, I'm a bit peckish. I say we strap on the old feed bag, then retire to the room to try and grab some untroubled slumber before tonight's festivities."

"If I might make a suggestion, sir, since Keezo has not thus far been well received in public, perhaps we should repair to the room and order the food to be delivered."

Even without understanding most of that sentence, Keezo could still readily second any motion having to do with food. "Food. Food. Okey dokey."

They climbed an inside hill that Pelie called stairs. Then they walked down a long tunnel. Finally, they entered a smaller space with two of the huge soft things like the one Keezo had woken up on in Pelie's flat place.

Bandy said, "Regrettably, sir, the hotel is nearly full for the Alliance Day festivities. You will have to share the room with myself and Keezo. Hopefully, it will be for only the one night."

"Not to worry, Blandings. This is how co-conspirators should be housed. Quite exciting, what? Now how do we go about ordering supper?"

"As it turns out, there will be no need, sir. The room contains a replicator."

"Excellent. After a day like this, I'd like to start with an Amurru fizz."

Bandy turned to the wall. "One Amurru fizz."

Something buzzed, and just as in Pelie's flat place, a cup magically appeared out of nowhere. Bandy presented it to Pelie.

"Would you like something, Keezo?" Bandy asked.

"Keezo is want nuts."

"Very good. One bowl of native Danánn nuts."

A disembodied voice came out of the wall. "Please specify bushnuts, pitakia nuts, or teeko nuts."

Keezo ran behind the side of one of the huge soft things and changed color to match it. "Who is say that?"

Bandy said, "It is only the replicator, Keezo. Remember the one in the flat? What kind of nuts would you like?"

Keezo remembered. "Teeko nuts."

Bandy said, "One bowl of teeko nuts."

The buzz sounded again, and a small bowl appeared, at the sight of which, Keezo changed to black. Bandy passed the bowl to Keezo. The nuts were good, like fresh off a tree, and Keezo chomped them down greedily.

Pelie said, "How about an egg, Blandings?"

Bandy said, "One egg, poached."

"And bowl teeko nuts," Keezo said, chomping down the last nut from the first bowl.

With a buzz, a plate and a bowl appeared. Bandy handed the plate to Pelie and the bowl to Keezo. Keezo gobbled down the new batch of nuts.

Bandy said, "Soup, creamy ratooshi with chive pepper."

"And bowl teeko nuts," Keezo yelled.

Two bowls appeared. Bandy passed one to Keezo and kept the other.

"Bowl teeko nuts," Keezo said. Another bowl appeared.

"Bowl teeko nuts," Keezo said again. Yet another bowl appeared.

Bandy held up a hand. "Replicator, shut down for now. Start up again only on my voice pattern."

"Bowl teeko nuts," Keezo said. But no more nuts came.

Then for a long time, they did nothing.

Bandy stared at a flat thing he called a book. Pelie stared out the winno, which was like the winno on the white pointy thing with wings that had brought them there but much bigger. Keezo hopped up to the winno and looked out too, watching the Bigs pass by below.

A large blue sun hung low in the sky. With all the other things to look at that day, Keezo had barely noticed it before. Who knew suns could be blue? First the huge ringed Nuggies in Pelie's sittee. Now a blue sun.

After a while, the sun set, and it grew too dark to see the Bigs out the winno. Keezo hopped down and went to sleep on the woolly ground beside Pelie.

And then Keezo felt Pelie shaking one of Keezo's legs, "Wake up. It's time."

Keezo sat up and blinked at Pelie and Bandy, who were standing. Keezo stood and followed them along the tunnel, down the inside hill, and out into the night. Huge moons hung in the night sky. Keezo counted them. One-two. Two moons

— another detail to remember for stories around the fire. Two moons and a blue sun. This was a strange plan-it.

It had by now also become a cold plan-it. Keezo wrapped tentacles around to stay warm. "My feets is cold."

Pelie said. "No wonder with you walking around barefooted. It is a touch chilly this evening, Blandings. Should we take an automated carriage?"

"I shouldn't advise it, sir. Doing so would leave an electronic record of us going to the house. It would be safer to walk."

They walked and walked. It was very far, and the smooth, flat rock was tiring to walk on. And cold. Keezo's feet ached from the chill, and soon he began lagging behind the others. Finally, Bandy picked Keezo up and walked on.

They made their way back to the place with the low outside wall. Bandy sat Keezo on top of the wall. Across a stretch of ground, stood one of the places the Bigs live in.

"That is flat?"

"Not exactly, Keezo," Pelie said. "It's called a house. It's like a flat but a single family lives there."

"Houz," Keezo remembered Pelie saying that word earlier. "Is like mound?"

"I suppose it is. Now, Keezo, do you see that door over there?"

"What is … door?"

"Not this again." Pelie waved toward the houz. "That. That's a bally door, Keezo."

Keezo tried to follow the direction of Pelie's top limb. It pointed toward a bush, another bush, and the wall of the houz. Which one of those was a door?

Pelie said, "Keezo, the door is the glass part of the wall. See it?"

"What is … glaz?"

"The shiny section of the wall," Bandy said.

Keezo nodded. Yes, there was a shiny part.

Bandy said, "That opens. A door is an opening. Go to the door and press the button with the one on it. Do you remember what the one looked like?"

Keezo nodded.

Pelie said, "Then take the leg lamp."

Keezo said, "What is … lamp?"

"The leg, Keezo, the big leg."

Keezo nodded. "I is take leg."

"That's right. Now off you go."

Keezo jumped to the ground on the other side of the wall and took a step toward the houz. Uncertain of everything that was expected, Keezo looked back to Pelie. Pelie gave an encouraging nod. Keezo took another cautious step, then another.

Finally reaching the door, Keezo struggled to remember what to do next. Something about legs. Keezo lifted one leg. Was that it?

In a whisper from the other side of the short wall, Bandy said, "Press the button with the one."

That was it. Keezo remembered now. Keezo searched around for a button. On a shiny metal plate, Keezo found many buttons. Keezo slowly scanned them all. Finally, seeing the button marked with a one, Keezo pressed it.

A *click* sound came from the door followed by a long *squeak* as it swung slightly away from the rest of the wall. Now Keezo understood. A door was an opening. That was what Bandy said. But not like the opening of a mound. A door could also be closed. A door was a sometimes opening.

Pelie called out in a whisper, "Go on, Keezo. Go inside. Grab the big leg thing."

Yes. Keezo was to take somebody's leg. Keezo did not like that part but would try to do it for Pelie.

Keezo slipped through the gap between the door and the wall. It was dark inside except for a glow coming from somewhere on the other side of the space. Between Keezo and the glow, stood many furnsures and other things.

Keezo stepped in and gazed around at everything. There were no Bigs with legs to take, no Danánn with legs to take. That was good. Keezo didn't want to take anybody's leg. But many of the things here did have legs. The furnsures had legs. Some of the things on top of the furnsures had legs too. Which leg was Keezo supposed to take?

Then stepping around one bulky piece of furnsure, Keezo saw it. The glow Keezo had seen came from a huge leg thing standing in the corner. It was bigger than all the other legs. This must be the leg Pelie wanted.

Keezo moved to it. Afraid that the glowing leg must be hot like fire, Keezo stretched out one tentacle and gave it a quick tap. The leg was warm but not hot and only above the knee. Keezo wrapped a tentacle around the lower part of the leg, then stretched up to wrap two tentacles above the knee. As Keezo lifted it, the leg lurched forward, and Keezo had to step back and to the side to keep it from crashing onto the ground.

Unfortunately, with the backward step, Keezo's back slammed against a piece of furnsure. It screeched across the wooden ground of this space. Many little things that were on the furnsure — things with wheels — rolled off and clattered to the ground. Keezo froze.

A deep voice came from somewhere in another space not far away. "Hello?"

Keezo didn't answer. Gripping the big leg, Keezo slowly began backing toward the door. But after a few steps, the big leg jerked to a halt. It ripped from Keezo's tentacles, in the process knocking Keezo to the ground. The leg also fell to the ground with a *thump*. Keezo sat up, looked at the leg, and saw the problem. A vine extended from the bottom of the leg across the space. Footsteps sounded from nearby. A Big was coming.

Keezo yanked on the vine, trying to pull it free from the leg. It would not come loose. Keezo stood and dashed to the other end of the vine to try and free it on that end. But Keezo's foot came down on one of those little wheeled things and fell with a *thud*.

"Who's in there?" the voice called.

Keezo stood and took another step, the other foot now coming down on another of the wheeled things. Keezo pitched forward and slammed into a one-legged furnsure. Keezo again fell, this time onto a woolly patch of ground that was red with gold and blue swirls.

The one-legged furnsure rocked backward, then forward, then back again. Something slid off it onto Keezo's lap. In the faint light coming from the glowing leg stretched across the ground, Keezo saw that the figurine was kind of like a Big, only little. It had one-two top limbs and one-two legs. It wasn't nearly as furry as a Big, though, and had much longer legs. It wore pink with a clear round thing over its head.

Then a door opened in one of the walls, and light flooded in. A Big filled the opening — a really big Big, who blocked most of the light except for some that fell directly on Keezo. Keezo froze in place and tried to blend into the surroundings. But Keezo's fur got confused by all the different colored swirls in the red woolly ground and couldn't change.

The Big looked straight at Keezo and said, "What in the world?"

Keezo glanced at the Big, at the opening in the wall that led to Pelie, to the little pink figure in Keezo's lap. It had legs. It had one-two legs. Maybe this was what Pelie wanted after all.

Keezo thought that was a good thought because it meant Keezo could leave the big leg that was caught in the vine and take this and run now. Keezo jumped up and sprinted toward the door, the pink figurine clutched in Keezo's tentacles.

In the next instant, much light came on in the room. Keezo shot through the door. Light from inside streamed out through the glaz across the ground. Keezo kept running. The heavy footsteps of the Big thundered close behind. Just ahead was the wall where Pelie and Bandy waited. But then the huge top limb of the Big came down and pinned Keezo to the ground.

The Big said, "Gotcha, you little thief."

Chapter 22

A Doleful Retreat and a Disagreeable Plan

In the eternal psychological battle between fight and flight, Haplors instinctively come down solidly on the side of flight. And for good reason. Not only are they smaller than most intelligent species in the galaxy, Haplors are also smaller than many of the native creatures of the planet Haplor, most notably creatures with long teeth and sharp claws, such as roonaceroses and crocoraptors, who historically — or rather, pre-historically — found Haplors tasty.

Buried deep in the Haplor psyche lies an ancestral memory of — and propensity toward — scurrying off in the face of danger. It is one reason why Haplors developed such good running skills. Or one might say, those Haplors with genes for fast running tended to be the ones who survived long enough to pass on those genes to the next generation.

So while Pelham sincerely wished to rush out and fight to help Keezo, he found that impulse being overridden by a flight response, which perhaps counterintuitively in this case, took the form of cowering behind the wall in terror.

He gawped at his valet, who also had ducked behind the stone barrier, and said in a strained whisper, "What should we do, Blandings?"

Blandings rose enough to peer over the wall into the yard. Pelham joined him. From the light shining out of the study, they could see Gubbins standing in the middle of the yard, holding Keezo at arm's length by the scruff of the Danánn's neck, Keezo's legs dangling high above the ground.

Gubbins' baritone voice sounded across the dark yard. "What are you, anyway?"

Keezo, eyes wide, said nothing.

Blandings whispered, "I very much doubt, sir, whether even both of us working together could free Keezo from Mr. Gubbins' grip."

"But … but," Pelham said.

Another figure burst from the study. It was Sallow, a dressing gown wrapped around his stocky frame. He scowled around at the scene and cried out, "My Barbie!"

"What's a Barbie?" Pelham whispered.

Blandings nodded toward the small figurine in pink lying in the dirt at Gubbins' feet. Sallow swept it up and cradled it in his arms.

The vidcaster glared at Keezo. "What is that?"

"The burglar," Gubbins said.

"That thing? I don't believe it. Scan the grounds for accomplices."

Pelham and Blandings ducked back behind the wall.

Sallow said, "When you've checked the grounds, Gubbins, bring the creature inside. If it can talk, I want to question it."

"Blandings?" Pelham said.

"Sir, I think the best option is to withdraw to a safer location and devise a new plan."

"We can't leave Keezo."

"We will return, sir. But for now, you must follow me, and please, keep your head down."

With reluctance, Pelham nodded.

In a crouch, they moved along the length of the wall. When they reached the end of the block, they straightened and walked on into the night, their path lit by the two moons glowing in the sky.

"Well, that didn't exactly go to plan, eh, Blandings?"

"Most regrettably, sir, it did not."

"What do we do now? Do we break in ourselves and try to smuggle out both Keezo and the lamp?"

"I would advise against any such move, sir. We do not know where they will be keeping Keezo … or if they will turn Keezo over to the city guards. In addition, Mr Sallow is sure to be on heightened alert following the incident. He will most likely reset the lock on the door."

Pelham sighed. "But dash it all, Blandings, we can't just leave the little guy … and by guy, of course, I mean—"

"I do know what you mean, sir, and I agree. We must rescue Keezo somehow."

"Righto. Glad we're on the same screen, as it were." Pelham took a heavy breath in the thin air. "I don't mind telling you, Blandings, this evening's events have shaken me to the core."

"I confess, sir, I am considerably distressed myself."

"You, Blandings? I thought you were unflappable. I say, it *is* growing cold out here."

"Yes, sir. As I understand it, the temperature will continue to plummet through the night to the point where it would not be safe to be out of doors. One more reason for a temporary retreat."

"If you say so, Blandings." Pelham glanced back over his shoulder. "I'm heartbroken over little Keezo … all alone now … with that blister Sallow. I'm … I'm disconsolate. Doleful. I feel a great deal of shame."

"Yes, sir."

"Blandings, have I ever mentioned my great granddad, old Eustace C. Totleigh?"

"The explorer, sir?"

"That's the one. You know, back in his day, he mapped the great jungle of Tharsis."

"So I have heard, sir."

"The family stories say it was quite the trying experience. There are a lot of dangers out in the jungle, you know, Blandings."

"So I should be disposed to imagine."

"Large animals prowling about. Dangerous insects swarming."

"Yes, sir."

"Swollen rivers. Perilous mountain peaks."

"Yes, sir."

"But enough background. Here's my point. Old Eustace passed an adage down to his children and grandchildren, which in due course was passed down to me. Do you know what that was, Blandings?"

"I would not hazard a conjecture, sir."

"Never leave a Haplor behind. That was it, Blandings. Never leave a Haplor behind. It became a sort of maxim in the family. I once overheard Aunt Agutha muttering it under her breath when she had to bail me out of jail."

"Indeed, sir."

"And Blandings, though Keezo is not technically a Haplor, I feel confident my distinguished forebear would approve of extending the dictum to cover the little critter."

"I would assume so, sir."

"So you can imagine the degree to which it stings a Totleigh such as myself to be walking in the opposite direction and leaving Keezo to face Sallow alone."

"I understand, sir. However, rushing in without a plan could easily end with us arrested as co-conspirators in the attempted robbery."

"What of it, Blandings? It was Aunt Agutha who told us to undertake the burglary. She surely couldn't get too annoyed."

"I would point out, sir, that from a jail cell, we could do nothing either to free Keezo or to obtain the lamp. Further, a public arrest on Unara of the nephew of the Sonus governor would unquestionably lead to a public spectacle and an embarrassing interstellar incident for the governor."

"Ah, well when you put it that way, Blandings, I can see how the ancient aunt might not be entirely pleased."

"Most assuredly, sir."

They had left the residential area and were now walking through the city center. Pelham looked up to see them passing by the curio shop. "There it is, Blandings. The proverbial scene of the crime, as it were. Or the scene of the purchase, at least. I suppose we've just vamoosed from the crime scene. If only I could have slipped into the shop and back out again with the lamp before that blighter turned up. And by blighter, Blandings, I mean one Oswald Sallow."

"I had inferred as much, sir."

"Then none of this would have happened. But I suppose there's no point playing what if at this juncture, eh, Blandings?"

"No, sir."

"What we need is a plan — a scheme to free Keezo without landing ourselves in the old consommé, eh?"

"Yes, sir."

"Has anything sprung to mind so far?"

"Only that we need more information, sir, such as Keezo's current location and the security arrangements being employed."

"How in the blazes are we going to learn that?"

"I believe, sir, it will require making a formal visit to the house."

Pelham's chest tightened. "Visit old Sallow? Infiltrate enemy lines?"

"Yes, sir. In a manner of speaking."

"Who? Or should it be whom?"

"It depends on the construction, sir?"

"What construction, Blandings? Do we need to build something as well?"

"I was referring to the sentence construction, sir. But in answer to your initial question, it is likely we will both need to go. That way one of us can engage in social interaction while the other searches for Keezo."

Pelham scoffed. "Social interaction? If you had been present at the curio shop during my first encounter with Sallow, Blandings, you would hardly characterize it as social interaction. More like the comments section of an inflammatory network post. Sallow hates me, and I, for my part, am not exactly wild about him. Going there would be far from a pleasant experience. What it would be is dangerous. Don't forget that his daughter wants me to propose marriage solely to give the old stinker the pip. She's liable to bring it up herself, given half a chance."

"I do recall that, sir. However, if you wish to free Keezo, I see no other way."

"Hmm. Well, for Keezo then."

"There may be some difficulty for me as well. Previously, I presented myself at their door as Mr. Horace Smythe-Pucket."

"Yes, that does present a problem. How are you going to explain away the uncanny resemblance?"

"I have not as yet decided, sir."

"Evil twin?"

"That would not be my first choice, sir. I should not wish to disparage twins, very few of whom are evil."

They walked on in silence. When they reached the hotel, Pelham collapsed onto one of the beds.

Blandings began rummaging through the cabinets and drawers. "Sir, I regret to say that the only way to make tea appears to be with the replicator. Would you like some?"

Pelham shook his head.

Blandings requested tea for himself and sat down in a chair with the cup. Somewhere outside, a bell tolled.

Pelham rolled over on the bed and pulled a pillow over his head. "What's that blasted ringing?"

"I do not know, sir. If you wish, I will inquire about it tomorrow."

"Probably tolling the death knell of our fortunes, Blandings, now that both the leg lamp and Keezo are held captive in the recesses of the Sallow compound."

Blandings took a sip. "Hmm."

Pelham removed the pillow and raised his head from the covers. "You hmm-ed, Blandings?"

"I did, sir."

Does that mean you have come up with an idea?"

"Not fully, sir. However, I do have an approach in mind."

"What is it?"

Blandings hesitated. "I fear you may not find the plan overly agreeable, sir."

Pelham sat up on the bed. "What, Blandings?"

"I believe, sir, you should apologize to Mr. Sallow."

"What?" Pelham leaped from the bed and began pacing. "I mean to say ... what? Apologize to that rotter, that menace, that smudge on the landscape? I think not. Really now, Blandings. One must draw the line somewhere. How can I apologize when the offense is entirely his?"

"Sir, given Mr. Sallow's animosity toward you, I judge it is the one approach that will gain us admittance. You must do it for Keezo."

Pelham whirled on his valet. "Wait. Wait. Did I tell you that Marigold gave me one of her handkerchiefs so I could visit on the pretense of returning it?"

"No, sir."

"What about that?"

Blandings studied the ceiling for some moments. Pelham waited in silence as Blandings considered the possibilities.

Finally, the valet shook his head. "It is far from certain, sir, that the handkerchief would gain us admittance. Mr. Gubbins is likely to merely take it from you and dismiss us at the doorstep."

Pelham slumped onto the edge of the bed. "You're right, Blandings. Blast! But I don't bally well want to apologize. I've done nothing for which an apology is needed."

"I should point out, sir, that you will not be begging pardon for the incident at the curio shop."

"No? Then what? That was my sole encounter with that black hole of a Haplor ... fortunately."

"You will be apologizing for me, sir."

"For you, Blandings?"

"Yes, sir. You will have just learned tomorrow morning of my failed attempt to impersonate a collector of Earth artifacts in an effort to obtain the lamp for you."

"I did … I mean, I will?"

"Yes, sir. Naturally, you will be mortified at my behavior."

"What?"

"And determined to apologize face-to-face."

"I still don't like that part."

"While I, no doubt, am sent off to the kitchen, allowing me an opportunity to explore the house in search of Keezo."

Pelham rubbed his chin and nodded. "I see. Yes. Are you sure this is the only way?"

"I believe it is, sir."

Pelham smiled. "Hmm. Well, Blandings, now that you mention it, I am more than a bit shocked by your recent actions. Frankly, it is quite beyond the pale, not the done thing, what?"

"No, sir."

"It is an embarrassment to both of us."

"For which I am deeply sorry, sir."

"Nothing for it but to march over to old Sallow as soon as poss with hat firmly in hand."

"Yes, sir."

"Good thinking, Blandings."

"Thank you, sir. I endeavor to give satisfaction."

Chapter 23

The PELIE Plot

Oswald Sallow leaned back in his chair at the kitchen table and crossed his arms. A cup of tea sat on the tabletop in front of him beside the Earthling doll, now cleaned of dirt. Sallow reached for the cup but hesitated. His arm instead swung to the doll, from which he brushed another smudge he had just noticed. He tsked. How much more work would it take to return the figurine to mint condition?

He regarded the creature sitting across the table from him. A cargo strap secured the small, black-furred body to the chairback. The alien didn't struggle against the restraint. All it did was sit there, blinking occasionally and staring around at the room. Sallow had never seen a being like this, and Sallow had made a thorough study of alien life-forms. Whatever it was, it hadn't come from Unara. The planet had no such creatures.

The thing looked frightened. Good, Sallow thought. Fear was useful. Fear could give the truth a sharp elbow to the ribs and shove it out into the open. Sallow needed to learn the truth, though he already had a strong suspicion about what was going on here.

He lifted the teacup from the table and took a slow sip. Lowering it, he stared into the alien's two large eyes. "All right. What are you, anyway?"

The alien blinked at him.

"You heard me," Sallow said in a more threatening tone. "What are you?"

The creature blinked again.

Gubbins, leaning against a nearby cabinet, said, "Maybe it doesn't have translator bots. Maybe it's a mute animal."

Sallow set the cup back in the saucer with as much calm as he could muster under the circumstances. "No, I need to find out who sent it."

"But, boss, if it doesn't talk—"

"No!" Sallow brought a fist down onto the tabletop with a *thud* that thundered through the room and rattled the cup and saucer.

The little alien's eyes grew huge. Its fur faded to the brown of the chair.

"Whoa," said Gubbins. "Do you see that? It has superpowers."

Sallow shot his assistant a glare. "No. It does not. The word *superpower* implies superiority. This creature merely possesses an adaptive defensive mechanism to make up for its lack of size and intelligence. On the whole, this is an inferior species." Sallow turned back to the alien. "I asked you what you are?"

The alien blinked again.

Sallow snatched up the cup and took another sip. "Are you hungry? Talk to me, and I'll give you some food."

The alien's fur shifted back to black. It nodded its head.

"Ah-ha," Sallow said. "It understood me. Do you have a name? Tell me your name, and I'll get you some food."

The voice came out in a timid squeak. "I is Keezo."

Sallow grinned, a sight from which the creature immediately recoiled and again camouflaged itself.

"Now we are getting somewhere," Sallow said. "Keezo. Is that your name or your species? Or perhaps a rank?"

"I is Keezo. Who is you?"

"Oh, I think you already know who I am. That's why you broke in, isn't it? Who sent you?"

The creature blinked again.

"Who told you to steal my property?"

"Pelie. Pelie is say take leg."

"Of course."

"Of course, what?" Gubbins asked. "Who's Pelie?"

"It's not Pelie as a name," Sallow said, "but PELIE as an acronym. P-E-L-I-E. The People Entirely in League with Interstellar Extraterrestrials. It's a dangerous fringe group, Gubbins — Haplors intent on taking over the governments of Haplor worlds with the help of alien conspirators. This all makes sense now."

Gubbins scratched at the back of his head. "Not to me. What would a group of insurrectionists want with an Earth doll?"

"To try to embarrass me, of course, Gubbins. They think if they reveal that I collect Earth artifacts, it will somehow show that I have a double standard when it comes to aliens. They're plotting against me. They're plotting against us all. But of course, they completely misunderstand why I collect Earth objects. I grasp what many refuse to see. That in the long run, the Earthlings will become our greatest threat. I study their culture to learn their weaknesses. One must understand one's enemy to defeat them."

Gubbins' face formed into a question. "You're saying you collect Earth toys so you can learn how to save Haplors from Earthlings?"

"Exactly, Gubbins."

The alien's fur changed once more to black. "You is has food?"

Gubbins said, "What was the part about the leg?"

"What leg?"

"The alien said PELIE told it to take some leg."

"Isn't it obvious?"

"Um ..."

"You is has food?"

"It means they want to cut my legs out from under me, Gubbins ... metaphorically speaking."

"It does?"

"Of course, it does. I'm one of the few people holding back their diabolical plot. They want to discredit me, to knock me off my feet, so to speak. But we won't let them, Gubbins. And this Keezo is the very thing we need to fight back."

"Why?" The big Haplor straightened. "What are you going to do to it?"

"I'm not doing anything *to* it. Not yet anyway. I'm going to feature it in a vidcast. When are we slated to record again?"

"Zahnsday. You're scheduled to interview the author of a new book on Haplor history."

"Do I agree or disagree with this one?"

"You like this one."

"Then I don't want to postpone him."

"Her."

"What?"

"The author is female."

Sallow's head jerked around to stare at his engineer-slash-bodyguard. "And I approve?"

"That's what you told me."

"Whatever. All right, we'll record a special episode tomorrow. This Keezo will be our featured guest, exhibit A in my proof of the alien threat. The idea that one of them could fly into Unara without ever once being questioned by the authorities and then break into the home of a private citizen, that should alarm every Haplor on every world."

"How do you know the alien was not questioned by the authorities?"

Sallow rolled his eyes. "Call it a working hypothesis, Gubbins, a reasonable assumption, a piece of unassailable logic. It is patently clear that if anyone had competently interrogated this ... thing, they would have uncovered its connection to PELIE and stopped this outrageous attack."

"Should I check with the guards to confirm that?" Gubbins asked.

"Absolutely not. There's no point. For all we know, the guards may be in on it." Sallow took a moment to play with the thought. "Yes, a conspiracy involving the law enforcement elite. No. A conspiracy down in the ranks. That's even better. Agents put in place by alien worlds." He smiled his unattractive smile at Keezo. "Who is your contact in PELIE?"

"What is ... contact?" the alien asked.

"Who do you talk to?"

"I talk to Pelie. You is has food?"

"Yes, yes. But who — who within PELIE?"

The alien blinked.

Sallow said, "Who brought you here?"

"Bandy is carry Keezo here when Keezo tired."

"Bandy, eh? Gubbins, search for a Haplor named Bandy."

Gubbins pulled a device from his pocket and tapped on it. "What do you think the alien means by *carry*?"

"Who knows? It's probably talking about an automated carriage or even a spaceship. This creature is clearly of subnormal intelligence. It's this Bandy who is important."

Keezo said, "We is look for Tunna. Is you see Tunna?"

"Who is Tunna?" Sallow asked.

"Tunna is Tunna."

"See, Gubbins. Inferior intellect. No reasoning abilities."

The imager said, "I can't find any Bandy on the network, as either a given name or a surname."

"Are you searching for Haplors only? Widen it to aliens."

"There's Ban DiVeran, the Pardiun pop singer."

"There you go."

144

"I don't think so. We would know it if Ban DiVeran was on Unara. Everyone in the galaxy would know it."

"Hmm. Then Bandy must be an alias, a code name. This is truly a dark conspiracy. What ships have landed here recently?"

Gubbins tapped some more. "Two Rhegedian starliners today and a Gray cargo ship yesterday."

Sallow leaned forward. "Rhegedians and Grays. Either of them could be involved in PELIE. It would be just like them."

"So if you're going to use Keezo in your show tomorrow, what should we do with it tonight? We can't leave the poor little thing tied up to this chair."

"You is has food?" Keezo asked once more.

"Poor little thing?" Sallow said. "Gubbins, this alien broke into my study and nearly destroyed it."

"Yeah. Well, some of that may have been me."

"In that case, you can clean up the mess. Do it before you return to bed. But as for the alien, it has already shown us its camouflaging abilities. It will need to be locked up lest it escape. Do we still have that cage for the moon owl Marigold used to have?"

"I think so. It may be out in the garden shed."

"Good. Deposit the alien inside it."

"We can't stick it out in the shed. It'll freeze."

"It would serve it right for breaking into my house."

"But then you couldn't put it in the vidcast."

Sallow harrumphed and waved an arm toward the back of the kitchen. "Fine. Keep it in the pantry."

"Yes, Mr. Sallow."

"And then straighten up my office."

"Yes, Mr. Sallow. And I'll get Keezo some food too."

Sallow shot him an incredulous look.

Gubbins said, "You promised."

"All right, if you must."

Sallow rose from the table and headed toward his bedroom. He hoped he could fall asleep again after all the excitement. He had a big day tomorrow — a script to write and shoot. And this might just be the most important vidcast of his career.

Chapter 24

A Not So Sincere Apology

The next morning, Pelham and Blandings took an automated carriage to the home of Oswald Sallow. They stood on the doorstep, shivering in the early morning cold and looking up at the face of Gubbins, who stared at them from the open doorway.

"You were the one at the shop," Gubbins said, pointing a meaty finger at Pelham. His eyes darted toward Blandings. "And you were the one who came here yesterday — Smythe-something."

"Yes," Pelham said. "That is all true. Well, the Smythe-something isn't totally in accordance with all the facts. But that is what we would like to discuss with old Sallow."

Gubbins's thick eyebrows descended over his eyes. "What do you mean?"

"It is something of a private matter." It was going to be hard enough, Pelham thought, to choke out an apology to that menace Sallow. He certainly didn't want to go over it all with the henchman as well. "Suffice it to say that he will be interested in what we have to say. And if you don't mind, could we step inside? It's freezing out here."

"Yeah, it gets that way. All right. Come in. I'll see if he wants to receive you."

They entered the house and waited in the hall while Gubbins disappeared into the back. Within a few moments, Pelham heard footsteps coming their way. He looked up expecting to see the unpleasant face of Oswald Sallow. Instead, Marigold sailed in as if on a strong spring wind. All in all, Pelham had to admit, she was a much more appealing sight than the old yak himself, though under the circumstances, hardly a more welcome one.

"Mr. Totleigh, what a pleasure. I see you're taking me up on my offer. I am positively elated."

"Well … um … not entirely," Pelham said. "By the by, this is my valet Blandings. Blandings, Marigold Sallow."

Blandings inclined his head. "A pleasure to meet you, ma'am."

"Charmed." She turned back to Pelham. "But what do you mean by not entirely?"

"Not … um … at all … actually. I'm here to talk to your father about another matter. I am not asking for your hand in marriage."

She stared at him for a few moments with an inscrutable grin on her face. Then she laughed gaily and said, "Don't be silly. Of course, you're going to ask to marry me. You want that hideous leg lamp, don't you? Help me, and I'll help you. I'll make arrangements to bring Cecil here. Then we can spring the trap. Don't go anywhere." And with that, she barreled off into another part of the house.

"Blandings?"

"Sir?"

"Could you rewind that last bit of conversation and explain it to me? It seems to have veered off in a trajectory rather different from what I intended."

Before Blandings could reply, Sallow appeared from another direction, tying the belt of a dressing gown as he walked. He scowled at Pelham. "What do you want, Totleigh?"

"And a good morning to you too, Sallow," Pelham said, putting on a cheery tone. "I say, we didn't pull you from your bed, did we?"

Sallow harrumphed. "No. No, I … well, I did arise somewhat later than usual … only because I was up in the middle of the night."

"So was I, as it happens. But here I am, dressed and ready to take on the day."

"What were you doing up late? Frequenting some seedy saloon?"

Pelham's mouth went dry as chills squirmed across his skin. He dared not give Sallow cause to suspect that he had anything to do with the attempted smash-and-grab of the previous evening. But if he said he was out at some pub in the wee hours, Sallow might ask which one, and Pelham didn't know any on this planet. He chortled out a nervous laugh.

Blandings said, "Mr. Totleigh has been suffering from space lag."

Pelham gazed at his valet with a flutter of admiration. "Righto, Blandings. Frightful nuisance getting used to a new time zone on a different planet, what?"

Sallow scrutinized the valet. "He called you Blandings? I thought your name was Smythe-Pucket. What are you doing with Totleigh?"

"Ah," Pelham said. "That is precisely the reason we called."

"Oh?"

It seemed to Pelham that Sallow had somehow managed to cram into that one syllable — those two small letters — a level of bile and intimidation worthy even of Aunt Agutha. It threw him off his game.

"Ah …. Ah … Ah …"

Sallow glared. "Well, don't just stand there saying 'ah,' Totleigh."

"Ah …."

Blandings once again came to the rescue. "The fault is entirely mine, sir."

"What do you mean, Smythe-Pucket … or Blandings … or whatever your name is?" Sallow's eyes narrowed.

"It is Blandings, sir. I am Mr. Totleigh's gentleman's gentleman."

Sallow glared at Pelham. "You have a valet? Of course, you do. Your kind would."

Pelham found his voice. "My kind? Now see here, Sallow—"

Blandings cleared his throat, stopping Pelham from continuing. "May I explain, sir?"

"Somebody should," Sallow said. "What's this all about?"

Blandings said, "Late yesterday morning, Mr. Totleigh returned to me in what I can only describe as a despondent state, the reason for which, I soon learned, was his failure to obtain the Earth lamp now in your possession."

Sallow chuckled. "It broke him, did it?"

"I confess it did seem to me, sir, to have that effect."

Sallow shifted the smirk to Pelham, who responded by heaving what he hoped was a convincing forlorn sigh.

Blandings continued, "It grieved me to see Mr. Totleigh in that condition. Therefore, I contrived to come here under false pretenses in an attempt to purchase the item for him."

"Is this true, Totleigh?"

Pelham sighed again.

Blandings said, "Naturally, when Mr. Totleigh learned of the scheme, he was, if I may say so, sir, appalled."

Blandings made eye contact with Pelham, which Pelham took to be his cue. "Yes … um … appalled. And shocked. Shocked and appalled. And abashed. One might almost say aghast." He was finding his footing now, warming to the topic. "Yes. I must say, I was outraged. This sort of underhanded tactic is something I will not tolerate. The besmirching of the grand old name of Totleigh. At the moment, I can barely stand to lay eyes on him. I insisted that we come here first thing this morning to offer you … um … um …" The next words seemed to catch in his throat. He dropped his voice. "… a sincere … apology."

Sallow's smirk grew wider. "What was that, Totleigh? I couldn't quite make out that last part."

"I said … I said … I wanted to … to apologize … for Blandings. Sorry and all that." Over his young lifetime, Pelham had often had reason to wear contrite expressions — mostly in front of Aunt Agutha and assorted judges. He slapped one on now.

Sallow, meanwhile, took on the most annoyingly smug facial expression Pelham had ever seen. "May I assume that you have dismissed this person from your service?"

Pelham's jaw dropped. "What? You mean, fire him? Fire Blandings? Hand him his hat and tell him to turn in his key?"

"That's what I said."

Pelham scoffed. "Not likely."

The wrinkles at the edges of Sallow's eyes deepened, and not, Pelham thought, solely because the rotter was on the wrong side of middle age and subject to that sort of thing. Sallow was obviously enjoying this.

"I would think, Totleigh, it would be the least you could do … to show your sincerity … and to punish him for his misdeed. One has to keep employees in check."

"I … I suppose … but if you saw what he can do with a trouser crease …" Pelham waved a hand up and down his leg as proof of what he was saying.

"Crease or not, I demand that you fire him. I'm the offended party here."

"But … but …"

Blandings emitted a respectful cough. The others turned to him. "I have, in fact, tendered my resignation. However, Mr. Totleigh recently advanced me a small sum of money and is now requiring that I stay on until I can repay him with labor."

"Is that right, Totleigh?" Sallow asked.

"Oh, absolutely. One can hardly give him the boot while he's in arrears, as it were."

Sallow studied Blandings. He scrutinized Pelham. "Do you have any proof of this?"

Blandings said, "I sent Mr. Totleigh my notice this morning. Sir, if you would open your personal device, you will find it among your messages."

"What?" Pelham pulled an electronic tablet from a pocket and began tapping on it.

Blandings leaned over to watch him. "Go into that app, sir. No, not that one. Exit that. This app. Yes. Then tap there ... and there. There it is, sir. You might wish to show that to Mr. Sallow."

"Yes," Pelham said. "This appears to all be in order."

He held out the screen. While Sallow squinted at the resignation message, Pelham shot a furtive wink in the valet's direction. "I must say, Blandings, you seem to have thought of everything."

Sallow nodded slowly. "All right. Well, gentlemen, I appreciate the apology." He held out an arm to sweep them toward the door. The next moment, he dropped it. "You know, Totleigh, now that I think of it, how would you like to see the leg lamp one last time ... in its new home?"

Pelham knew Sallow was not motivated by any spirit of magnanimity but rather by the base desire to rub it in. He started to decline the offer, but then he realized that refusing to view the bally thing would be an admission of defeat on his part. An idea came to him. "Why not, old chap? Much obliged."

Sallow led them to the study where the leg lamp stood in the corner glowing warmly. Sallow stepped to it and patted the lampshade, causing the fringe to swish around in a way Pelham found somewhat distracting.

Forcing a note of joviality into his voice, Pelham said, "Hmm. What was I thinking? Now that I see it here in situ, as it were, Sallow, clearly the thing is a trifle tacky, what?"

Sallow tutted. "So you say. It didn't stop you from bidding it up in the shop."

Pelham snickered. "Merely a lark, old son. I thought the lads back home might derive a giggle or two from it. I was thinking of donating it to the club just to see how long they'd keep the bally thing out on display. I can see now that it wouldn't last a day."

Pelham shot a glance at Blandings and was gratified to see on the valet's placid face the barest hint of a smile.

Meanwhile, Sallow had reddened and was on the verge of snarling out a comeback when Marigold swept into the room. "Hello, Mr. Totleigh! Don't you look sharp today!" She moved to Pelham and slipped her arm in his. "Couldn't stay away, could you, you charmer?"

"What?" Pelham said.

The redness in Sallow's face deepened. "What are you doing, Marigold?"

"I'm saying hello to a winsome visitor, Daddy. Won't you stay for lunch, Mr. Totleigh?"

"Well ..." Pelham said.

"But ..." Sallow said.

"Wonderful," Marigold said. "It's settled. I'll tell Chef."

Through gritted teeth, Sallow said, "Now, darling, I'm sure Mr. Totleigh has more important things to do than wait around here all morning. He came all the way from Sonus."

She beamed at Pelham. "What about it, Mr. Totleigh? Is there somewhere else you simply must be?"

Pelham said, "I mean ..."

"See, Daddy. He'd love to stay."

Sallow said, "But ..."

"I insist," Marigold said. "We never have interesting people over, do we, Daddy?"

"I beg to differ, my dear. We have some remarkably interesting visitors from time to time — some of my vidcast guests who travel here, leaders of business and popular movements."

Marigold rolled her eyes in a dramatic fashion. "Boring. All they ever talk about is politics. Mr. Totleigh is obviously a person who loves art and knows about the galaxy. Have you traveled much, Mr. Totleigh?"

"Oh, here and there," Pelham said. "I was on Vogus some time back and—"

"Don't tell me now. Save it for lunch. I want to hear all about it. Daddy, you can entertain him until then, can't you?"

"But I've yet to dress."

"Well, if you'd rather I take him for a walk through the garden, just the two of us, arm in arm ..."

The red in Sallow's face turned ashen. "No, no. You go on about your day, dear. It won't take me but a few minutes to dress. You'll wait here, won't you, Totleigh?"

"I ... I suppose," Pelham said.

"Thank you, Daddy. You're a dear," Marigold said. "Ooh, Mr. Totleigh. I'm terribly excited to have you here."

She swept out again, leaving everyone in stunned silence.

After several moments, Pelham managed to say, "I ... I must say, Sallow, though nippy this morning, the weather is remarkably nice. Tell me, do you ever have tornados on Unara ... other than her, I mean?"

Chapter 25

Heard it Through the Grapevine

Nearly all the worlds in the civilized galaxy, a term which is generally meant to include all spacefaring species other than quarantined worlds such as Earth, share access to a decentralized matrix of data and computers known simply as the network. With detailed facts and photos of people, places, and events, it is the largest compendium of information anywhere. And unlike certain other electronic networks, it is almost completely free of pictures of cats, restaurant entrées, and people making duck faces (except, of course, among the duck-billed Alashiyans). Some people have noted with alarm that the Grays have recently begun posting cat memes from Earth, dubbing them adorable and hilarious.

But even the galactic network, Blandings often thought, could not hold a candle to the exchange of information shared by staff and domestic help who work for the wealthy. No valet or gardener or nanny would dream of accepting an offer of employment without first checking with the community of hired help to find out what working with that particular employer might be like.

Of course, unlike the galactic network, none of the data in the domestic rumor mill was written down in any form. Its vast wealth of knowledge was shared exclusively by word of mouth and absolutely in confidence.

Because of that, Blandings was anxious to slip away from the study and meet the hired staff of the Sallow household to try to learn what had happened to Keezo following the Danánn's capture and more importantly, what might happen next.

When Marigold left the room, she had seemingly left Sallow and Mr. Totleigh in something of a daze. Sallow, still in his dressing gown, dropped into a chair and stared off into space. Mr. Totleigh, meanwhile, was gazing intently at his shoes. A cold and awkward silence reigned between the two of them.

Blandings looked for a reason to slip out but could find none. So instead, he remained in place, practicing the Danánn-like skill known to all domestic staff of making themselves invisible.

He expected that Sallow would soon, as he had previously announced, move along to get dressed, thus opening the way for Blandings to find and interview the staff. However, the thought seemed to have completely slipped the older Haplor's mind.

Might there be some way to hurry things along, Blandings pondered? He doubted it. He was in no position to mention Sallow's pajamaed form to him. Not only would the statement be improper, but it might very well lead to him being ordered from the house.

Blandings cast his eyes toward Mr. Totleigh, hoping to wordlessly communicate the situation to him. But Mr. Totleigh was still fiercely studying his shoes.

Then Sallow dropped a hand to one leg and seemed to realize he was touching sleepwear. The hand froze in place. Sallow stared down at it and blinked. Pulling the dressing gown tighter, he stood. "Um … Totleigh, if you'll excuse me, I'll need to find my day clothes."

"Certainly. Certainly," Mr. Totleigh said. "Don't worry a thing about me."

"Why don't you sit here on the couch while you wait."

"Ah. Thank you. Most considerate of you."

Sallow frowned. "I'm not making the offer out of concern. I don't want you touching any of my things. Sit there, and don't move." Sallow waited for Pelham to sit before marching from the room.

"Sir," Blandings said, "If you do not require anything else at this time, I will slip away to look for Keezo."

"Righto, Blandings. Feel free to trundle off. And good luck."

Blandings glided from the room. He headed toward the back of the house and found the kitchen, where a tall, furless female with honey-colored skin stood at a cooktop. With one hand, she stirred something in a pot. Using the other wrist, she pushed her hair from her eyes, revealing a forehead dotted with bumps.

Interesting, thought Blandings, that Mr. Sallow, who was so opposed to other species moving to Haplor worlds, would employ a Gallican chef. Sallow evidently saw her as no danger to Haplor society. Of course, people were often like that, Blandings reflected, thinking one thing about an entire group while thinking the opposite of a specific member of that group.

As Blandings entered, she looked up with a pinched expression. "Are you the unexpected guest?"

Blandings inclined his head politely. "No. It is my employer, Mr. Totleigh. He offers his regrets for any inconvenience his presence will cause."

"I bet he does." She shook her head and heaved an exasperated breath. The chef moved to a cooler, pulled out a loaf of replicated protein, and slapped it onto a cutting board. "Now I have to add more of everything to the stew." Picking up a wide chef's knife, she carved off several pieces, added them to the simmering pot, and resumed stirring.

Blandings knew it would, of course, be easier for the chef to simply use the food replicator to instantly create complete individual servings as opposed to replicating the ingredients and cooking them by hand. But he could venture a guess as to why she did it this way. She was Gallican, a culture that prided itself on its cooking. That and because he assumed if she did not actually cook, she would probably soon find herself out of a job. Anyone can stand in front of a replicator and name dishes.

Her eyes shot up to glower at Blandings. "I suppose you'll be wanting tea."

"That would be lovely," he said.

She pointed the knife toward the replicator. "You can tell it to the machine."

"If it wouldn't be getting in your way," Blandings said, "I would prefer to make it fresh. I would be happy to prepare a cup for you as well."

She stared at him for a moment or two while Blandings struggled to read her expression. Then a gentle smile made it to her face. "That is exactly what I need. Everything is in that cabinet beside the cooler.

Blandings pulled out the kettle, teapot, and tea and set to work. "Cream and sweetcane?"

The chef looked up from the pot. "Just cream, thanks."

She opened a cabinet, pulled out a container of cumberbeans, and poured some into the pot. Moving back to the cooler, she brought out a bundle of asparachokes, which she chopped and also added.

The kettle boiled, and Blandings poured the water into the teapot. While it steeped, he said, "It smells wonderful, whatever it is you are making."

"Bactaren stew with Haplorian vegetables. I'd like to say you can have some, but with an extra guest ..." She left it at that.

"Don't worry about me. I can replicate something for myself. How long have you been working for the Sallows?"

She hesitated a few moments before answering. "Two years."

Blandings poured the tea, added the cream, and handed her a cup. She took a sip, sighed, and leaned back against the counter. She took a second sip and then set down the cup and returned to work. "Thank you for the tea. It's divine."

"Do you enjoy it here?"

This time she didn't answer at all.

Blandings said, "Please allow me to apologize for my employer adding to your workload. May I assist in any way?"

"Maybe. Under the circumstances, I think they can put up with replicated desserts. Could you handle that?"

"I would be most pleased to do so. I assume Mr. Sallow prefers Haplorian sweets?"

She answered with an eye roll.

Blandings moved to the replicator. "Trifle with blue fruit and meido fruit, please." He glanced over to the chef. "Three portions? For Mr. Sallow, Ms. Sallow, and Mr. Totleigh?" She bobbed her head, and Blandings turned back to the replicator. "Three portions."

The cups appeared, and Blandings moved them to the cooler.

She dipped a spoon into the pot and tasted. Her head tilted to one side. She dipped her fingers into a bowl of seasoning and sprinkled it over the stew. "Thank you. This has been a trying day. More so than usual."

Blandings carried his cup to a nearby table. "I am sorry to hear it. How so?" He sat and took a sip.

"I came in this morning to find the kitchen a shambles. It seems the old guy was up in the night."

"I understand that many older Haplors suffer from insomnia."

"No, this was different. There was a break-in."

"Oh my. Was anything taken?"

"I don't think so. The thief tried to raid the old guy's knickknack collection. Well, I say thief. It was some kind of strange animal — an alien animal."

"Interesting." Blandings forced a surprised expression to his face. "Were the city guards able to catch it?"

"They didn't need to call the guards. Gubbins caught it. He's the bodyguard and vidcast engineer and general lackey for Sallow."

"Yes, we have met."

"They questioned it in here, of all places. There was so much mess, it looked like they threw a party. Males never clean up after themselves." She threw an apologetic glance toward Blandings. "Present company excepted."

"What did they do with it — the alien?"

The chef made a sour face. "That's another thing making my life difficult today. It's caged up back in the pantry. I had to go back there to fetch a cutting board. Creepy little beast. It has no arms, for Zahn's sake. I was afraid the thing would bite me."

"May I see it?"

"Help yourself. But watch out. It has these appendage things." She wiggled fingers from her jaws to illustrate.

Blandings stood and pointed in question toward a door at the end of the kitchen. The chef nodded.

He passed through the door into a small room lined with shelves. On one shelf, next to a stack of brown matter cubes used for replicator stock, stood a small cage. Keezo sat inside, leaning listlessly against the wires.

Keezo's eyes shifted toward the door, then lit up with excitement.

"Bandy!" Keezo jumped to a standing position. In the process, the alien's head bumped against a perch hanging down from the top of the cage. "Ow!" Keezo sat back down, rubbing tentacles over the sore spot.

"Shhh," Blandings said. "Pretend you don't know me."

Confusion passed across Keezo's face. "Okey ... dokey. I is Keezo. Who is you?"

At that Blandings nearly smiled. "Hello, Keezo. I am pleased to meet you. Has anyone brought you food?"

Keezo's head shook back and forth. "Not since I is go in cage."

"Are you hungry?" Blandings thought the question unnecessary but asked it anyway.

Keezo's head bobbed with vigor.

Blandings said, "I will return with something."

He stepped back into the kitchen where the chef was tossing a large bowl of salad.

Blandings said, "May I help?"

"I think I can manage it."

"If you do not require the replicator at present, I would like to make some food for the creature. It appears to be hungry."

The Gallican shrugged. "If you want to. Help yourself."

Blandings moved to the replicator and said, "One large bowl of teeko nuts."

"How do you know it eats teeko nuts?"

"Call it a hunch."

Blandings moved back to the pantry where Keezo devoured the nuts.

"Is you find Tunna?" Keezo asked.

"Not as yet. First, we need to find a way to free you from this cage."

Blandings jiggled the cage door and was about to open it when he heard footsteps. He turned to see Gubbins shoulder his way into the tiny space.

"What are you doing back here?" he asked gruffly.

"Remember, you don't know me," Blandings repeated to Keezo in a whisper. He inclined his head toward the bodyguard. "Good morning again, Mr. Gubbins. I don't believe we have been formally introduced, at least not with my true identity. My name is Blandings. I am Mr. Totleigh's gentleman's gentleman."

"Are you now? I asked what you were doing back here."

"I am seeing that this creature gets something to eat."

Gubbins' brows furrowed. "What's it to you?"

"It was hungry."

"Well, don't make it sick. If anything happens to it, it'll be my head."

"I certainly would not want that to happen. If I may ask, what is Mr. Sallow going to do with it?"

"He's going to put it in his vidcast this afternoon. It's supposed to serve as an example of the alien threat."

"Goodness," Blandings said with a low chuckle. "This little thing a threat?"

He had hoped to be able to free Keezo when the chef left the kitchen following lunch. That now appeared to not be feasible.

Gubbins said, "It broke in and made a mess … somehow. I still don't see how it got in without hands." He eyed the valet.

Blandings changed the subject. "I hear you are the engineer for Mr. Sallow's vidcast."

Gubbins shrugged. "That's the job title … if you want to call it that."

Blandings raised one eyebrow. "What would *you* call it?"

"More like glorified imager and audio technician. I'm paid to point a camera and punch buttons."

Blandings gave Gubbins a sympathetic head nod. "Dealing with employers is often challenging, is it not?"

Gubbins took an audible breath but said nothing.

"Still," Blandings said, "vidcasting sounds quite fascinating — researching a topic, selecting the content, structuring the show in the best way to present it all."

"If I did any of that," Gubbins said, staring at the floor.

"I take it your voice is sometimes not heard when it comes to more creative input."

"I is Keezo," Keezo said.

Gubbins looked up. "Anyway, you shouldn't hang around back here."

"I understand," Blandings said. He followed Gubbins out, turning to wave to Keezo as he left.

As they entered the kitchen, Marigold breezed in from the other door. "Oh, Chef, I wanted to tell you that we'll have one more for lunch."

"You already did." She nodded toward Blandings. "His boss."

"Yes, yes. Mr. Totleigh was invited earlier. But I've just now confirmed that my friend Cecil will also join us. Thanks. Bye."

As Marigold skated out, the chef reached once more for the knife. She brought the edge of it down hard, embedding the tip into the cutting board. Blandings glanced at Gubbins, who rocked on his heels in silence.

Chapter 26

It's the Pits

Meanwhile, Pelham fidgeted alone in the study, trying to pass the time while he waited for Sallow to dress ... or for Blandings to return ... or for something —anything — to happen. Ordered to stay on the couch and not wanting to violate the dictate lest he and Blandings be tossed from the house before they located Keezo, he sat and gazed around the room at Sallow's many trinkets, though he couldn't see much of them from a sitting position.

When that lost his interest, he stared out the glass door to the patio and the yard beyond. After that, he slid to the other end of the couch and goggled up at the shelves to read the framed reviews of Sallow's vidcast, which nearly made him ill with their fawning praise.

When he could sit no longer, he stood, clasped his hands behind his back to keep himself from touching anything, and paced. He was examining the leg lamp when Sallow marched through the door.

"I thought I told you to sit." Sallow scanned the room. "You didn't handle anything did you?"

"No." Pelham whirled away from the lamp, taking a few casual steps in the direction of one of the shelf units. "Are all these Earth objects?"

"Yes."

"Fun fact, I met an Earthling once."

Sallow crossed his arms. "No, you didn't."

"I did."

"Pah!"

Pelham tutted. "I should think I would know better than you the things I have done."

"Did it have any superpowers? I understand some of them have superpowers."

"I didn't notice any. Well, he was pretty snappy with the wisecracks. Does that count?"

"Where did you meet this alleged Earthling? You didn't break the Earth quarantine, did you?"

"Me? No. Never been within two systems of the place. The Earther in question was at Girsu space port. He helped me out of a jam."

Sallow's nostrils flared. "Who let an Earthling out into the civilized galaxy?"

"Oh … um …" Pelham thought it would be just like this Sallow blister to lodge a formal complaint with the galactic alliance. He certainly didn't wish to land anyone in the soup. "I don't think he told me."

Then to change the subject, Pelham picked up a random item from a shelf, a black ball with a number eight on it. "Ooh, what's this?" He casually turned the ball over in his hand, and letters appeared as if by magic, which his translator bots rendered as: *Very doubtful.*

"Aaaaah!" He dropped the ball to the floor with a *thud.*

"I told you not to touch anything, Totleigh."

"It … it gave me a message. What is that thing?"

Sallow glared at him. "It's a toy."

"A toy? Not … not some mystical intelligence communicating over space and time?"

"A toy."

"Then the message?"

"Toy."

"Oh."

Pelham slipped the black ball back onto the shelf. He stepped to the table full of tiny vehicles and studied them. They were a little like automated carriages in that they each had four wheels, but there the resemblance ended. These were built much lower to the ground and bore bright colors. Some had shiny silver bits poking through here and there.

He reached out a finger and pushed one. It wheeled across the tabletop. Pelham shot out his other hand to stop it but missed, accidentally launching several more of them off the table and clattering to the floor.

Sallow cleared his throat in an aggrieved manner.

"Oops," Pelham said. "Frightfully sorry." He reached down and set the vehicles back in their places. Then he backed away, nearly bumping into the leg lamp.

Sallow let out a low grumble. "All right. Come along, Totleigh. I suppose I should show you the grounds. It's better than having you in here wrecking the place. What do you know about Unaran plant life?"

"Oh, this and that. Not much, actually."

"Why am I not surprised?" Sallow walked out the glass doors onto the green stone patio. The sun had risen above the surrounding houses, and the day had warmed from chilly to cool.

Sallow said, "These patio slates were mined not far from here. Unara exports these around the galaxy."

"Fascinating," Pelham said. "Chipping your world up and rocketing it off somewhere else, eh? That makes sense. What will you do when you've shipped away the last bit."

"What are you jabbering on about? It's business, another subject with which you obviously are unfamiliar."

For a moment they stood and glared at each other.

Sallow stepped off the patio to continue the tour. "These are all native Unaran plants. Nothing else could survive the temperature extremes. Both the blooms and the fronds close up at night to protect the plant from the cold. They have only now opened for the day."

He moved to a bush as tall as a Haplor with wide fronds and bright red flowers. "We call this Unaran jasmine because of the scent." He stood an arm's length from the shrub and fluttered his hand to waft the fragrance in his direction. "It has a pleasing scent."

Pelham stepped closer to the bush and bent over to sniff at a bloom.

"Not so close," Sallow barked. "Not if you like having a nose."

"What?" Pelham jerked his head back just as the bloom snapped shut.

"Keep your distance, you dimwit. They're hungry in the morning. They'll close upon and eat anything that comes too near."

"Egad!"

"The plants can't get enough nutrients from the soil. It's a marvelous adaptation."

Pelham scoffed. "Righto. Splendid feature. Carnivorous plants."

A smell of sulfur reached Pelham's nostrils. He turned and spotted a bubbling puddle of mud in the corner of the yard. "I've heard about these mud thingies. Blandings says they're all over the planet." He walked toward the pool. "Interesting to see one up close with the steam and all."

162

Bubbles of various sizes rose one after another to the surface of the steaming mud, popping and putting out a noxious odor.

Sallow came up beside him and pointed to a group of bright orange creatures hopping in and around the mud. "Copper mud frogs. They live in the sulfur pools."

"Why would they want to reside in such a stinky place?"

"Because no predators go there."

Pelham nodded. "I bet they don't. Who would want to come somewhere like this for dinner? It would be like a restaurant built at the sewage treatment plant."

One of the frogs hopped out of the mud bath across the cracked ground. Pelham took a step closer to it, but Sallow yelled, "Stop, you idiot!"

"Now see here, Sallow, enough with the insults."

"Don't you see the cone?"

"Hmm? Oh yes. Now that you mention it." A yellow cone stood to one side of the mud pool. On it in big black letters was a single word: *PIT*. "What of it?"

Sallow said, "Unara has a fair amount of tectonic activity. Sometimes fissures open underneath the sulfur pools and drain them. If they drain quickly enough, you'll end up with a pit."

"I don't see any pit around here," Pelham said.

"No, you don't. Because if they drain slowly, then the top layer, no longer being heated by the bubbling sulfur, will cool to a brittle crust while the pool underneath drains away. What you end up with is a hidden pit, what we call a dropout. Walk across that, and you're likely to break through and plunge down who knows how far."

Pelham said, "My word. I say, on Sonus, we may not have much in the way of natural oxygen, but at least you can trust the ground you walk on."

"The dropouts aren't that difficult to avoid if you know what to look for. There won't be any plants growing over one. And as you can see, the ground shows cracks and takes on an orange cast." Sallow nodded toward the yellow cone. "And whenever people spot one, they mark it with cones like this. You'll find them in and around town and even out on the open plain. Watch for them when you're strolling about."

"I doubt I'll take many strolls if there's a chance of falling down a hidden hole and breaking my neck."

"Suit yourself."

One of the orange frogs hopped over to the toe of Pelham's shoe. He bent down for a closer look.

"And don't touch the frog either," Sallow said. "Its skin has a toxin."

Pelham straightened and jammed his hands in his pockets. "This is quite the planet you have here, Sallow. Everything's trying to kill you."

"At least we don't need pressure suits like you do on Sonus." He pulled out a device and scowled at it. "Looks like it's time for lunch. Let's get it over with."

"Ah, Unara," Pelham muttered to himself, "where the hospitality is as noxious as the flora and fauna."

Chapter 27

The Dark Lunchtime of the Soul

Pelham followed Sallow back to the house, stepping in the other's footprints to hopefully avoid anything else trying to kill him. They entered through the study and moved across the hall into a dining room with green striped wallpaper above white painted wainscoting.

Sallow was glowering down at the white-clothed table set for four when Marigold cruised in with Cecil Cakewood in tow.

"Oh, so that's who the fourth place is for," Sallow grumbled. "What are you doing here, Cakewood?"

"Um … um … Hello, Mr. Sallow," the skinny shopkeeper stuttered out, seemingly intrigued by the carpet.

Marigold said, "Daddy, you told Cecil he should come over and see your leg lamp."

"Did I?"

"Mr. Totleigh," Marigold said in a gushing voice. She moved to Pelham and took his arm. "Did I see you out in the garden with Daddy? What did you think?"

"Oh, it's quite an enjoyable spot," Pelham said, "especially for someone with a death wish."

Marigold laughed at the comment while Sallow and Cecil glared at him. Pelham assumed Sallow's glower was for the snide comment about his yard. He thought the Cakewood stink eye was more likely due to the sight of Marigold hanging on his arm.

Pelham tried to shake her off, but she clung on and raised her eyebrows at him. She muttered, "Stick to the plan, Totleigh." Then she smiled at Cecil and shot him a wink that caused the poor goop to blink several times and look like a fish floundering on land.

"Sit, everyone," Marigold said.

Sallow took his place at the head of the table. Cecil grabbed a chair at the foot. Pelham and Marigold sat on opposite sides between them. Pelham threw her what he hoped was an imploring expression. She returned to him an icy, bullying smile.

Sallow rang a bell beside his plate. A few moments later, Blandings floated in carrying four bowls on a silver tray.

"What are you still doing here?" Sallow asked, his eyes like slits. "Why is my house suddenly infested with shopkeepers and deceitful butlers and … and Totleigh."

"If I might be permitted to correct the misapprehension, sir," Blandings said, "I am a valet, not a butler."

"Though I'm sure he could buttle with the best of them, what?" Pelham put in.

"But to answer your question, sir," Blandings said, "I am assisting Chef with the additional lunchtime workload. With your permission, of course."

Seeming to take on the mantle of the magistrate, Sallow pursed his lips and stared at Blandings for several moments before passing judgment. "I'll allow it."

Blandings acknowledged the consent with an incline of his head. "We will begin with salad, followed by bactaren stew, and finishing up with trifle." He served the salad bowls and glided out.

Marigold reached across the table and rested her hand on Pelham's. "So Mr. Totleigh, what brings you to Unara?"

Pelham thought he heard a sad moan coming from Cecil's side of the room and a low, unnerving snarl emitting from Sallow's. He snatched his hand back, covering for the movement by reaching for his water glass. "Oh, trying to help someone in need."

"How noble! Tell me more."

He couldn't help feeling buoyed by the compliment. "See, I was overseeing a shipment of power whatchamacallits, and well, come to find out, a little creature had hidden in with—"

He froze mid-sentence with the sudden realization that he was talking about Keezo, a person he shouldn't admit knowing in this company.

Oswald Sallow had also become immobilized, his spork halted halfway to his salad bowl. "What sort of little creature?"

Pelham read the suspicion in his eyes. "What?"

"I asked you what sort of creature you found?" Sallow stabbed at his salad as if it were crouching to attack him.

"Creature? No, I said … I said reacher. My assistant, Munson is his name, he made a little reacher — do you use the word *reacher* here on Unara? No? Handy little term. Means to reach."

Cecil looked puzzled. "Why don't you just say reached instead of made a reacher?"

"Oh, I don't know. Slang, what?"

Sallow groused. "I don't believe in using slang. But do continue with your story, Totleigh."

"Well, not much to it really. Munson made a … um … reacher, as I say, to grab one of the power thingamabobs and threw out his back. Not as young as he used to be, old Munson. Such a shame. He was planning to come here to discuss trade between our two colonies, but alas. I had to make the trip in his place."

Pelham focused intently on sporking a bite of salad, studiously avoiding any eye contact that might invite follow-up questions.

Marigold said, "Well, picking up the slack for a co-worker, that's noble too. Don't you agree, Cecil?"

"Hmm," was all the response Cecil made.

They lapsed into awkward silence, and Pelham began listing in his head all the places he would rather be lunching. He thought of that little bistro near the atmospheric plant on Sonus where he often met the lads on days off. There was the lovely mid-flight service they had served him that time he rode the *Girsu Express* — before all the unpleasantness. Even eating lunch at work with Munson slurping soup at the next desk was preferable to sitting here with Marigold's flirtations and the constant scowls from Sallow and Cakewood.

Marigold said, "Cecil, you must let me show you the leg lamp after lunch. There are some things I want to explain … related to it. You really shouldn't worry … about the lamp. Daddy, what will you be doing this afternoon?"

A glint flashed into Sallow's eye. "I'll be recording what I think will be a pivotal vidcast. I have incontrovertible proof of the alien threat."

"Oh?" asked Cecil.

"A creature …" Sallow directed the word at Pelham with a suspicious glance. "A creature broke into my study last night and tried to make off with some of my collection."

"What kind of creature?"

"I don't know. It's small. Has no arms. Covered in black fur with weird tendrils hanging from its head."

"Tentacles," Pelham said.

"What?"

"Plants have tendrils."

"How do you know so much about it?"

"Blandings and I were discussing the difference ... purely by coincidence."

Marigold said, "Maybe it wandered in by accident ... or was trying to get out of the cold."

Sallow scoffed. "It was captured making off with my dolly."

The conversation was interrupted by Cecil, who at that point seemed to choke on his salad. He pulled his napkin up to his mouth and stared down at his lap while rocking back and forth.

Blandings appeared again, exchanged the salad bowls for crocks of steaming bactaren stew, and once more withdrew.

Pelham asked Sallow, "I take it you're going to tell your vidcast viewers about the incident?"

"I'm going to do more than that. I'm going to display the alien, let everyone see how odd and grotesque it is."

Cecil said, "Sounds like a Danánn."

"What does?"

"The creature. I think it's a Danánn, the native species of the planet we colonized."

Pelham said, "Ha! I wonder if the Danánn talk about the threat of alien invasion in reference to us?"

"I've never heard of them," Sallow said, glaring at Pelham. "But it would be just like the Danánn settlers to pick a planet with life already on it. Talk about asking for trouble."

"As I understand it," Pelham said, "they didn't know they were there. Not at first."

"We did it the right way here," Sallow said. "Unara had no native fauna other than microscopic life."

Pelham said. "I suppose after you do the vidcast, you'll let the little guy go, what?"

Sallow scoffed. "So it can break in again? I have no intention of doing that."

"Then what? You wouldn't file criminal charges against it, would you?"

"I could. I haven't decided yet. It's not very intelligent. Right now, I don't know whether to charge it in my own court or turn it over to animal control."

"Could I see the Danánn?" Cecil asked. "I've had some of their art in the shop. It's amazing what they can do without hands."

"Art? This thing couldn't produce art."

"Oh, they do. Basket weaving. Rock painting."

Sallow scoffed. "Pishposh. But if you want to see it, Cakewood, come to the recording."

"Thank you, Mr. Sallow. I would like that." The shine of buttering up beamed on the shopkeeper's face.

Marigold said, "Pelham … Can I call you Pelham, Mr. Totleigh? Pelham, you were going to tell us all about your trip to Vogus."

She leaned across the table toward him, her eyes sparkling with apparent interest. Pelham watched Cecil's face grow red, and he was almost certain he caught the sound of grinding teeth coming from the Sallow end of the table.

"Oh, righto," Pelham said. "Interesting place, Vogus. They trowel on the glitz and glamor there by the bushel. You might like it, Sallow, seeing as how it's modeled after Earth and all. Of course, the Zurks run the place, and they can be stinkers sometimes. But all that may be changing."

"Smug, arrogant Zurks." Sallow spit out the words like they were something produced from a malfunctioning food replicator. "They think they're better than everyone else in the galaxy."

That was when Pelham and Cecil both seemed to choke on their stew.

Chapter 28

The Keezo Show

While Pelham recounted his exploits on Vogus, lunch progressed, the trifle following the bactaren stew. Marigold appeared captivated by his adventures, the males not so much. Sallow, who glowered through most of Pelham's tale, excused himself as soon as he finished dessert with the excuse that he needed to prepare for the vidcast. Shortly thereafter, Marigold said she wanted to speak with Cecil alone, and they left.

Pelham was still there, sporking up the remaining bites of his trifle and ruminating over the present situation when Blandings came in to clear the table.

"Excuse me, sir. If you are still eating, I can come back later."

"No, Blandings. Come on in. Take a seat, in fact."

"It would not be proper for me to do so, sir."

"No? Well, as you wish." Pelham mechanically slid the spork around the dish for one last bite. "Blandings, we seem to have slogged our way into the soup yet again."

"Sir?"

"Apparently, Keezo will be featured prominently in the next episode of Sallow's vidcast, playing the role of alien invader."

"So I understand, sir. I was able to locate Keezo in the pantry. Mr. Gubbins informed me of this afternoon's recording session."

"How is Keezo?"

"Well enough for the moment."

"We'll see what happens after this afternoon's matinee. Old Sallow is threatening to chuck Keezo in the pokey for breaking and entering."

"Yes, sir. I happened by chance to overhear some of the luncheon conversation while moving between the kitchen and the dining room."

"I need not point out, Blandings, that Keezo's incarceration would put the kibosh on our attempts to reunite the missing Tunna with the aforementioned."

"Indeed, sir."

"Not to mention, we still don't have that leg lamp. I can hardly return to Sonus without it."

"No, sir."

"Aunt Agutha would be vexed, to say the least."

"Yes, sir."

"If one can refer to a volcanic eruption as a mountain being vexed."

"I do take your meaning."

"And now Marigold is flirting with me, visibly raising the blood pressure of both Sallow and Cecil."

"So I observed, sir."

"I don't suppose you see a way for us to extricate ourselves from this mess?"

"I am giving the matter consideration, sir."

"Well, ponder as quickly as poss."

"I will, sir."

"Anything to suggest at present? Perhaps a step in the right direction, as it were."

"I have one recommendation, sir. I understand from Mr. Gubbins that Mr. Sallow has invited some local people in to watch his recording session. It seems he felt that an audience response would help him convey his message. I recommend you attend as well. Should the crowd have an adverse reaction, you may be needed to shield Keezo from attack."

"Act as hero, you mean."

"If necessary, sir. Often a single dissenting voice can stop a crowd from taking extreme actions."

"Righto. And where will this performance be taking place, Blandings?"

"On the patio outside Mr. Sallow's office, sir. And quite soon, as I understand."

Pelham stood. "Then I should totter around there and find my mark."

"Yes, sir."

"Not too close to any of the murderous shrubbery."

"No, sir."

"Oh, one other thing I've been curious about, Blandings."

"Sir?"

"We've met father and daughter Sallow. Is there a mother? A partner? A co-parent? Judging by Marigold's behavior, I wouldn't be surprised to hear she was part steamroller."

"I understand that there is a mother, sir."

"Where is she?"

"According to the chef, she is visiting relatives on Haplor."

"I see."

"It seems she has been visiting them for the last three years."

"Ah," Pelham said with meaning. "I see. Well, who can blame her with Sallow being ... well, Sallow?"

"Yes, sir."

Pelham returned to the study and slipped out the door to the patio. A table covered by a blue tablecloth stood near the wall. At the outside edge of the slates, two rows of chairs had been set and were in the process of being filled with Haplors coming in at the gate. Pelham selected a seat in the back row behind one of the more wide-bodied visitors as a precaution against Keezo spotting him and shouting out his name in front of everyone.

To get a sense of the crowd, he eavesdropped on some of the muttered conversations going on around him. Some were excited for an opportunity to hear Sallow speak. Others spoke of what else they hoped to accomplish that afternoon and openly wondered how long all this was going to take.

Cecil came out through the study door and sat beside Pelham.

"What ho, Cecil."

The shopkeeper repaid the friendly greeting with a cold look. "Marigold told me about her plan for you to propose."

"Um ... about that," Pelham said. "As you correctly labeled it, this was her idea. It was all her doing, don't you know."

"Hiding behind a female, eh?"

"What?" Pelham detected an unexpected note of derision in Cecil's tone.

"Don't think I can't see what's going on, Totleigh."

"Good ... I think. Wait. What is it you believe is going on?"

"Marigold may be playacting, but it's obvious you aren't. You're falling in love with her."

"I'm what? No, I'm not."

"How could you resist those goo-goo eyes she's making at you? She's ... she's a dream. And now you're trying to steal her from me."

"What? Wait. What? Nothing could be further from my thoughts, old chap."

"Don't call me old chap."

"All right. If that's your preference. But Cecil, old … Cecil, you seem to have grabbed the wrong end of it."

"What I intend to grab is your throat, Totleigh."

"My dear fellow. There's no need to—"

"And I am not your dear fellow. I know what you're up to. I tried to warn Marigold, but she wouldn't listen."

"I haven't had much luck getting her to listen to me either. But I say, really." Pelham pulled a handkerchief from a pocket to pat his brow.

Cecil glared at it. "MS? She gave you her hankie?"

"What?" Pelham rammed the cloth back into a pocket. "Again, that was her idea … merely as a means for me to gain admittance to the house."

"And yet you hang onto it even after being admitted."

"Well, I sort of forgot about it."

"You forgot about it," Cecil said mockingly. "I see the glow of affection shining in your eyes when you talk to her."

"The what in my who?"

"I know love when I see it."

"Ah!" Pelham seized at the statement like a life preserver. "I think I see now where you may have gone wrong, my lad." He leaned in conspiratorially. "What you may not realize is that I have a bit of stage experience, treading the boards, as they say. I once played Townsperson Number Two in our school's production of *Waiting for Gort*. I still remember my line. 'Watch out! He's got a blaster, he has.' Some still speak of my moving portrayal. But despite my convincing performance, I assure you I have no interest in Marigold."

"Rubbish. She's a lovely lass."

Pelham nodded. "That she is."

"Aha! I knew it."

"Dash it all," Pelham said. "I don't want to marry Marigold. Ha! Marry Mari. Get it? That's a corker, what?"

Cecil didn't have an opportunity to answer because, at that moment, Sallow walked out through the patio door.

He raised one arm to the crowd and was rewarded with a spattering of applause. With the other arm, he carried something covered by a cloth, which he set on the table.

Pelham craned around to spot Gubbins at the back of the crowd, pointing a camera toward Sallow. At his side stood Blandings. Gubbins panned the camera over the crowd. Pelham waved at it in the event any of the lads back home happened to be watching.

Sallow cleared his throat and said in a commanding voice, "Welcome, friends, to a very special live episode of my vidcast. As you can see, I have invited some of the leading citizens of Unara to join me because I want witnesses for the shocking evidence of alien invasion I will show you today."

Sallow walked to the cloth-covered shape on the table and patted it. "You know, people like to make fun of Oswald Sallow. They say he's an alarmist. They say he exaggerates and takes things out of context. Well, they won't be saying that after today. I have conclusive proof of a systematic, high-level conspiracy against our species."

He whipped away the cloth, revealing Keezo in a cage. Keezo blinked twice at the crowd. The crowd responded with a heartfelt, "Aw."

Someone shouted out, "He's a cutie, he is."

Sallow scoffed and raised a hand to quiet the crowd. "This species is clearly inferior. As you can see, it lacks arms. It possesses limited intelligence. But this creature is not as harmless as it seems. This, friends …" He pointed a dramatic finger at Keezo. "… is a thief and an agent of those who want to destroy Haplor culture."

Someone in the crowd called out, "What does any of this have to do with Alliance Day?"

Sallow scowled. "What?"

"Today is Alliance Day."

Sallow lifted his chin in haughty disdain. "I do not observe Haplor joining the galactic alliance … except in mourning."

"Morning? Why, what did you do this morning?"

"Quiet!" Sallow bellowed.

Which elicited a sharp intake of breath by several and a frightened *erp* from Keezo. The Danánn's eyes widened, and its fur faded to the blue of the tablecloth. This was followed by more gasps from the audience and a general round of applause.

"Hey, that's great," someone said. "What other tricks does he do?"

"No, no," Sallow said. "This isn't a performance."

"Are you going to have him at the festivities tonight?"

"No, I am not. This—"

Sallow was interrupted by more applause. He turned to see Keezo, who seemingly encouraged by the crowd's reaction, had faded back to black and was now waving tentacles around to form geometric shapes.

Sallow turned back to the crowd and spoke more quickly. "This creature was captured last night breaking into my study and trying to steal my possessions."

Keezo stood on one leg and hopped around the cage, followed by a headstand, followed by tentacle pushups. Sporadic giggles kept breaking out, interrupting Sallow.

"As I have mentioned … I say, as I have mentioned a few times … history is … history is my fascination and … and I am a collector of alien artifacts."

Keezo extended a tentacle up and wrapped it around the bird perch hanging from the top of the cage. With a pull, Keezo rose into the air and casually spun around in a circle. People in the crowd nudged each other and pointed in delight.

Sallow tried to continue. "It was one of my alien artifacts that … that this creature attempted to take. Not anything to … not anything to eat. Not an …. not an artifact from its own culture. Why … I say why then did it … take it?" Sallow whirled on Keezo and bellowed, "Quit it. Stop that now."

Keezo shuddered and again faded to blue, prompting another round of applause from the crowd.

Pelham, who until now had been watching the show from behind a hand he held over his face, now leaned around the Haplor in front of him to get a better view. Which was when he and Keezo made eye contact.

"Pelie!"

"There you have it, folks," Sallow said, shaking a finger. "PELIE. You heard it from the creature's own mouth. PELIE, the People Entirely in League with Interstellar Extraterrestrials, a terrorist organization bent on undermining our proud culture with influences from alien worlds."

Someone shouted out, "That little guy? A terrorist? You're barmy."

Sallow glared back. "It's the truth."

Keezo shut both eyes and changed colors from black to brown to green to dark red and then back to black. The crowd hooted.

Gubbins called from the back, "Boss, why don't you cover the cage again? Then you can explain the plot without interruption. You might even take it from the top."

Sallow waved an angry hand. "Be quiet, Gubbins. Don't interrupt the recording."

Gubbins frowned back at him.

Sallow began pacing around the makeshift stage area. "I have reliable information that this creature is a Danánn, meaning that its kind has already infiltrated our Danánn colony."

Cecil leaned over to Pelham and whispered, "That's not what I said. They didn't infiltrate. They were already on the planet."

Sallow just happened to stop pacing at a point that blocked the view of Keezo for most of the crowd. "And now we find one of their kind here on Unara. Where will they show up next? On Sonus? On Haplor itself? What is their agenda? Is it to plunder our valuables as was done here? Or is it even more insidious? Is it ..."

Sallow stopped as several in the crowd were giggling. He glared back at them. Pelham could almost see steam rise from the old rotter like mist from a mud pool.

It was clear to Pelham that the source of the laughter was Keezo's tentacles stretching out the sides of the cage and waving in the air beyond the width of Sallow's body. Which given the width of Sallow's body, Pelham thought, made them prodigiously stretchy.

Sallow's eyes shifted left and right, seemingly straining to see behind him. He may have caught a glimpse of the movement because his face scrunched up like a dried-up meido fruit, and he whipped around to face the alien, giving the audience a view of the line of red creeping up the back of his neck, which made them chortle all the more.

"Keezo." He stretched the syllables out like a spring pulled to its limit.

Keezo said, "Hello. I is hungry."

Full-on laughter swept over the crowd. People elbowed each other and slapped their knees. Pelham glanced at Cecil and saw him biting his bottom lip in a seemingly desperate attempt to maintain composure.

Pelham leaned over to him. "You know, for someone with no sense of humor, old Sallow makes a tolerably convincing straight man. This routine would kill in the music halls of Sonus."

Chapter 29

Comforting Daddy

Oswald Sallow sat in his favorite replicated leather armchair, brooding in the darkened study. It was the chair where he began all his vidcasts. All except this one. Perhaps that had been the problem. He should have introduced the topic from this chair. It would have put his mind on the right track and lent more of a sense of continuity. Not that he wanted to invite all those people into his study … or to ever see them again, for that matter.

And yet he would see them again. This was, after all, a small colony. He let his head flop against the seatback.

Of course, he could still record an opening here in this chair. And with skillful editing, the whole fiasco might yet be fixed … or at least salvaged … provided Gubbins could edit out all the giggles and perhaps edit in some impressed murmurs.

Sallow grimaced at the memory of the debacle. The peals of laughter had been the last straw. How could he continue in the face of that? Mortified, he had stormed off the patio into this room, sweeping the drapes closed behind him.

He gazed across at the glowing leg lamp, the only light source currently on in the room. At least he had that … and the rest of his prized collection.

He had, at times past, had entire theaters full of people cheering him, hanging on his every word. Today, he couldn't even hold the attention of a handful of rustic townsfolk who would rather see an alien acrobatic act than listen to his calls of warning. They would thank him one day. If only enough people believed him in time.

And he would show that little alien a thing or two. He would convict it of robbery and ship it off to the penal camp in the jungles of Haplor.

"Daddy?" It was Marigold outside the hall door.

"What?" he barked.

"I have a cup of tea for you."

Sallow took a moment before answering. A cup of tea would cheer him up, though he wasn't at all sure he wanted to be cheered up.

"Daddy?"

"Fine. Come in."

She bustled in and over to him. "How are you, Daddy? I heard what happened."

He snorted. "I will be all right."

She patted his head. "I'm sure you will be."

He jerked his head away from her hand. "You said something about tea?"

Marigold nodded to Blandings, who had slipped in behind her unseen. The valet stepped forward and handed Sallow a cup.

The vidcaster took a sip. "Mmm. This is excellent." Under different circumstances, he might even have smiled.

"Thank you, sir," Blandings said.

"He made it from scratch," Marigold said. "Now let's turn on some lights in here."

"I prefer the dark," Sallow said.

"Daddy."

"If you insist."

Marigold motioned again to Blandings, who turned on a lamp at the desk and another one across the room and then retreated inconspicuously to a corner. A knock sounded on the glass patio door.

"Now what?" Sallow said with a snarl. "Who is it?"

The door swung partially open against the curtains, and Cecil Cakewood stuck his head through the opening. "Me, sir. I ... I was wondering if I could do anything?"

"Yes. Go away."

Sallow watched the words slap the shopkeeper across the face, which he found deliciously enjoyable.

"Yes, sir." The head started to withdraw.

"Wait, Cakewood. Have you seen Gubbins?"

Cakewood pushed through the drapery to step inside the room. "Y ... yes. I spoke with him after the ... the program. He said he was going to see if he could do anything with ... I mean, enhance ... the recording ... with editing."

"What did he do with the alien?"

"Nothing. He left it on the table."

Sallow shook his head toward the heavens. "Of all the irresponsible … We can't leave it out where someone could walk off with it. Someone from PELIE may be out there."

"Oh no, sir," Cakewood said, standing taller now. "I was guarding it myself."

"You were until you came in here," Sallow muttered. "Get out there and bring it in."

Cakewood ducked back out the door. He re-entered a few moments later carrying the cage and followed by Pelham G. Totleigh.

"What's he doing here?" Sallow growled.

Totleigh grinned idiotically. "Oh, I thought I'd come along to help guard the dangerous alien invader, what?"

"I found him standing beside the cage," Cakewood said, giving Totleigh the evil eye. "It looked to me like he was about ready to make off with it."

Totleigh made what he probably hoped would be a dismissive scoff. It came off more like someone having a coughing fit. "Cecil, your words wound me. I thought we were bonding out there."

Cakewood glared at him and set the cage down on the desk.

From inside it, Keezo said, "Hello. I is Keezo."

"Don't leave that thing there, Cakewood," Sallow grouched. "What if it … wets?"

The curio shop proprietor snatched up the cage. "Then where …?"

"Take it back to the pantry. I'll call the city guards this afternoon and arrange for a speedy trial."

"I'll be glad to, Mr. Sallow." Cakewood started across the room. Then with Marigold's next words, he stopped mid-step.

"Hello, Pelham," she said with a lilt in her voice. She moved to him and touched him on the arm.

"Oh … um. What ho," Totleigh said.

"I'd love to hear more of your stories."

Marigold shot Totleigh a conspiratorial look that Sallow couldn't interpret. What were they plotting? Probably some scheme to persuade him to approve of their budding relationship.

Well, it wasn't going to work. Totleigh was an even worse match for her than Cecil Cakewood. The shopkeeper might be an underachiever and a simpering toady, an obsequious fawner who would do anything to ingratiate himself with

Sallow, but at least he wasn't an imbecile, a vapid dandy like that Totleigh. What could Marigold possibly see in him?

But at the same time, it was amusing to see Cakewood stew as Marigold showered attention on Totleigh. He thought it might be fun to play the two against each other.

"Totleigh," Sallow said.

The twit physically startled and goggled at him in apparent alarm. "What? What?"

"You know, Totleigh, I realize we may have a common acquaintance. Spencer Rainsby lives on Sonus. He's a fellow collector. Recently got into Earth artifacts."

A panicked look flooded Totleigh's face. "What? Who? Never heard of him."

"Surely you have. He's the governor's spouse."

"Um … no … doesn't ring a bell."

What a dolt this Totleigh was, Sallow thought. This was hardly likely to provoke Cakewood. He would have to try something else.

"Tell me how Sonus is coming along in its terraforming process."

Totleigh gawped. "Oh, you know … jolly well and all that. I think I saw a cloud the other day, so the atmosphere is starting to form."

"Fascinating," Sallow said, studying Cakewood for a reaction. "And I think you said you have something to do with the imports that keep the process moving forward."

"Righto. I inspect them. Well, generally my assistant, Munson — I think I mentioned him earlier — he performs most of the inspecting. But I have to sign off on it all."

Cakewood cleared his throat at a louder volume than necessary. "Speaking of imports, I'm expecting some Fornaxi sand art in a few days. Have you ever seen their sand art, Mr. Sallow? I think it would look wonderful on that wall."

"Sand art?" Totleigh said, a confused expression on his face. "Wouldn't the sand slide right off?"

Marigold giggled. "Oh, Pelham, you're hilarious."

Her words elicited a satisfying glower from Cakewood.

Sallow had had enough for now. "What are you still doing here, Cakewood?" he said, relishing the gruffness. "I thought I told you to take the alien to the pantry. Off you go now."

Cakewood shot an appealing glimpse at Marigold, but she only said, "Go on, Cecil."

The shopkeeper sighed and slouched out.

"Pelham," Marigold said, "what are we going to do about those horrible people who laughed during Daddy's recording session?"

Totleigh shrugged. "Do? I mean to say, what can you do? You aren't considering retaliation, are you?"

"Perhaps," Sallow said.

"No," Marigold said, throwing a disapproving look at her father. "I mean, what do we do about Daddy's reputation."

"Oh, I wouldn't worry about that awfully much," Totleigh said. "You may not know this about me, but people have laughed at me a time or two."

"You're kidding me," Sallow said, his voice dripping with sarcasm. "How could that be?"

Totleigh did a slow burn. "The point I was attempting to make was that I don't think it ever did me any lasting harm. People move on, don't you know."

"That's your advice?" Sallow scoffed. "Do nothing?"

Marigold said, "But Daddy is an important vidcaster and a magistrate."

"I certainly haven't forgotten that," Totleigh said, shooting Sallow a sideways glance, "especially the magistrate part."

"People can't be laughing at a magistrate," Marigold said.

"Can't they? I've met a few funny ones."

"Oh?" Sallow asked accusingly. "You've had occasion to meet magistrates?"

Totleigh gave a nervous chuckle. "Oh, now and again."

"Socially?"

Totleigh opened his mouth, then closed it, then opened it again. "Not … um …. exclusively."

"I didn't think so. You met them in a professional capacity, you mean."

"A bit."

Marigold said, "Be serious, Pelham."

"Oh, believe me, I had to be. All I did was giggle at one of them one time, and the stinker doubled my fine. But I ask you, he had a high-pitched voice … like those blokes on that planet with all the helium in the atmosphere. Whatever slight snicker, which may or may not have been snicked, was hardly my fault."

"You're veering off topic, Pelham," Marigold said. "We're looking for an idea to help Daddy."

"Sorry. Hmm. Let me give it some thought." Totleigh frowned. "Let's see. Let's see. You want to boost him up a bit in everyone's eyes. You want to win the people over. Have him rise in their estimation."

"Exactly," Marigold said.

Pelham snapped his fingers. "Well, now that you mention it, I heard a few people outside talking about how they hoped Keezo ... the alien, that is ... would perform tonight at the festivities in the park."

Sallow harrumphed. "Are you unhinged, Totleigh? That's what got us into this mess. Another performance would only cause further embarrassment. It's out of the question."

From the corner, Blandings coughed softly.

Sallow swung around to glare at him. "Are you still here?"

Totleigh said, "He sort of shimmers in and out, evaporates and whatever the opposite of that is."

"Materialize, sir," Blandings said.

"Not dis-evaporate or something?"

"No, sir, and I assure you, I do not possess such powers."

"So you say. Anyway, something to add to the conversation?"

"If I may, sirs and ma'am, I would like to point out that far from causing embarrassment, allowing the alien to perform tonight would likely bolster Mr. Sallow's reputation."

"Ah," said Totleigh, "then you like my idea."

"I do, sir."

"How would that help me in the least?" Sallow demanded. He hadn't forgotten the Smythe-Pucket deception this valet had tried to pull and was not about to be tricked again.

"It is the difference, sir, between laughing *at* someone and laughing *with* someone. Should you allow the alien to perform, it would demonstrate that you also find humor in its antics despite the disruption of your vidcast. It would prove that you are secure in your identity and emotionally mature enough to take yourself lightly."

Marigold said, "To be honest, Daddy, there have been some ... a few people ... who have called you ... imperious ... overbearing ... pompous."

"You've made your point," Sallow grumbled.

"I'm only saying that I can see how this might help people relate to you better."

"Yes," Totleigh said, "a person of the people, what?"

182

"I might further suggest," Blandings said, "that you have Mr. Gubbins record the performance, especially shots of you enjoying it. He could then edit parts of it into the vidcast."

"What would be the point?" Sallow asked.

"You might suggest that this alien, while itself harmless, is a pawn of nefarious forces."

Sallow sat forward in the chair. "By Gort, you're right. People don't have to see this Keezo as the villain. The real scoundrels are the people in PELIE and the galactic alliance and those pushing the galacticization conspiracy. This little alien is but a dupe, a patsy. That's why it was sent here — to lure us into complacency about the real alien threat. Putting on a little show tonight might be exactly the thing needed. People can be sympathetic to this Keezo and still see the danger it represents. You know, it might make them even more angry at the real villains because of how they are exploiting poor Keezo. All right, we'll do it. Stick around, Blandings. I forgive you for trying to trick me yesterday. That devious mind of yours just came in handy."

Chapter 30

Blandings Advises Cecil

Blandings left the study feeling less than sanguine about the preceding conversation. True, he had succeeded in persuading Mr. Sallow to allow Keezo to perform at the festival that evening, which at least would postpone legal proceedings against the Danánn. If all worked well, it might even set in motion an opportunity for Keezo to be freed, allowing them to resume the search for Tunna. However, it bothered Blandings that Sallow had so easily been able to fit the suggestion in with his preconceived conspiracy theories. He did not wish to be a party to any of that.

The remaining piece of business was trying to acquire the leg lamp. Judging from her actions, it appeared the young Ms. Sallow was fully committed to her scheme of using Mr. Sallow's antipathy toward Mr. Totleigh as a lever to pry out an approval of her engagement to Mr. Cakewood. She had promised to somehow procure the lamp for Mr. Totleigh if he went along with it. Blandings, however, now thought he could see a way to obtain the lamp without Mr. Totleigh needing to take the risk of proposing marriage.

He stepped into the kitchen, where the chef was chopping replicated asparachokes.

"May I be of any assistance?" Blandings asked her. "It would appear that Mr. Totleigh will be here for the evening meal as well."

At Blandings' words, a small moan emanated from the direction of the table. He turned to see the forlorn figure of Cecil Cakewood, slumped in a chair and staring at the wall.

The chef raised her eyebrows, shook her head, and glanced toward the shopkeeper. The effect of which was to communicate that Cakewood had been like that for some time, that she didn't know how or want to deal with him, and that the only help she wished of Blandings was for him to do something about him. It was a great deal of communication to pack into one expression, but she somehow managed it.

Blandings moved to the table. "Would you like a cup of tea, sir?"

The shopkeeper looked up at him with a blank expression. "Oh … um …"

"Tea? I make it fresh."

Cakewood sighed and shook his head. "I should head back to the shop. I might have customers." He didn't stir from the table.

"Sir?"

Cakewood spoke as if to himself. "I just … I thought this would be my chance. I was invited to lunch. I hoped I would impress Sallow with my wit and charm." He blinked. "Turns out I don't have any wit and charm. Not enough to compete with a galaxy-trotting, high-ranking colonial leader like Totleigh."

"Oh, sir, I would not concede the race for Ms. Sallow's affections so early as this."

Cakewood looked up and searched Blandings' face. "You wouldn't?"

"No, sir."

"She was fawning all over him."

"Tea? It will only take a few minutes."

The shopkeeper mechanically nodded his head.

Blandings steered around the chef to the sink. He emptied and refilled the tea kettle he had used earlier. While the water heated, he rinsed the pot and dropped in fresh tea leaves. Pouring the boiling water into the pot, he then moved to the replicator and requested three blue fruit scones. All the while, Cecil continued to gaze vacantly, switching up his view of the blank wall from time to time with that of the tabletop.

While the tea steeped, Blandings slipped back to the pantry with one of the scones and found Keezo in the cage.

"Bandy. Hello, Bandy," Keezo said.

"Good afternoon, Keezo." He held out the scone. "Hungry?"

"I is." Keezo stretched out a tentacle, took the pastry, and devoured it.

"This evening, Keezo, you will be brought to a large gathering where you will perform tricks."

"Okey dokey. The Bigs is enjoy Keezo tricks."

"Yes, they do, Keezo. But keep this in mind. If you see an opportunity to escape from the cage, take it. Run and hide somewhere. Then watch for Mr. Totleigh and me. We'll look for you. Can you do that?"

"I is run and hide and look for you."

"Excellent. I need to go now."

Blandings returned to the kitchen, thinking through the plan. Keezo escaping the cage would be only the first step. They would still have to get the Danánn off this planet before Oswald Sallow mobilized the guards to stop them. If only there were a way to render the threat of legal action moot. An idea came to him.

He poured the cups and brought them along with the two remaining scones to the table, where Cecil Cakewood was now staring at his hands. It went against Blandings' nature and all his training to sit in the presence of anyone other than another person in service. But this was a time for exceptions. He pulled out a chair, sat, and slid a cup and plate toward the shopkeeper.

Cakewood looked at him as if seeing him for the first time. "Who are you?"

"My name is Blandings, sir."

"You served lunch, right?"

"I did, sir. Have some tea."

Cakewood took a sip and uttered an almost contented sigh. He cradled the cup in his hands. "I haven't seen you around here before."

This was the point at which Blandings normally would have identified himself as Mr. Totleigh's gentleman's gentleman. But he thought such an admission might not be conducive to the goals at hand given the shopkeeper's animosity toward his employer. Instead, he said, "I have only recently come here."

"Nice to meet you. Though I doubt you'll be seeing much more of me. I seem to be getting drummed out of the picture."

"I take it, sir, you are referring to your relationship with Ms. Sallow?"

Cakewood nodded silently.

Blandings took a sip before continuing. "It is, of course, not my place to meddle, sir, but I wonder if I might be able to offer you some advice."

"You know a lot about females, do you?"

Blandings tilted his head. "Less than I do of tea and scones. However, in my years of service, I have come to learn a few things about people. My observation is that your problem is not with Ms. Sallow but with her father."

The other shot him a deadpan stare. "That's no great revelation. Marigold would have married me ages ago if not for the threat of being cut out of his will."

"Yes, sir. Forgive me for stating the obvious. Nevertheless, I wonder if you have stopped to consider what behavior would induce Mr. Sallow to view you in a more favorable light."

"I've thought of little else. I made sure he acquired the lamp. I guarded the alien for him. Nothing I do seems to impress him."

"Try the scone, sir."

Cakewood shook his head. "I don't feel like eating."

"You do need sustenance, sir. Just a bite."

Cakewood broke off the tip of the scone and popped it into his mouth. "Mmm. This *is* good."

"Thank you, sir. Consider, for example, the recent challenge to Ms. Sallow's affections from Mr. Totleigh."

"What about it?"

"In the study, I noted how you attempted to verbally disparage Mr. Totleigh and compete with him."

The shopkeeper chuffed out a bitter sigh. "For all the good it did."

"May I suggest that verbal sparring is unlikely to raise you in Mr. Sallow's estimation."

"No? What then?"

"Mr. Sallow seems to me to be a person of strong emotion and firm opinion who values swift and decisive action."

"Such as what?"

"That would depend entirely, sir, on your personal inclinations. However, it occurs to me that fisticuffs might be something that could gain his favor."

"Fisticuffs?"

"It is something to consider, sir."

Cakewood took another bite of scone and chewed it thoughtfully. He swallowed. "Give Totleigh the old left hook, you mean."

Blandings gave a slight shrug.

"But ... but what would Marigold say? If she's in love with Totleigh, she would surely object to me giving him a fat lip. Wouldn't she?"

"The question is whether she is in love with him."

Cakewood shook his head. "She says she isn't, but I'm not convinced. Did you see the way she touched his arm, how she laughed at his inane jokes?"

"And how does she feel about her father?"

"Oh, she absolutely adores him. Sure, she gets frustrated with his hardheadedness, but she won't hear a word spoken against him from anyone else."

"Then perhaps she would follow her father's lead."

"You think so?"

"I think it likely."

Cakewood nodded slowly. He took one last swig of tea and then shot up from the table. "Mr. Blandings, you have given me much to think about. For now, I need to return to the store, but don't be surprised if you see me at the Alliance Day fete tonight."

Blandings stood with him. "I look forward to it, sir."

Cakewood tossed the rest of the scone into his mouth and strode out.

Chapter 31

Busy Making Other Plans

Pelham sat back and closed his eyes. He had at last found a quiet and pleasant corner of what he thought of as "this blasted house." It was a small glass-lined sunroom extending from the back of the Sallow residence, and it featured a well-padded swivel chair in which he was now seated. For some minutes he had gazed out over the back garden as the late afternoon sun cast everything in a shade of blue that made even the malicious plants and dangerous pits look bucolic — if *bucolic* was the word he wanted.

The true highlight of the room, however, was its notable lack of Sallows and Gubbinses, which allowed him, after taking in the view, to close his eyes and breathe out a deep cleansing sigh.

Pelham let his mind wander to simpler, happier times — school days, the glories of the cheeseball pitch, nights out with the lads. His revels were interrupted by the sound of strident footsteps clacking across the tiles. Pelham kept his eyes shut, hoping whoever was there would see him resting and respectfully tiptoe off. He had no such luck.

"There you are, Pelham." It was Marigold's voice. "Why can't you stay in one place?"

"I was trying to," he said through closed lids.

"We may have a problem."

He opened one eye. "Oh? With what?"

"With my plan of getting engaged to Cecil by flirting with you. Of course, you've done a great job of getting Daddy to hate you with all your talk about magistrates you've laughed at and your pointless stories and your unceasing, ridiculous twaddle."

He opened the other eye. "My what?"

"But your man Blandings may ruin it for us."

"I highly doubt that. I couldn't count all the times Blandings has saved the day."

"Well, he's about to lose this one. That was an excellent plan he devised about letting Keezo perform at the Alliance Day festivities tonight. Now Daddy thinks he's the best thing since food replicators. And because Blandings works for you, Daddy seems to be starting to view even you in a more positive light."

"I do have a way of growing on people."

"Well, stop it. Do you know what Daddy just said?"

"No, and I would prefer not to."

"He said you must be smarter than you look if you had the sense to hire Blandings."

"He's not the first to make that observation."

"It worries me. If Daddy starts to like you, he's liable to be pleased rather than horrified when you ask for my hand in marriage."

"Speaking of that. I still don't think—"

"And then I'd be stuck with you. Wouldn't that be a revolting situation? By the way, do you have my hanky?"

"Oh, that." He patted a pocket, then another pocket. "Cecil was none too happy when he saw I had it."

"Oh, for the love of Gort. You can't do something like that to Cecil. He has a sensitive nature. Hand it over this instant."

Pelham produced the hanky and presented it to her with a flourish. "M'lady."

She snatched it away. "Now, you need to engage with Daddy again. And this time, do something totally pinheaded."

"Well, of course, I can try. But I can't turn it on at will, you know. It just … it sort of comes out sometimes."

She shot him a look worthy of Aunt Agutha and pointed toward the door.

He gawked. "What?"

"Go. Go find Daddy and make him loathe you again."

"You mean now? Couldn't it wait? This is a jolly pleasant spot."

"Now."

"You want me to deliberately start a conversation with old Sallow."

"Yes."

"Seems a bit akin to voluntarily attending a Donovian poetry reading, what? Or a younglings' dance recital." He shuddered to think of it.

She shot him a steely glare and continued to point down the hallway.

All things considered, staying there with Marigold didn't seem frightfully pleasant either. Pelham rose. "Righto. I'll be tottering off then."

He wandered off through the house, checking last in Sallow's study since it would be the most likely place to locate the blighter. He found him sitting at his desk, tapping something into a tablet. Pelham knocked on the doorframe.

Sallow looked up. "Ah, there you are Totleigh. Come in. I wanted to ask you something."

"Oh?" Perhaps Marigold had been right. Pelham wondered if somehow his stock had risen in the old yak's eyes. Sallow seemed inexplicably chummy. At least that was better than being insulted. He took a step into the room.

"Totleigh, I want you to be in charge of having the alien do tricks tonight. I'll be there, of course, but mainly to be seen laughing and clapping along with the rabble. For obvious reasons, I don't want to work directly with the creature myself. You can do that, can't you? Run the alien through its paces. Then when it has done enough tricks, introduce me and take the thing away so it doesn't distract anyone this time while I talk."

"Why me?" Pelham asked.

Sallow grimaced. "Because I don't have anyone else. Gubbins will be imaging the performance. I don't want to involve Marigold. And I still don't completely trust that Blandings fellow. He's too smart by half."

"Blandings certainly excels at braininess, though I don't quite see how anyone could be too smart."

"Will you do it?"

Pelham thought this might be just the chance he needed to free Keezo. As soon as the act ended, he could snatch the little Danánn from the cage and make a discreet getaway. "Certainly. I think it's an excellent idea."

Sallow's eyes narrowed. "You do, do you? What exactly do you mean by excellent?"

"I mean ... I don't know ... I suppose ... I mean ... excellent? Blandings could define it for you. Something goodish."

"You're wearing an odd look, Totleigh. It's like you're thinking."

"Well, people think, don't they?"

"Normal people do, but I suspect it's more than you could manage."

There it was, Pelham thought. The rotter's feelings could not be classified as thoroughly pro-Totleigh. Marigold would be pleased.

Sallow said, "After the show, bring the alien back here and put it in the pantry. Gubbins will help you in case it tries to escape."

Pelham's hopes crumbled before his eyes. Having Gubbins around would ruin everything. "Don't you need him to stick around and image your speech?"

"I do. All right, take the alien to the back of the crowd and cover it up with something until Gubbins is free."

"Sounds a bit risky, don't you think? People might still glance back at Keezo."

"Oh, I think not. I can hold an audience."

"You didn't this afternoon."

Sallow glared at him. "As long as you keep that thing out of sight, everything will be fine."

"I mean, I'm sure I can handle carting around one small space invader."

"You?"

"Yes."

"Without adult supervision."

"I am an adult."

Sallow stared at him for a moment, then burst out in laughter. "Good one. Ha. You almost had me there, Totleigh. You an adult. You handling something on your own. Right. Right. Ha." Sallow's eyes went back to his tablet.

Pelham turned to go but stopped when he remembered he was supposed to do something stupid. But did he really need to? The crumb had just laughed at him. And yet, it wasn't the derisive, contemptuous laugh he had received at the curio shop. This laugh had been worryingly similar to the way he and the lads all laughed at each other's foibles with affability and warmth. Perhaps it wouldn't hurt to do something to take the bloom off the Pelham rosanthemum.

The trouble was that it was dashed difficult to come up with anything thickheaded to do apropos of nothing, not to mention embarrassing to do something foolish on purpose. It was all well and good to pull a bloomer by accident to start the lads' heads wagging. But to do so willingly … well.

"What are you doing?" Sallow asked.

"What? Nothing. Why? What am I doing?"

"You're standing there like a tin soldier."

Pelham twisted around to face him. "Oh. Um."

"It's annoying."

"Sorry."

"Did you forget something? Lose something?"

"Don't think so."

"Then get out of here, you twit."

The insult was curiously comforting — just the thing Marigold would have wanted.

"Righto." Pelham scuttled off, feeling satisfied that he had fallen out of favor enough for the nonce.

Passing through the entry hall, he found Blandings sitting in a chair beside the stairway while reading from a tablet. "What ho, Blandings."

The valet, always impeccable in etiquette, stood. "Sir."

"Reading something personally enriching, I suppose? Histories of ancient civilizations? Some sort of philosophy? One of those deep, symbolic novels?"

"No, sir. I was perusing a report by the Grays on the topic of Earth breakfast foods. I remembered how much you enjoyed the Earth waffle you once had."

"That I did, Blandings. I recall it fondly. Have you found anything else I might like?"

"Quite possibly, sir. The Earthlings seem particularly fond of a substance known as bacon. It is a meat product, but the Grays are offering a replicator recipe of it for sale."

"That's the Grays for you. Always trying to make a fast bill or two. Would they by any chance have a waffle recipe?"

"As of yet, I have not come across one."

"Drat."

"The Earthlings also do a surprising number of things with a plant-based food called a potato. They make hash browns, casseroles, potato pancakes, roasted potatoes, and more. And those are only the listings in the breakfast category."

"Sounds like a dashed handy foodstuff, Blandings."

"Indeed, sir. I am told the Earthlings even named a town after the vegetable."

"Astounding. A town called Potato."

"If the Grays' reports are to be believed."

"Well, they've been there, and we haven't. In any case, I approve of your reading material. I won't keep you from it but a mo. I was wondering if there might be a chance of liberating Keezo from captivity before tonight."

"I highly doubt it, sir. The chef is back at work in the kitchen, preventing me from taking action."

"Too bad. Well, hopefully tonight then."

"Yes, sir. The festival, with its crowds and many activities, may provide us with our best prospect for doing so. I have advised Keezo to get away if possible."

"Good. Sallow asked that I emcee Keezo's performance, which I thought might give me means and opportunity as well as motive."

"A credible premise, sir."

"Unfortunately, he's also planning to assign Gubbins as security."

Blandings pursed his lips. "Most disheartening, sir."

"I'll say, it is."

"Still, there may be a way. And in the confusion of the crowd, anything could happen. I will give the matter some consideration."

"Excellent, Blandings. And by excellent, I mean excellent, splendid, brilliant … in case you were wondering."

"I was not, sir. But thank you for elucidating."

"Meanwhile, Marigold is worried that old Sallow may be coming around to see one Pelham G. Totleigh in a more friendly light, which would ruin all her plans. She blames you Blandings, you and your impressive intellect."

"I am not certain how to respond to that, sir."

"She insisted I do something exceptionally goofy to make sure the old blister continues to hate me. Which leaves me all a trifle flummoxed. I mean to say, the times I happen to do something silly, I rarely plan it. Although a moment ago, I may have done a bit to squelch the stinker's alleged growing warmth toward me — astoundingly, merely by standing still."

"Fascinating, sir."

"But I'll have to keep it up, which is a burden. It's difficult to dream up ways of looking foolish."

"I shouldn't worry overly much about it, sir."

"No?"

"I'm sure something will come to you."

"I hope so. Otherwise, I could end up affianced to that cyclone of a female. And between you and me, Blandings, she reminds me far too much of my Aunt Agatha."

Blandings nodded. "The two are in some respects similar."

"Not to look at, mind you."

"No, sir."

"But to listen to her." Pelham shuddered. "Well, I'll let you resume your reading."

"Sir, there is one other thing. If you should happen to see Mr. Cakewood this evening—"

"You mean Cecil, purveyor of leg lamps and other alien sundries?"

"Yes, sir. If you should encounter him, I believe it would help with Ms. Sallow's scheme if you were to taunt him concerning her feigned affections toward you."

"Rub it in, you mean. Poke the snufflerus, as it were."

"Yes, sir."

"You think that will help turn old Sallow against me? To be honest, Blandings, I don't see how it would. Given the lout's acerbic personality, I dare say it would do the opposite. He's likely to regard me as something of a kindred spirit, what?"

"Nevertheless, sir, I would advise it."

"Well, you're seldom wrong, Blandings."

"Thank you, sir. It is kind of you to say so."

"Not at all. And Blandings, be sure to look into this potato and bacon business."

"Yes, sir."

Pelham strode off, hoping Marigold had vacated the sunroom, and he could sit there to prepare for his upcoming ringmaster duties. But as he was approaching the door to his oasis from other people, he heard a gruff voice behind him say, "Hey!"

He turned to see Gubbins striding toward him.

"What ho," Pelham said, staring up at the hulking Haplor.

Gubbins said, "I hear you're going to be in charge of the alien tonight."

"That is the plan."

"Well, all I wanted to say is I'll be watching you. Don't try anything funny."

Pelham shot him his best impish grin. "Oh, I don't know. I was thinking a joke or two would go nicely with Keezo's gymnastic routine. Have you heard the one about the Avanian, the Donovian, and the Kolrabie who walked into a bar?"

Chapter 32

A Twist of Fete

Alliance Day is celebrated across the galactic alliance on the anniversary of the day each world joined the coalition. Which means there are many different Alliance Days all around the galaxy. There are also many different ways of celebrating the day, with traditions ranging from solemn observations to rowdy merrymaking.

Of course, people of any species enjoy a good party. A hardy few have made it a goal to try to drop in on every Alliance Day ceremony, especially the more raucous celebrations, hopping from one planet to the next. However, with each world having different lengths of both years and days, the math involved in doing so is extremely complex, and it's not uncommon for revelers to show up days either early or late.

In the case of the bubble beings, who live high in the atmosphere of the gas giant Nahuatl, their planet's annual trip around its star takes the equivalent of four hundred thirty-five Haplor years. As a result, they aren't scheduled to celebrate their first Alliance Day for another Haplor century. They have, however, already formed a planning committee.

The planet of Haplor along with all its colonies celebrate on the same day, or as closely as they can coordinate it. As Pelham made his way through the streets in the company of families and groups of people filing along in a festive mood, he thought of how at this moment, Aunt Agutha would probably be giving her traditional tedious speech, to be followed by a reception featuring bland biscuits and a bowl of disappointingly tame punch.

Things appeared to be done a little differently here on Unara. Tents and tables were set up in the park along the river. Under lights strung between the trees, people were selling baked goods and homemade crafts to a buoyant crowd. A band was playing a peppy tune on a stage. At one booth, people tried to win prizes by throwing balls at plates embossed with the galactic alliance emblem. Inside a tent, people cheered on contestants in a pudding-eating contest.

Pelham watched the progress of the contest until it became clear that the amount of pudding required to win would be far more than he wanted to witness anyone ingest. He turned away and followed the sound of laughter through the crowd to a beverage stand where he ordered a pint of whatever the barman was pulling for everyone else.

As he waited for the drink, he shivered in the cooling evening air. "I say, it's getting chilly, what?"

"What?" the barman yelled over the noise of the crowd.

Pelham raised his voice. "It's a bit nippy."

"You ain't seen nothing yet, mate. It'll be freezing by the time we pack up."

"Have you ever thought of holding the festivities earlier in the day?"

"No, it's the whole point. Here we are, settlers on a planet that can kill you from exposure any given night of the year. This is the one night we thumb our noses at all that to show that we're as hardy as our ancestors."

"Good for you," Pelham said.

"Within reason of course." The bartender shook a warning finger at him. "Don't stay out past the ringing of the town bell."

"I may have heard that last night. What is it?"

"It's the warning of when the temperature starts to plunge." He slid the mug over to Pelham.

"I'll keep it in mind. Toodle-pip."

Pelham wandered off through the crowd, enjoying the merriment. Younglings zigged and zagged around people as fast as they could go. A group of middle-aged male Haplors wearing funny hats and ribbons tied to their legs was performing a rhythmic dance. A knot of older males was playing a game where they tossed balls to see how close they could come to another ball.

"Totleigh!"

At the sound of his name, Pelham scanned the crowd. He spotted Gubbins waving at him from the front of a tent. The engineer-slash-bodyguard was standing in a huddle with Blandings and a well-dressed Haplor female. As Pelham headed in that direction, the female shook hands with the other two and then slipped away into the crowd.

"Who was that?" Pelham asked Blandings as he reached them.

Before the valet could answer, Gubbins said, "Hey, you're going on soon. Get rid of that drink. The boss doesn't approve of that sort of thing."

"Of course, he doesn't." Pelham disposed of the drink in the best way he knew — by finishing it. "What *does* Sallow approve of ... besides toys from other planets, that is? Where's Keezo?"

Gubbins pointed to a raised platform at the back of the tent. "The cage is already on the stage. I set a chair up there for you. I'll give you a signal when we're ready to go."

Pelham turned to hand Blandings his empty cup, but the valet had disappeared. He handed it to Gubbins instead, then ambled to the front of the tent past rows of folding chairs, nodding at the Haplors who were beginning to find seats. He heard one male tell two small younglings beside him, "I hear this thing is amazing."

Pelham found the chair on the stage beside a table holding something covered by a silky, red tablecloth. He leaned over to it and whispered, "Keezo, are you in there?"

"Pelie!" a muffled voice said. "I is Keezo."

"I thought as much. How are you doing, old turnip?"

"What is ... turnip?"

"Just a bit of slang, Keezo. I meant chum ... friend. How are you?"

"Okey dokey."

"Are you ready to put on another performance with feats of skill and dexterity, changing colors and all that?"

"Okey dokey."

From the back of the tent, Gubbins, standing on a ladder, was holding his recording device with one hand while pointing into the upper recesses of the tent with the other. He brought his arm down to point at Pelham.

Pelham goggled back at the imager. What was that gesture supposed to mean? Gubbins shook his hand at him. Pelham pointed at himself in question. Gubbins returned a dramatic nod and switched to a rolling motion with his arm.

Pelham jumped from the chair and walked to center stage as a hush fell over the crowd. He looked out from the stage. Few chairs were empty. Expectant faces stared up at him — mostly Haplor faces along with a spattering of alien heads with feathers, scales, or skin of various colors.

"Um ... righto. Um ... good evening. My name is Pelham G. Totleigh. As it happens, I'm a visitor to your fair planet. I hail from the moon of Sonus. But I suppose none of that matters."

"No, it doesn't," someone in the crowd yelled. "Bring out the alien."

"Um … well, anyway, it is my privilege to introduce to you a fantastic little extraterrestrial …"

Pelham noticed Sallow about halfway back sitting on the center aisle. He was attempting to point at himself without anyone else seeing it.

"What?" Pelham asked.

Sallow mouthed, "Introduce me."

"What?"

Sallow hissed, "Introduce me."

"Ah. Yes. By the by, our alien friend is appearing tonight courtesy of Mr. Oswald Sallow, who is currently holding Keezo captive …" Sallow shot him a glare. "I mean … I mean, Keezo is a guest of the Sallows at present."

Sallow leaned forward in his chair as if about to stand.

Catching the suggestion, Pelham said, "Won't you stand, Mr. Sallow?"

Sallow rose and gave the crowd one of those little wrist-twisty waves. Clearing his throat, he said, "I was delighted, folks, to learn of all the tricks this little creature can do, which is why I have brought it here tonight for your entertainment. And I invite you to stay a few moments following the show as I explain to you some disturbing news directly related to this alien, which threatens the safety of your family and all you hold dear. You will not want to miss it." With one more wave, Sallow sat.

Pelham said, "Of course, you all know Mr. Sallow from his vidcast. Funny, I don't think I ever caught its name. What is it? *Oswald's Earfuls*? *Sallow's Sermons*? *Histrionics of a Haplor*? The crowd, excepting Sallow and Gubbins, laughed.

"It's *The Sallow Report*," Sallow said in a grumpy tone.

"Well, without further ado …" Pelham paused and blinked a couple of times. "Ado. Ado. You know, I've never understood what ado is. What exactly is ado? How do you do ado? Blandings would know." He scanned the crowd for the valet but didn't see him. "I mean, one hardly says, 'and now for the ado portion of our program' or 'the performance included some frightfully fine ado, what?'"

"We came to see the alien," someone called.

"Ah, yes, the alien. This alien — name of Keezo — is a Danánn from the planet Danánn, which now that I say it, only makes sense. I mean to say, our ancestors were all Haplors from Haplor, eh? Here's something I bet you didn't know. The Haplors who settled Danánn — the planet, I mean, in this case —

originally thought the Danánn — the species, that is — were mythological. You'll see why directly."

Someone shouted out, "I'd like to see now."

"Yes, quite. Which reminds me of a humorous story. You see a youngling came home from school one day and said, 'Mum, we started working on the school play today.' And his mother said … Well, I should have mentioned that this was a Dieran lad, and the mother was Dieran also. The whole family, in fact, and—"

Scattered boos came from the crowd.

Sallow glowered at him. "Would you get on with it, you dimwit?"

He spotted Marigold standing at the back of the tent. She gave him a thumbs up, then waved and strode out into the night. Well, Pelham thought, at least one person approved of his performance, though he suspected it wasn't for any of the proper reasons.

Pelham said, "I'll …" He moved to the table and picked up a corner of the red tablecloth. "So do I just … um … tug?" From the crowd, Sallow made an exaggerated eye roll. Gubbins nodded vigorously.

Pelham pulled the cloth to reveal Keezo inside the cage. As the crowd burst into applause, Keezo's eyes grew wide. Keezo's fur morphed to a deep red to match the cloth that Pelham had dropped in a wad beside the cage. The crowd gasped.

Pelham said, "That is but one of Keezo's many tricks and abilities."

This time the cage had been fitted with a set of three rings hanging above the alien's head. Pelham said, "Keezo, why don't you …" He raised his arms and waved them back and forth as if he were swinging from rings.

With a puzzled expression, Keezo waved two tentacles in the air.

"No, Keezo. On the rings … the circle thingies, don't you know." Pelham pointed.

"Keezo do," Keezo said. A tentacle stretched up to the far ring and wrapped around it. Another tentacle seized the middle one. Keezo's body lifted into the air. Giggles came from the crowd. For a moment, Keezo simply hung there. Then the Danánn began swinging from ring to ring.

Keezo released one ring and swung to the third, then back. The crowd went wild. Out in the audience, Sallow made a show of nodding to Haplors around him while pointing toward the stage and laughing.

Keezo moved from the rings to the bird perch and hung upside down, making faces to get laughs. Keezo let go, flipped in the air, and landed back on the floor of the cage.

Someone shouted out, "What other colors does he do?"

Pelham scratched his head. "Oh, I've seen a jolly convincing blue. Keezo, would you turn blue?"

Keezo blinked.

Pelham turned back to the crowd. "Apparently, Keezo needs to have the color at hand — or at tentacle, as it were — to work with. Is anyone wearing blue? Anyone? Ah, you there, lad." Pelham pointed to a youngling wearing a bright blue jacket with matching shorts and cap. "Would you come up here and hold the cage." The crowd applauded as the embarrassed lad slipped from his seat and shuffled forward.

Pelham pulled his chair around to the front of the stage. "Sit there." He handed the youngling the cage. "Hold this on your lap. Righto. You have it. Now change colors, Keezo."

Keezo blinked again.

"Hmm. Keezo tends to do it only when alarmed. Let's see." Pelham placed a hand on the youngling's shoulder. "Why don't you say, 'boo?'"

The lad tried. Keezo didn't respond.

Pelham said, "Um … Sallow could you say something threatening? You're good at that sort of thing."

"I am not," Sallow said gruffly. "And leave me out of this. Totleigh, one more word of poppycock out of you, and by Gort I'll come up there and—"

He was interrupted by applause as Keezo's fur transformed to a bright blue that was an exact match to the jacket and shorts.

Somebody yelled. "Where did he go? I don't see him."

Pelham said, "Oh, Keezo's still in there. If you tilt your head, you might see sort of an outline."

"I still can't see it," someone said.

"It's a trick," another person called out. "You hid the creature somewhere."

"No, really. Keezo just changed colors. I'll show you." Pelham unlatched the cage door and reached in, bringing Keezo out. He held the little alien in one arm.

As the crowd applauded, Keezo changed back to black. Pelham took a bow. It was at that moment that Keezo jumped from Pelham's arm to the stage floor.

Amid gasps from the crowd, the Danánn hopped off the stage to the ground, dashed up the aisle, and disappeared out the back of the tent.

Over the shouts of the startled audience, Pelham could hear Sallow bellow, "Totleigh!"

Chapter 33

Fade Runner

Pelham gaped after the fleeing Keezo, frozen in place with astonishment. Audience members, on the other hand, jumped to their feet, shouting, pointing, pushing this way and that, knocking over folding chairs in the process. The entire tent descended into pandemonium.

Sallow shook a fist at Pelham and bellowed, "You dolt. Why didn't you hang onto it?" He started down the crowded aisle after Keezo, yelling at everyone to get out of his way. "Let me through. Let me through. The alien can't escape."

"I think it just did," a male Haplor answered, chuckling at him.

Another male said, "Hey, Sallow, I thought you were going to share a few words with us after the performance."

"I'll give you some words," Sallow growled. "Get out of my way." He waved a signal to his assistant. "Gubbins, after it."

Being already at the back of the tent, Gubbins was able to quickly pocket his camera and sprint out the opening into the darkness. Sallow fought his way past the last audience members and followed.

Spotting a loose flap in the side of the tent near the stage, Pelham bypassed the mob and exited that way. He saw the other two ahead and put on as much speed as he could to catch up. It didn't take long to pass Sallow, Pelham's relative youthfulness easily besting Sallow's age and keg-like physique. Gubbins, who moved surprisingly fast for someone his size, was another matter.

It was not difficult to track Keezo's movement across the festival grounds as people kept yowling, "Oi," and, "What's that?" and making sudden surprised movements when something small and dark brushed past them.

The Danánn sprang onto a table selling baked goods, quickly gobbling down two donuts before turning and seeing Gubbins plowing through the throng in that direction. Keezo jumped to the ground and dashed away as Gubbins launched himself through the air. The big Haplor crashed down onto the table, sending pastries flying every which way to the delight of anyone who didn't mind picking one up off the ground and to the shock of everyone else.

Pelham wove through this scene of destruction as best he could and shot off after Keezo. Sallow stopped only long enough to call Gubbins a few choice names, leaving to others the job of helping the large Haplor to his feet.

Meanwhile, Keezo had passed from the circle of booths and out into the unlit park. Pelham now led the trio of pursuers, with Sallow and Gubbins contending for second place.

One of Unara's moons was full, the other a glowing semicircle. Both hung huge in the sky, lighting the landscape in muted colors and deep shadows. Pelham had never seen moons this large, and he had spent a fair bit of his life living on one.

As they ran through the park and out into the barren landscape beyond, the sulfur smell from the mud pools became stronger. More than once, Pelham had to make a hasty turn when he spotted steam rising ahead of him or one of the dropout warning cones sticking up from the ground.

"Keezo," he called out in a stage whisper. "It's Pelie. Where are you?" He hoped he might locate the alien, and they could slip away together into the night.

At that moment plodding footsteps and desperate wheezing sounded behind him. Pelham looked over his shoulder to see Gubbins and Sallow coming up on his position. "Never mind, Keezo. Hide."

"Do you ... see the ... alien?" Sallow yelled to him between gasps.

Pelham shook his head. "I hardly think we'll be able to find a small black extraterrestrial in this darkness. Might as well give up, I say."

"Rubbish. We can see perfectly fine." Sallow paused for a moment to shovel in some air. "We may have lost some color differentiation here in the moonlight, but that scarcely hampers us since the alien can fool us with color anyway. We have plenty of light to spot its movement. Look, there's something there." Sallow pointed at a shadow that had shimmered in front of a rock. "Come out, Keezo. I won't hurt you. We'll take you back to my warm house."

Undeniably, the warm house was a consideration, Pelham thought. The night air had already slid past cool into biting and seemed to be making a beeline toward downright cold. If they didn't find Keezo, could the little alien survive a night out here? The Danánn had talked about living in a mound. Perhaps Keezo would burrow into the sandy soil. Better yet would be to head back into town and find somewhere warm to huddle.

Pelham wished Blandings were here so he could ask his opinion. Where was Blandings anyway? Probably off with that well-dressed female, he thought. His valet should be here at his side, helping with the search and coming up with a scheme to divert Sallow and Gubbins while they located Keezo themselves. Without him, it would be up to Pelham G. Totleigh to save the day.

Gubbins' voice boomed, "Over there." He shot off between two dark bushes.

Sallow and Pelham trotted after the imager, catching up to him at the base of one of the funnel-shaped, bushy-topped trees. Gubbins gazed up into the branches, weaving his head back and forth.

"Is it up there?" Sallow asked.

"I thought I saw it scramble up the trunk," the big guy said, "but I can't spot it up there now."

"Climb up and see."

Gubbins shot his employer an aggrieved look. Sallow returned the same. Grumbling to himself, Gubbins backed up, ran for the tree, placed a foot on the trunk, and sprang up toward a branch. His arm missed, and he crashed to the ground. Gubbins lay there for a few moments. Then he rolled to his feet and tried it again. The second time, he managed to grab the branch and hang on. He swung his legs up into a divide in the trunk and pulled himself into a sitting position.

It was then that a small popping sound erupted from the base of the little tree — one pop, two more pops, four after that. The whole thing began a slow-motion tipping over. With the leaning and the cracking, it reminded Pelham of someone popping their back, except the tree never righted itself and just continued to pitch further and further.

Gubbins threw his arms around the rough bark and rode the creaking trunk to the ground. From the upper — or now, one might say, the further — branches, something black darted off into the night.

"Up, Gubbins," Sallow commanded. "It's getting away."

Gubbins stood and glared at Sallow while he brushed pieces of bark from his front.

Pelham said, "Why don't you just let Keezo go?"

"Oh no," Sallow said, propping his hands on his knees, "I can't let a dangerous alien run around loose on our planet. Get after it, Gubbins."

The big Haplor nodded and jogged off into the dark.

"But Keezo isn't dangerous," Pelham said.

Still trying to catch his breath, Sallow flashed a sneer. "All aliens are dangerous."

"What? What? No, they aren't. I've met any number of non-dangerous ones — Bononians, Okcho, Rhegedians, Javidians — mind you, the Javidians appear a bit menacing with their spiky tails and the barbs running down their backs, but they aren't — Axans, Kolrabie, Srathans. All right, I'll give you Srathans. They can be a bit dangerous. But, Sallow, you really should get out more. Meet some people. Most of the species are quite charming."

Sallow shook his head. "You don't understand, Totleigh. Aliens aren't dangerous because of spikes or claws or because a giant one might step on someone or a carnivorous one might eat somebody. It isn't any of those things. It isn't what they might do to one of us or some of us. They are dangerous because of what they will inevitably do to all of us."

"What are you talking about, Sallow? What will they do to all of us?"

"They will change us. They will destroy who we've always been. You see it happening already. Haplors are wearing alien clothes, using alien technology, celebrating alien holidays, for Gort's sake."

"So?"

Pelham couldn't see the harm. Aunt Agutha had once insisted he travel to Delusia for their Shed Sweeping Day. He had found it to be a good deal more fun than one would expect for a holiday dedicated to cleaning up storage buildings. All the sweeping had been accompanied by big block parties with delightful music and amazing food.

Pelham struggled to fathom how a festival or an imported gadget or two could make much difference in who Haplors essentially were. Then again, he had never found it easy to think this late at night, a shortcoming that had led to him getting into more than a few scrapes. Here in this numbing chill, he could barely think at all except about how cold he was.

"So?" Sallow repeated. "You ask, 'So?' So this. Who we are is who we are. If we lose who we are, then … well, who are we then?"

Pelham ran the words over in his mind, trying to make sense of them. Had alien influences changed him? He had to admit they had. His favorite drink, the Amurru fizz, was an alien concoction. Without it, he would probably relax of an evening with some Haplorian ale. And he did enjoy wearing some alien styles … when he could slip them past Blandings' hidebound notions of fashion. He harbored hopes of that Gray captain acquiring for him an Earth fedora. He thought he would look quite smart in one.

But were those changes bad? He couldn't see how. He would bring this all up with Blandings, who would surely have some insights, probably driving home his points by quoting some poet.

"Well?" Sallow asked with an impatient look on his face.

Pelham realized he had fallen silent amid his thoughts. "Frankly, I haven't the foggiest. I'm not even sure I understand the question. But I can tell you this much, Sallow. It's an excellent question, and one deserving of more than a knee-jerk, black-and-white answer. It can't be all one way and not the other."

Sallow scowled. "Pah! What do you know? This is all your fault, Totleigh. You just had to let the alien out of the cage."

"I didn't mean to. The audience had questions. I was trying to answer them."

"Pah!"

From the darkness, they heard Gubbins' voice. "Over here."

Pelham and Sallow trotted toward the sound. Out here the trees were fewer and further apart. Boulders and scrubby plants of various sizes dotted the landscape. They were a considerable distance from town. Pelham looked back the way they had come. The settlement was now only a glow of light on the horizon, a mere promise of a town. A town with beds and heat and warm drinks. He rubbed his hands together in the cold.

They found Gubbins, and he signaled for them to follow. They moved slowly and carefully, eyeing around every boulder, scanning for movement. Now and again, they would see Keezo standing against a plant. Then Keezo would spot them, fade to blend in with the surroundings, and shimmer off.

Gubbins waved his arms to the sides to signal them to spread out. They did, Pelham hoping that would give him a chance to find Keezo himself and be able to scoot away with the little alien.

They slogged on. The night air had now slipped from frosty to indisputably frigid. Pelham wrapped his arms around himself. How long were the others planning to stay out here?

"There," Gubbins said, pointing across the plain.

Something flashed in front of a rock, then cast a shadow as it passed by a plant, then glinted in the moonlight as it bolted across open ground. Pelham, Sallow, and Gubbins began to run, converging toward it.

Keezo jumped to the top of a boulder and looked back at them, eyes glowing white in the darkness.

"On that rock," Sallow shouted.

Gubbins put on speed. Sallow raced after him. They were now just a handful of steps away. Keezo leaped from the rock and darted across the landscape, Gubbins and Sallow close on the Danánn's heels.

The terrain here was practically barren, a solitary tree looming over exposed soil. The only other things standing up from the ground, the only possible places where Keezo could find cover, were two cones, pale in the moonslight, with indistinct lettering on the side. Keezo sprinted between them.

"No, wait," Sallow shouted, pulling up short.

But Gubbins had already thrown himself after the alien. He landed with his hands gripped around Keezo's legs.

And then they both vanished, a hole appearing where they had been a moment before.

Jagged fissures shot from the hole in every direction. Time slowed. The dirt began to crumble and drop away like so many dried cumberbeans pouring from a box. Sallow spun and took one step before the ground below his feet turned to dust. Fear etched across his face, he reached a hand toward Pelham and then dropped from sight.

Chapter 34

The Harder They Fall

Oswald Sallow lay on his back gazing up at the moons. They were so far away, the one a full two hours travel time by ion drive, the other three-and-a-half. The stars in the sky were even further — tens and hundreds and thousands of light-years.

But those weren't the distances that concerned him at present. Rather it was the relatively short span of pit wall that separated him from the surface of Unara. Short, yes, but fully long enough to trap him in this hole.

He heaved gulps of air in and out, watching the vapor of his breaths rise, condense into water droplets, and fall back onto his face and chest. He wiped his face with his hand, somewhat surprised that he had movement and feeling in his arm. He checked the other arm. He moved his legs. He thought he might be all right ... other than being in this pit.

From somewhere nearby, Gubbins groaned and coughed twice. "Are you injured, Mr. Sallow."

"I don't think so," Sallow said slowly. "Do you have the alien?"

"I'm fine," Gubbins said. "Thanks for asking. And for your information, the alien is here beside me. It appears unhurt as well."

Sarcasm was not what Sallow needed from his assistant right now. What he needed was a way out of this hole, preferably before what remaining heat there was on the planet's surface all drifted off into space.

He sat up and moaned, discovering a pain in his back he hadn't noticed before. That would ache for days, blast it. He brushed the dirt from his head fur. He pulled off his jacket to shake out the dirt, then quickly slipped it back on because of the cold. While it was warmer down in the hole than it had been above in the open air, the night was nonetheless frigid and growing colder with each moment.

Sallow made it to his feet and turned to find Gubbins on the other side of the irregularly shaped hole, also standing. The alien, invisible except for its eyes gleaming in the moonlight, sat huddled in the corner furthest from him.

"Gubbins, can you climb out?"

The big Haplor ran a hand along the pit wall as high as he could reach. "No way. No tree roots. No rocks sticking out from the dirt. And it crumbles if I try to dig a handhold. There's nothing to grab onto."

Sallow slowly scanned up the sides, confirming Gubbins' diagnosis. As his gaze reached the top, a head-shaped shadow appeared over the edge of the hole.

Totleigh's voice called down. "Well, well, well." With the moons behind him and the dark pit in front of him, the twit's face was cloaked in shadow. Sallow could only infer the smirk from the tone of voice.

"Totleigh," Sallow said, "quit snickering and go bring help. No, wait." After all the embarrassment he had suffered today — the laughter during his vidcast taping, the fiasco at the festival — the last thing Sallow needed right now was the public humiliation of everyone knowing he had fallen through a dropout. "On second thought, don't tell anyone. Run back to the house. You'll find a coil of rope hanging in the shed. Bring it back here and haul us out."

"He's not big enough to haul us out on his own," Gubbins said.

"He can tie the rope to the tree up there, and we can climb out." Sallow shook his head. Was he the only one who could think of these solutions?

"We've already seen how strong those trees aren't," Gubbins said.

"Then I'll climb up first."

"And then what?"

"Then we'll figure out something for you. We don't have time to argue about this. Totleigh, just go get the rope."

The shadow above them still loomed over the hole.

"Well?" asked Sallow. "What are you waiting for, you halfwit? Move! Hurry up before we freeze to death."

"Yes, yes," Totleigh said. "I'll be off soon enough. I was thinking though, Sallow."

"That's a first."

"Insults will get you nowhere. I was thinking how you've rather stepped in it this time … literally, what? Ha!"

"What are you prattling on about, you imbecile."

Totleigh shook a dark finger at him. "There you go again with your little terms of endearment. Imbecile. Halfwit. And what was the slur you unleashed against me earlier? Oh yes. Dolt. Such ugly, malicious words, don't you think? Not to mention hurtful. Such conduct, Sallow, is hardly conducive to your negotiating position."

"What negotiating position? What are you talking about?"

"I'm talking, you odious mud frog, you gourd-headed creep—"

"Now who's slinging abuse?"

"Never mind about that," Totleigh said. "As to your original question, I'm talking about how we can assist each other here."

"You can assist me by popping off immediately and fetching that rope."

"Yes, yes," Totleigh said. "Run back to the house. Fetch the rope. I have it all up here in the old bean." The shadow of an arm and hand tapped the shadow of a head. "But we have yet to touch on the topic of what you can do for me."

"What do you want?" Sallow asked bitterly.

"I was thinking you could release both Keezo and the leg lamp to me."

"Balderdash!" Sallow said. "I will do no such thing."

"Now, now, Sallow. You know, I can't help wondering if you're considering your situation here with the proper degree of seriousness. I mean to say, there you are in a deep pit several sprintspans from town. What are you going to do if I choose not to assist?"

"You're bluffing. You wouldn't dare leave us here. It would be tantamount to murder."

An annoying chuckle from Totleigh sounded down the sides of the pit. "Oh, I suppose you're right about that. I won't leave you here … not the entire night at any rate. The question is how long it will take me to find my way back? Will I be sufficiently motivated to hurry? Or will I find it necessary to first locate and slip into some warmer clothes or rustle up a nourishing bowl of soup to fortify me against the cold? You know, I really should track down Blandings before coming back. He's frightfully good in a crisis. It all could take quite some time."

"Go get the rope, Totleigh." Sallow could hear the strain in his own voice.

"First, you agree to give me the lamp and let Keezo go."

"We don't have time to talk about that now. Go. We'll discuss it later."

"Oh, I don't know. I have all the time in the world. I mean, it is growing a trifle cold up here. But it's nothing I can't handle. I live on Sonus, which has even less atmosphere than this. I expect the vigorous jaunt to your house and back — once we agree to terms, of course — will warm me up a fair bit."

"Look, you can have the alien, all right? Just get a move on. I can't feel my toes."

"And by 'the alien,' do you mean the one who calls himself Keezo?"

"Yes, yes, what other alien could I mean?"

"I haven't the faintest, but I'm working on the assumption that you will try to wiggle out of our agreement on some technicality. And you agree you won't prosecute Keezo for the attempted robbery?"

"Fine."

"Or anyone else?"

"What? Yes, yes."

"You agree?"

"I agree. No prosecutions for the break-in."

"Excellent. Now as to the matter of the leg lamp, by which, I am referring to the one you bought out from under me yesterday."

"Yes."

"The one from Earth."

"There isn't any other leg lamp, you numbskull."

"Now, now, now. Watch the derogatory language, please."

It would be a bitter thing, Sallow thought, to lose the lamp. It would be especially bitter to lose it to this brainless dimwit under these circumstances. He rubbed his cold nose with a cold hand, which left both of them precisely as cold as they were before. "Fine. I'll sell it to you for what I paid for it."

"My dear lad," Totleigh said, "I think at this juncture we're well beyond tawdry buying and selling.

Sallow huffed. "You want me to just give it to you?"

"Think of it as payment for services rendered. Totleigh's Rescue Service and all that."

Sallow couldn't believe he was being extorted like this by Totleigh, of all people. "All right, all right."

"Pardon? I couldn't entirely make that out from way up here."

Sallow spoke louder. "I said all right."

"You agree to my terms?"

Across the plain, they heard the tolling of a bell.

"Yes. Yes, I agree," Sallow said, spitting out the words. "Now go."

Totleigh laughed. "Righto. Be back in a jiffy." His head disappeared from view.

Feeling defeated but at least relieved that he would be rescued, Sallow moved with growing stiffness to the side of the hole. He sat down with his back against the dirt wall and breathed out a sigh.

A moment later he heard Totleigh's voice scream out, "Aaaaah!" It was followed by a *thump* and a muffled, "Oh, blast!"

Sallow groaned and rolled his eyes in Gubbins' direction. "The dope just fell through a different dropout, didn't he?"

In the faint light, he could make out the big guy sadly nodding.

Chapter 35

The Pit and the Pandemonium

Pelham's first thought as he found himself crashing through the brittle crust of mud and plunging headlong into the pit below was not one of fear or alarm but rather utter disappointment. Only moments before, he'd had Sallow exactly where he wanted him. He had haggled out an agreement to free Keezo and take possession of the leg lamp. He had achieved success on all fronts. Most remarkably, he had done it all without Blandings' assistance. It had been he, Pelham G. Totleigh, who for once had tied everything up in a tidy package.

And then one wrong step led to disaster.

He landed on his chest with a *thud* amid showers of dirt clods. When the rain of topsoil subsided, he checked his extremities. Everything seemed wiggle-able. He rolled over, stood, brushed himself off, and gazed up.

The sandy walls seemed to close in on him. This was far too reminiscent of that time during his school days when he had climbed into the air vents to try and break into the headmaster's office. He had ended up stuck in a cavity not much narrower than this with the opening at the end every bit as far away.

The slightly muffled voice of Oswald Sallow sounded out in the darkness. "Totleigh, you oaf ... you thick-witted sap ... you blithering idiot ... you ... you ..." The invectives came to a sputtering halt as if words had at last failed the odious vidcaster.

It was a surprise to Pelham to find Sallow stymied this early into his list of aspersions. At such a point in a harangue, Aunt Agutha would have scarcely begun to have warmed up, no doubt going on to call him a nincompoop, a simpleton, or even a bonehead. But in the present circs, Pelham saw no need to offer suggestions.

Then Sallow seemed to rally and continued in a sarcastic tone. "Oh, there I go again. I'm sorry, Totleigh. Did those words hurt your feelings? Did they wound you? Well, all I can say is I hope they did. You, Totleigh, are without doubt the most worthless Haplor I have ever had the misfortune to lay eyes upon. And now because of your incompetence, we're all going to die out here."

"For what it's worth," Pelham called back, "I would like to point out that at least I didn't fall into the first hole."

"Shut up."

Which was hardly the kind of sentiment to encourage further conversation. Silence descended over the two pits. Pelham paced around the hole, which took but a few steps. After a couple of laps, he sat on the ground. Finding it uncomfortable, he immediately stood once more and began waving his arms up and down — as best he could in the tight space — in an effort to keep himself warm.

Sallow spoke again. "By the way, Totleigh, you realize the deal for the alien and the leg lamp is off now."

"Yes, yes," Pelham said wearily. He didn't need to have it pointed out.

"Null and void."

"I get the picture."

"Our contract is canceled."

Sallow might have continued along those lines for some time, but Gubbins interrupted with, "What's the plan now?"

"Plan?" Sallow asked with derision in his voice. "We have no plan. Totleigh was our plan. No one knows we're out here. There's a chance Marigold will notice I'm gone, but she has no idea where to look for us. Or perhaps that Blandings fellow will miss Totleigh and begin a search. Sounds unlikely, I should say. If you were joined to Totleigh, and then one night he failed to appear, would you scour the countryside for him? I certainly wouldn't. I would simply celebrate my good fortune at being rid of him and move on."

"There's no need to get snippy," Pelham called out.

Sallow muttered something unintelligible, and the discussion lapsed back into silence.

After several moments Sallow said, "Gubbins, let me stand on your shoulders."

"What?" the imager asked.

"You heard me. Let me stand on your shoulders. Maybe I can reach something."

"You won't reach the top. We're too deep."

"I said *something*. I might be able to reach a root or anything and then be able to climb out from there."

"I don't see any root."

"That doesn't mean anything. It's dark."

It's not that dark. I can see shadows."

"Do you have a better idea, Gubbins? Help me up."

From his separate hole, Pelham lacked the visuals of the scene that followed. But with the aid of the dialogue reaching him, he could envision most of it.

"Come over here, Gubbins. Now stoop down. Further. Down, down."

"But it's muddy here."

"Don't be a baby. Now hold still. Wait. Move closer to the side of the hole where I can balance myself against it."

"First you want me down, then up, then down. Is here all right?"

"Yes, yes. Now stoop down again. Further, Gubbins. How many times do I have to tell you? All right, I'm stepping up now. First foot. Now … second foot."

"Ow! That's my head."

"All right, all right. I think this is your shoulder. Now, stand up, Gubbins. Wait! Not so fast. I can't … Wait. Hold still … oh oh oh!"

A dull *thud* sounded from the other hole.

"Ow! I said to slow down, Gubbins."

"Sorry."

"Try it again."

"This is not going to work."

"Again, Gubbins. There. Now stand slowly this time. Up … up … up."

"That's all the up I have."

"Well, it's not nearly enough."

"I tried to tell you."

"Maybe if I stepped up—"

"Hey! Not on the head."

"But I think if I climb just a little higher I could—"

"Not on the head."

"If you insist. Jump then."

"Jump?"

"Jump. I think I can reach the top if you jump."

"I can't jump with you standing on me. You're heavy."

"I am not. Jump! Jump!"

This time two dull *thuds* reached Pelham along with shouts of pain and a fair amount of colorful language. He chuckled to himself.

When things had quieted down, Pelham called out, "What about Keezo?"

"What about the alien?" Sallow asked. "We didn't land on it if that's what you're worried about."

"I'm glad to hear it, but that isn't what I meant."

"Then say what you mean, you dumb brick, before we all freeze to death."

"I meant that Keezo is a dashed good climber."

"So?"

"I bet Keezo can climb out and run for help."

"You've got to be joking."

"I am not."

"First, the creature is clearly too unintelligent to do anything so complex as run and bring back help."

"That's where you're wrong, Sallow."

"I don't think so. Look what happened when I tried sending you. And secondly, I'm not going to let that alien out of my sight. We chased it all the way out here to catch it ... after you let it go, I might add."

"You'd rather become an icicle?"

Sallow didn't answer right away. Then in a grumpy voice, he said, "All right, you can try."

Pelham called, "Hello, Keezo."

Keezo's voice came back. "Hello. I is Keezo."

"Yes, you are. I was wondering, Keezo, would you be a dear and climb out of the hole over there?"

"I is climb out hole?"

"Yes, Keezo, climb right up and out."

Keezo didn't answer, but Pelham heard Gubbins say, "Look at those tentacles stretch. Do you see that? It's pulling itself straight up. What's it possibly grabbing onto? It's amazing. It's like gravity doesn't even apply to it."

A moment later, a small dark head, framed by one of the moons, peered down at Pelham from above. "Hello. Is cold out here."

"Yes, it is, Keezo ... and growing colder. I want you to run and find Blandings. You know Blandings, right?"

"I is know."

"Find Blandings and tell him we are stuck out here and that he should bring rope and possibly someone to help yank us out of these holes. Do you have all that, Keezo?"

Pelham waited for an answer that didn't come. The shadowy head above him still hung there, a small furry eclipse against the moon. "I say, Keezo, can you remember all that?"

"I is think so. Go find Bandy."

"What was that?" Sallow called. "I couldn't make it out."

Pelham ignored him. "Yes. Righto. Find Blandings. But that's not all. What will you tell him when you find him?"

"You and mean Bigs fall in holes?"

"What did it say?" Sallow bellowed.

Pelham laughed. "Yes, that will do nicely. And then what should Blandings do about it?"

"Bring help and rope."

"Righto again. I say, Keezo, you're going to do a smashing job."

"What you is want Keezo smash?"

"What? Oh nothing. Sorry. Figure of speech. No smashing. Just Blandings and the rope."

"Okey dokey."

The difficult bit of all this, Pelham thought, might be finding Blandings in the first place. "Now, Keezo, Blandings might be at Sallow's house ... you know, the house of the mean Big."

"I heard that," Sallow shouted from the other hole.

"I not is like that place," Keezo said. "I not is like cage."

"I'm sure you don't. But Blandings will make sure no one puts you in a cage. If he isn't there, try the hotel. Can you find the hotel again?"

"I is try."

"That's all we can ask."

From the other hole, Sallow grumbled, "For the love of Gort."

"Shush," Pelham said. "Now, Keezo, if Blandings isn't at either of those places ... well, then alert anyone you can. We can't survive in this cold."

"I not is like cold. Keezo's mound never is this cold."

"We can chat about your mound later. Now off you go. Find Blandings. And don't dillydally."

"What is ... dillydally?"

"Just go."

The shadow disappeared from the top of the hole.

Pelham took a breath and let it out. He called to the others, "Keezo's popped off. Now we wait for the rescue."

Sallow scoffed. "Unless the alien simply runs off and leaves us … or forgets what it's supposed to tell your valet … or gets lost on the way there or back. I put the odds of success at around twenty-to-one."

In a bitter tone, Gubbins said, "That's still better than you trying to stand on my shoulders."

"Shut up, Gubbins."

Chapter 36

Rescue Me

Shivering from the cold despite himself, Blandings pressed the button at the front door of the Sallow mansion and spoke into the speaker grill. "Blandings here to see Mr. Sallow."

No one answered.

He tried again. "Pardon me. Is anyone home?"

Still no answer.

"Excuse me. If I may, I am worried about Mr. Totleigh. He seems to be missing. Is Mr. Sallow here, or has he gone missing as well?"

The voice of the young Ms. Sallow sounded in the speaker. "What did you say?"

"Good evening, Ms. Sallow. I said that Mr. Totleigh is missing. Is your father home?"

"No, he isn't."

"Then I fear they may both be missing."

"Missing? Together?"

"I do not know, ma'am. However, it stands to reason."

"No, it doesn't. They hate each other."

"Undoubtedly. However, they were last seen leaving the festival together. I wonder if you might be so good as to admit me so we can discuss the situation."

"Um … certainly. I'll be right there."

She answered the door with Cecil Cakewood standing beside her.

Blandings said, "Forgive the interruption, ma'am. I was unaware that you were entertaining company. Good evening, Mr. Cakewood."

"Nonsense," Ms. Sallow said. "If Daddy is missing, I want to know. Now come in before you freeze. We can talk in the dining room."

She led the way there and offered Blandings a seat. It was with some reluctance that he took it. He judged, however, that now was not the time for a strict observance of social norms. This could be a matter of life and death.

Ms. Sallow said, "You think Pelham and Daddy are together?"

"I do, ma'am. Mr. Gubbins as well. Did you attend the performance at the festival — the one your father arranged?"

"Briefly. I wanted to see how Pelham did." She grinned. "He exceeded expectations."

A low grumble came from Cakewood.

She patted his arm. "You know what I mean, Cecil. I wasn't there long, Mr. Blandings."

Cakewood said, "Marigold and I had arranged to meet."

"Then you were not present at the end?" Blandings asked.

She shook her head. "No. Why? What happened?"

"I was not there either, but I heard reports. The Danánn escaped, and your father, Mr. Totleigh, and Mr. Gubbins gave chase through the festival grounds and out into the park." Blandings paused. "It is possible they continued across the open country."

"No. Are you sure? Have you checked the pubs, the all-night diner?"

"I have, ma'am."

She stood and paced to the window, leading Blandings to reflexively rise as well.

"They could still be out there … with the temperature plunging."

"Yes, ma'am. I share your concern. I wonder how we might go about mobilizing the colony's search and rescue team."

She looked puzzled. "We … don't. Unara doesn't have one."

"It doesn't?"

"No … we never have. Remember we were founded by people who thought of themselves as rugged individualists. There is no fire brigade or rescue team. Everyone is supposed to take care of themselves."

"On the plus side," Cakewood said, "we have surprisingly low taxes."

"I see," Blandings said.

The shopkeeper flipped up a palm. "Though that does tend to be offset by higher insurance premiums."

"In that case," Blandings said, "since the rescue falls to us, I propose—"

He was interrupted by a squeaky voice coming through a speaker. "Bandy Bandy Bandy Bandy Bandy."

Ms. Sallow jumped.

Cakewood said, "What in Gort's name is that?"

Blandings rushed from the dining room toward the front door. He returned moments later carrying Keezo, frost hanging from the alien's tentacles.

Keezo eyed the other two Haplors suspiciously and might have changed colors if not for the fact that Keezo's black fur already matched Blandings' black suit jacket.

Blandings said, "It's all right. These people are friends. Do you know where Mr. Totleigh is?"

Keezo nodded, eyes wide. "Big hole. Pelie and mean Bigs fall in holes."

Ms. Sallow drew a sharp breath. "Oh no."

Blandings asked, "Do you mean Mr. Sallow and Mr. Gubbins? They are with Mr. Totleigh?"

Keezo shrugged tentacles. "I think I is hear those names. The mean ones who is catch me and put me in cage."

"Are they all right?" Ms. Sallow asked.

"They not is hurt. But they not is happy. They is yell … a lot. Pelie is say find Bandy and bring rope and others to help."

"Mr. Totleigh sent you?" Blandings asked.

"Yes, yes. He is say go find Bandy."

"Can you lead us there, Keezo? Can you take us to the holes where they fell?"

"I can take."

Cakewood said, "We'll need to bundle up … and bring some blankets for them."

Ms. Sallow said, "Cecil, there's rope in the shed. I'll find blankets and coats for us all. Mr. Blandings, I know you don't like to replicate tea, but just this once. We need to hurry. It will be dangerously cold before long."

The hike out was laborious and grueling with everyone dressed in heavy coats and weighed down by blankets, rope, extra clothes for the others, handlamps, and canteens of hot tea. Even Keezo was wrapped up in a tiny coat that Ms. Sallow had worn as a very small youngling and wearing socks that made the little alien walk awkwardly, legs rising to the side with each step.

Keezo led the way with Cakewood right behind, steering the others away from any mud pools and warning cones he spotted. They walked in silence, lamplights

222

bobbing up and down through the darkness, their breath billowing out ahead of them.

Cold was seeping into Blandings' bones, and he was beginning to become seriously worried for the safety of all when finally, Keezo stopped and pointed at two open pits. "They is there."

"Mr. Totleigh?" Blandings called.

"What ho, Blandings," came a familiar voice from a hole.

"It is heartening to hear your voice, sir."

"Daddy?"

A weak voice answered. "Marigold? Muffin? Is that you?"

She rushed forward to the edge of the hole. "Are you all right, Daddy? I'm here with Cecil and Blandings. We have rope."

Blandings was already tying the rope around the base of the lone tree that stood near the holes. He pitched the other end of the rope down into Sallow's pit along with two pairs of gloves.

Blandings said, "Sir, slip on the gloves and take hold of the rope." He shone his handlamp on them. "Mr. Cakewood and I have this end. Try pulling yourself up while we walk backward."

From behind them, Mr. Totleigh called, "I say, Blandings, be careful not to stumble into the hole over here. It's frightfully easy to do."

"Yes, sir. Thank you."

With the help of Gubbins pushing and Blandings and Cakewood pulling, Sallow emerged from the hole. Fortunately for all concerned, Gubbins was able to scale the pit wall with the aid of only the rope and with just a few creaks sounding from the tree trunk.

After wrapping them in blankets and handing them tea, Blandings and Cakewood turned their attention to the second hole and brought Mr. Totleigh to the surface. Blandings draped a blanket around his employer's shoulders and passed him a steaming cup.

Keezo cried, "Pelie!"

"Hello, Keezo," Mr. Totleigh said. "I say, good job, what? Hey, Sallow, it must be a bitter pill to have your life saved by an alien."

"Nonsense," Sallow said. "Blandings and Cakewood pulled us out."

"Ha! They found us only because of Keezo. Where would we be without Keezo's skills at climbing and trekking? What's that old saw about the contributions of diversity and all that?"

Sallow scowled at him over his tea but said nothing.

Blandings said, "We should get everyone back to the house."

"Wait," Sallow said sharply. He looked from Mr. Totleigh to the little alien and then back again. "Totleigh, why did it say, PELIE when it saw you?"

Mr. Totleigh said, "Oh ... um." He glanced at Blandings, who shook his head. Mr. Totleigh gave Sallow a shrug. "I haven't the foggiest. Keezo says some funny things, you know. What was his word for a bakery? Bakie, I think. What a corker, eh?"

"Don't change the subject. You're connected with the PELIE organization, aren't you? I should have known."

Gubbins laughed out loud.

Sallow turned to him. "What?"

"Isn't it obvious?" Gubbins asked.

Blandings said, "We really should be moving. We have a long walk ahead of us, and it is growing colder."

"What's obvious?" Sallow asked.

Gubbins shook his head. "Pelie — Pelham."

Sallow's jaw dropped. "You mean Totleigh *is* Pelie?"

"Of course, he is. This isn't some vast conspiracy. It's only him."

"You mean Totleigh was — I can scarcely say it — the brains behind the robbery?"

Mr. Totleigh gave a modest shrug. "Well ..."

Sallow snapped at him. "I will see that you are arrested and charged."

Mr. Totleigh waved a finger. "Ah ah ah. You agreed not to prosecute anyone."

"That was the deal for you to rescue us ... before you fell into a dropout and had to be rescued yourself."

"Granted, but ..."

Blandings cleared his throat.

"Yes, Blandings?" Mr. Totleigh asked.

"One can make the case, Mr. Sallow, that Mr. Totleigh's efforts did indirectly bring about the rescue. I understand that sending Keezo was his idea."

"There you go," Mr. Totleigh said. "I was the one who submitted the winning entry."

"Poppycock," Sallow said. "I intend to convene a jury tomorrow morning. Both Totleigh and the alien will go on trial for robbery. I may even charge them with attempted murder for luring me out here."

Mr. Totleigh's eyes bulged. "Luring? You were chasing."

Gubbins said, "Now really, Mr. Sallow."

"You stay out of it," Sallow said in a gruff tone.

Gubbins looked to Blandings. Blandings responded with a single nod.

The bodyguard said, "I think you may have a hard time proving your case."

Sallow snorted. "The murder charge is a stretch, admittedly. But we caught the alien in the act of burglary."

"We did, but you can't testify. You'll be acting as magistrate."

"That doesn't matter. We have your testimony, Gubbins."

Gubbins cocked his head. "No, you don't. I won't testify against either of them, not after they helped save us from freezing to death."

"Codswallop. They're the reason we were in the hole in the first place."

Gubbins shook his head. "Sorry."

"Gubbins, you'll testify, or I'll fire you."

"No, you won't. Because I quit."

"Don't be ridiculous. You can't quit. We have an episode we need to drop."

"I quit."

Marigold Sallow moved to Mr. Totleigh and took him by the arm. With the other hand, she began straightening his head fur, which was matted with mud and in disarray.

Cakewood glared. "Marigold."

Mr. Totleigh smiled at Blandings and then tossed a smirk in Cakewood's direction.

"It's all right, Daddy," Marigold Sallow said. "I'm sure Pelham can engineer your vidcast for you. You'd love to work more closely with Daddy, wouldn't you, Pelham?"

Unfortunately, Mr. Totleigh was at that moment taking a sip of tea. He choked, erupting in a spit take and nearly toppling over in the process. He threw his arms around Ms. Sallow for balance.

It was like someone had thrown a switch. Cakewood's face darkened. He strode toward them. "That is enough … too much, in fact. Totleigh, kindly remove your hands from her person."

"Sorry," Mr. Totleigh said. "I went a bit weak in the knees there when she suggested I work for old Sallow. I only meant to—"

"Oh, I know what you meant to do, and I won't stand for it." The spindly store owner hauled back a fist and punched his romantic rival squarely in the face.

Chapter 37

Bringing Home the Bacon

Pelham staggered back as much from the shock of being hit as from the force of the blow from the skinny shopkeeper. He sat down hard on the ground, clutching a hand to his nose. It hurt like blazes. "Ow! What? What? Smack dab on the snuffer! Oh, I say, really!"

Blandings knelt beside his employer and fussed over the damage.

Meanwhile, Cecil stood over his victim, hands still clenched in fists, huffing impassioned breaths.

Marigold, eyes wide, said, "Oh oh oh!"

Keezo hopped up and down. "Pelie. Pelie."

For his part, Sallow was pointing at Pelham and roaring with laughter. He moved to Cecil and held out his hand. "You're all right, Cakewood. I didn't know you had it in you. Way to stand up for yourself for once. Let me know if the twit attempts to press assault charges against you. I'll see that they're dropped."

Cecil stared at the offered hand for a few moments before un-fisting his own to shake it. "Um … thank you. Thank you, Mr. Sallow."

"Call me Oswald, son." He slapped the shop proprietor on the back, nearly knocking him over.

"Um … right. Well … um … um … a Haplor has to do what a Haplor has to do."

Marigold cleared her throat pointedly and raised her eyebrows.

Cecil glimpsed the expression on her face and added, "Not that I approve of fighting as a rule, of course."

Marigold said, "May I assume then, Daddy, that you have no objections to Cecil calling on me?"

"Eh? Well … why, no, I don't." Sallow's face beamed. "Drop by anytime, Cakewood. I say, that was quite a punch. Enjoyed it immensely."

Marigold moved closer to Cecil. "Wasn't there something else you wanted to ask Daddy?"

"Hmm? Um ..." He cast her a questioning look.

She wiggled the fingers of her ring hand.

"Oh! Um ... and ... and, Mr. Sallow, if I'm not being too forward ... um ... I um ... well, I was thinking ... or rather, I'd like to ask you ... if you would approve of an ... um ..."

"What is it, Cakewood?" Sallow asked "Spit it out. We don't have all night to stand around in the cold."

"An ... engagement, sir ... between Marigold and myself."

The default scowl returned to Sallow's face. "Engagement? That's awfully fast, don't you think?"

Cecil's voice shot up about an octave. "Not ... not really, sir. I've had feelings for her for some time now. I promise to always take care of her."

Sallow looked to his daughter. "What do you think of all this, muffin?"

In answer, she wrapped her arm around Cecil's and leaned her head on his shoulder.

Sallow glanced at Pelham, who was still holding his nose. He threw back his head and chortled once more. "Certainly, lad. You two have my blessing. Say, I wish I had a vid of that punch. It would be gratifying to watch it over and over in my old age. You didn't get that, did you, Gubbins?"

"No," the former imager grunted.

Blandings said, "If I may interject, we must return to the house."

They made way their way across the dark plain back to town, Sallow, Marigold, and Cakewood walking together in one group while Pelham, Blandings, Gubbins, and Keezo formed a separate huddle. When they reached the Sallow residence, Marigold insisted they all stay for the night. Blandings prepared more tea, and they drank it down with hands wrapped around the warm cups.

A medic was summoned who examined everyone for signs of exposure and Pelham for the swelling around his nose. With the application of an ice pack and a medicinal Amurru fizz, Pelham was soon feeling better. He retired to a guest room and slept soundly through the night.

He awoke to daylight streaming through the window, blinked twice, rolled over, and slept some more. When he finally arose, it was with something of a sense of accomplishment. True, his nose still hurt. If anything, the schnoz hurt worse now than it had the night before, and it was difficult for Pelham not to take umbrage at being used as a punching bag.

Yet through the unanticipated help of Gubbins, he had at last won Keezo's release and was assured that he himself would not be prosecuted. The leg lamp was still a concern, or more specifically, what Aunt Agutha would say should he fail to acquire it for Uncle Spence. But he hoped Blandings would devise a plan for that. He could hardly propose to Marigold now that she was already engaged.

Pelham dressed and trundled down to the dining room in search of breakfast. He was met with a delightful and tantalizing scent. Poking his head through the door to the kitchen, he found Blandings assisting a Gallican chef. "I say, Blandings, what is that delightful aroma?"

"Good morning, sir," Blandings said. "As you suggested, I purchased that replicator recipe for Earth bacon. How is your nose this morning?"

"A tad sore, but clearly the sniffing part seems to be ticking along nicely. Tell me, does this bacon taste as good as it smells?"

"It does, sir. Ms. Sallow and Mr. Cakewood consumed several pieces. I do have some left."

"Bring it on. And could you see your way to plopping an egg on the plate beside it?"

"It would be my pleasure, sir. You may find a seat in the dining room."

Pelham grabbed a chair at the table and was served a brief time later. "Oh, Blandings."

"Sir?"

"Where is our friend Keezo?"

"Keezo is still asleep in the back of the kitchen."

"Caged?"

"No, sir. Keezo is asleep on top of a shelf of table linens."

"Good. I'm sure it must have been a long and stressful night for the little critter. I know it was for me."

"No doubt, sir."

"Running across the plains with people hot on his heels, falling into a pit, climbing out of said pit, then dashing back to find you, finally returning with the rescue party. It didn't seem much like it at the time, but I suppose I had the easier job of it. All I had to do was sit in the hole and wait."

"Indeed, sir."

"Not that waiting was easy or particularly enjoyable. It was dashed cold, and I had to put up with Sallow's grousing around." Pelham tried the bacon. "I say, Blandings, this is frightfully good. I could get myself on the outside of a fair-ish number of these things."

"I will replicate another batch, sir."

As Blandings was leaving the dining room, Marigold and Cecil entered from the hallway door.

"What ho," Pelham said, wiggling his hurt nose at the sight of the shopkeeper. "Where have you two been off to?"

"Strolling the grounds," Marigold said with a smile, "and making plans for our wedding."

Cecil said, "I'll see about replicating us cups of tea, dear. Would you like one, Totleigh? It's the least I can do."

"After punching me, you mean?"

"Well, that. But I was referring to what Blandings did."

Pelham stared at him. "Tea. Yes."

Cecil disappeared into the kitchen as Marigold took a seat at the table.

Pelham asked, "What did Blandings do?"

Marigold grinned at him. "Cecil said it was Blandings' idea for him to bop you. I must say, it worked like a charm with Daddy. He was downright friendly toward Cecil the entire walk back last night, and he put him up in the best guest room. We can't thank you enough."

"What? Wait. What? Let's back the carriage up a block or two. Did you say Blandings suggested that Cecil give me a wallop?"

"That's what Cecil says."

At that moment, the door from the kitchen swung open, and in walked Cecil with two cups, followed by Blandings carrying a third cup and a plate of more bacon. The valet set them both down beside Pelham.

"Blandings," Pelham said with what he hoped was an authoritarian tone.

"Sir?"

"I'd like a word with you."

"Sir?"

"What have you done?"

"Sir?"

"Don't stand there saying 'sir,' Blandings. I've recently been informed that the idea of Cecil bludgeoning me came from you. Is this true?"

Blandings coughed softly. "I merely suggested, sir, that a display of pugilism might be efficacious in gaining Mr. Sallow's favor."

"And was it ever!" Cecil said.

Pelham glared at the shopkeeper. "Blandings, did you, I wonder, stop to consider how I might feel about this scheme?"

"I did, sir."

"Oh, you did, did you? And you thought I would reckon it topping fun to have the Totleigh face deployed for target practice?"

"I deemed this scheme to be the best way to secure the leg lamp, sir. You previously indicated that you were willing to make certain sacrifices to obtain it."

"Financial sacrifices, Blandings. Not my nose. It was dashed painful." Pelham reached up and rubbed the snout with a wince.

"I am sorry for that, sir."

"Me too," Cecil said with a casual shrug.

Pelham gave the shopkeeper what he hoped came off as a withering look. "And besides, Blandings, how was me getting slugged supposed to win us the lamp?"

"That's where I come in," Marigold said.

But it was, in fact, the moment when Oswald Sallow came in ... to the room, at least. He scowled around at the gathering at the table. "What's going on here? You three haven't ended up on cordial terms, have you? Because I won't have it. This Totleigh fellow attempted to rob me whether I can prove it in court or not."

Marigold said, "Oh, absolutely not, Daddy. We aren't getting along at all. In fact, just before you entered, Cecil was berating Pelham for his reprobate behavior and lack of regard for private property. Isn't that right, Cecil?"

"Hmm? Oh ... yes. That's exactly what I was doing ... Oswald." Cakewood flinched a little as he said the name. "I was telling Totleigh ... how he ... um ... well, how he displayed a depraved character. I advised Blandings to check him into some kind of institution for treatment."

Pelham tsked. "Now see here. This is all a touch thick, what?"

"Sounds like a wise course," Sallow said. "See that you do it, Blandings. And make sure it's a place with locked gates."

"I will attend to it, sir," Blandings said.

"He will not," Pelham said.

"And I want you out of my house," Sallow said.

Pelham huffed out an offended breath. "Oh, believe me, I will be delighted to shove off as soon as poss."

"What's that smell, anyway?" Sallow asked.

"Bacon, sir," Blandings said. "It is an Earth food."

Sallow's lip curled. "Oh, we're eating Earth food now, are we? What's wrong with Haplor food?"

"What's wrong with a bit of variety?" Pelham asked, feeling the need to score a point or two after all the talk about chucking him into a home.

Sallow glared at him.

Marigold said, "Daddy, I've been thinking about my engagement gift."

He turned to her with a more pleasant expression. "Yes, dear?"

"As you know, according to tradition, I can ask for anything I want, and you have to give it to me."

"Well." Sallow stretched out the syllable. "That's the ancient custom, of course. The bride would most often ask for an heirloom or a family keepsake as a way of honoring her family. In modern times, people have tended to give more practical presents, such as money or food replicators."

"Yes, but I know how much you respect the old traditions, the pure, time-honored Haplor ways uncontaminated by interstellar influences."

"Well, yes, but—"

"I think I read somewhere that the switch to monetary gifts came about after Haplors learned of Cuneddan Tipping Day. Or maybe I saw it on a vidcast."

"Which vidcast?"

"Can you imagine? A whole day where everyone passes around small sums of money to everyone they meet. Customers tip shopkeepers, and the shopkeepers turn around and tip the customers right back."

"Well, naturally, if you'd prefer a keepsake gift—"

"I do, Daddy."

"I have your grandmother's brooch."

"No, I want the leg lamp."

"You want what?"

"The leg lamp."

"The leg lamp? But ... that's hardly an heirloom."

She held out her hand. "One leg lamp, please, Daddy."

"Are you sure? I thought you didn't like it."

She shrugged. "I didn't at first. But now, after all that has happened over these last few days, it will always remind me of how you and Cecil were brought together."

"Well … of course. Of course, when you put it like that. But … well, how would it be if, after I give it to you, you left it in my office? Cakewood can't have much room in his place."

"Oh, I don't think that will be a problem," Cecil said.

"I only mean that … well, if you left it here, then I could gaze upon it and think kindly of you … and Cakewood."

Marigold waved a dismissive hand. "No, silly. I have the perfect spot for it." She swiveled her head and shot Pelham a wink.

Chapter 38

Between You and Me and the Leg Lamp

A short while later, Pelham stood beside Blandings and Keezo outside the stone wall in front of the house, where they waited for an automated carriage that would take them to the hotel to pick up their bags and then on to the space port.

Pelham, still in a daze as to the conversation at the breakfast table, said, "So she's getting the leg lamp from old Sallow … and then what?"

"Psst." The sound came not from anyone in their group but from down the street.

Pelham glanced around and saw Marigold at the end of the block gripping the leg lamp around its fish-netted calf and pointing to it with a grin on her face. They strolled over to her.

She held it out to them. "Per our agreement. I told you I could get it for you."

Pelham shook his head in admiration. "I wish I could have seen the old blighter's face when he had to hand it over."

She frowned. "Don't call Daddy a blighter."

"Sorry. Didn't mean to offend. I only said it because … well, he is, in fact, a blighter."

She waggled her head. "You may be right, but I still don't like to hear it."

"We are much obliged," Blandings said. "It is not every fiancée who is willing to give up her engagement present."

"It's worth it to me to secure Daddy's approval of Cecil. That and to get this eyesore out of the house. It was a bang-up idea you had, Mr. Blandings."

"Bang onto my nose, you mean," Pelham said, sniffing and grimacing.

Marigold shrugged. "You wanted the lamp."

"That I did."

"Are you waiting for a carriage?"

"We are." Pelham leaned forward to look down the street. "It ought to be along any time now."

"Well, if you're going to be standing around holding the lamp, wait down here out of sight of the windows."

"Will do … and congratulations again to you and Cecil." With the leg lamp in hand, Pelham decided he could be magnanimous even for betrothals built upon his personal pain and suffering.

"Thank you." She waved her fingers and slipped back around the corner.

Blandings said, "I do apologize, sir, for the injury. I did not think Mr. Cakewood would strike you quite so hard."

Pelham touched his nose gingerly. "Neither did I, Blandings. For someone of the scrawny persuasion, old Cecil was able to pack a considerable punch when properly motivated."

"Yes, sir. I see now it was the motivation, which I failed to properly take into account."

"Yes. True love and all that. Well, water under the bridge, Blandings. It worked out all right in the end. We have the lamp. We even have Keezo. Though I must say, I was surprised at Gubbins turning on old Sallow last night. Granted, spending time in a dark hole with Oswald Sallow is bound to sour anyone's disposition."

"Yes, sir."

"Did you know that at one point in the proceedings, Sallow insisted Gubbins hoist him on his shoulders?"

"I did not, sir."

"He even tried to stand on the poor fellow's head. Now I ask you, if that wouldn't put one in a disagreeable mood, what would?"

"Indeed, sir. No doubt another factor was the understanding Mr. Gubbins and I reached yesterday evening."

"Eh? What sort of understanding was that, Blandings?"

A deep voice called to them, "Hello, gentlemen."

They turned to see Gubbins carrying two equipment cases out the front gate.

"Good morning, Gubbins," Pelham called. "Are you taking your leave of the Sallow house as well?"

"I am. And good riddance to that pompous old yak. Thank you again, Mr. Blandings." He headed toward them.

Pelham said, "Is that a reference to this mysterious understanding, Blandings?"

"It is, sir. Do you remember the other day when I mentioned my former employer Mr. Archibald Winton?"

"I think so. Was that the mattress tycoon bloke?"

"Yes, sir. Mr. Winton's daughter is now in charge of the firm, the Snoozer Mattress Company, as you may recall."

"Snoozer. Snoozer. Are those the chappies who claim you'll sleep like a hibernating crocoraptor?"

"Yes, sir. As the new president, Ms. Winton is overhauling the entire marketing strategy, including the development of a pithier tagline."

"I can see why she might want to. It doesn't exactly roll off the tongue, what?"

"No, sir."

"Nor is the thought of a crocoraptor, hibernating or otherwise, much conducive to restful sleep."

"I should think not, sir. In any case, I believe you saw Ms. Winton speaking with Mr. Gubbins and myself last evening at the fete."

"Oh, so that's who that was."

"Yes, sir."

"How about as soft as … um … as soft as … um … no, that won't work. I say, Blandings, this slogan business is harder than it seems."

"Yes, sir."

"Wait. I've got it. 'Don't be a loser. Get a Snoozer.'"

Blandings took a beat to answer. "Most ingenious, sir. I took the liberty of contacting Ms. Winton and suggesting she explore vidcasting as a new avenue for marketing."

"Or 'Feel like you're floating in space.' Yes, that's better. I say, Blandings, I'm getting the hang of it now."

Gubbins, who had joined them, said, "Except floating in space would kill you."

Pelham shrugged. "May need a bit of tweaking, what?"

Blandings said, "It seems Ms. Winton had been thinking along much the same lines herself and had been working on developing a vidcast to be called *Snooze Fest*. The show will discuss the physical, emotional, and psychological keys to sound sleep."

"'Give it a rest.'"

"I beg your pardon, sir?"

"What? Oh. No, I wasn't directing that toward you, Blandings. Another catchphrase idea."

"I see. I will pass it along. It seems Ms. Winton has nearly everything ready to go. She only needed to find someone to serve as engineer and share co-hosting duties."

"Or 'Sleep like ...' What? You say they needed ... Oh, I see. And you suggested Gubbins."

"I did, sir. Mr. Gubbins had confided in me that he was less than contented in his current employment. Ms. Winton was impressed with his credentials and offered him the position. And so with another job in hand—"

Gubbins put in, "With better pay and more of a voice in the production."

"Indeed," Blandings said. "It provided Mr. Gubbins with sufficient motivation to do the right thing regarding Keezo."

Gubbins said, "Blandings told me about what you were trying to do for Keezo. I was only too glad to help."

Pelham laughed. "Well done, Blandings. And you too, Gubbins. Without you standing up for us, I might well be sitting in the slammer right now."

"In addition, sir," Blandings said, "as a sales promotion, Ms. Winton is willing to offer a substantial discount on any orders coming from Sonus over the next year and to donate a new mattress specifically for the governor's residence to promote their products."

"I say," said Pelham, "that's snappy stuff."

"You did promise your aunt, sir, that you would work on trade deals during the trip."

"So I did. Blandings, you astound me. You think of everything. The aged relative will be delighted. Perhaps with a good night's sleep, she'll even be a tad less cranky."

"One can hope, sir."

Gubbins said, "Well, I need to hurry along. I have a *Snooze Fest* meeting."

Pelham chuckled. "Ha! I've had a few of those myself."

"How's that again?"

"Sorry. Merely a joke. Good luck."

As Gubbins walked away, their automated carriage pulled up. Pelham opened the door and climbed into the cab. Keezo jumped in after him. Blandings boarded last, holding the leg lamp awkwardly by the thigh. The carriage rolled off through the streets.

Pelham looked out the window at the passing sights. "Interesting planet, this Unara. Seems as if almost everything here was continually trying to kill me — the cold, the pits, the flora and fauna. I think old Sallow would have taken a shot at it himself, given half a chance. Hopefully, we can terraform Sonus into a more hospitable place."

"A worthy goal, sir."

Keezo said, "What is we do now?"

"Well, Keezo," Pelham said, "now we are free to continue our search for Tunna and your youngling. Blandings, what was our next stop? Tucana Three?"

Keezo jumped up and down with enthusiasm. "We is find Tunna. Tunna and little is somewhere. Pelie is find."

"Yes, we will, Keezo," Pelham said.

A muffled voice squeaked out from somewhere. "Keezo?"

Keezo's big eyes widened. "Tunna?"

A black head identical to Keezo's poked out from under the fringe of the lampshade. "Keezo!"

"Tunna!"

Tunna dropped from the leg lamp onto the carriage seat with an even smaller version of the two of them wrapped in Tunna's tentacles. They gave each other huge tentacle-y hugs and jumped up and down.

Pelham gawped. "The Grays. They brought the leg lamp to Unara ... on the same ship as Keezo."

"It appears so, sir," Blandings said.

Keezo asked, "Tunna, is you in that thing this whole time?"

Tunna nodded. "We is hide. We not is know where you is. Is warm in there, but we is has nothing to eat. We is hungry. We is walk home now, Keezo?"

Keezo made a sort of scratchy sound like metal being filed, which Pelham took to be a laugh. "No, silly Tunna. You not is understand. Home is very far. We is on different plan-it way out in stars. We not is walk. We is go home in big flying makeen in black space."

Tunna blinked. "We is on different planet?"

"We is."

"Which one is we on?"

Keezo's jaw dropped. "What is you mean, which one?"

"Which planet is we on? Haplor? Rheged Prime?"

"You is know about plan-itses, Tunna?"

"My parents is teach. What is your parents teach?"

"My parents is teach Keezo climb tree."

Tunna nodded again. "Keezo good at climb tree."

Pelham said, "Keezo is a jolly good climber. Saved my life."

"Who is these Bigs?" Tunna asked.

Keezo said. "This is Pelie. This is Bandy. They is help I find you. They is friends."

"We is thank you," Tunna said.

"Think nothing of it," Pelham said. "We Totleighs would never dream of turning our backs on a person in need."

"Is you has food?"

"We will be sure to find you some food. I am pleased to meet you, Tunna. This puts the bow on the box, what? Here we've been trying to locate you, and we've been trying to get the leg lamp. And as it turns out, you were inside the leg lamp all this time. Of all the cargo on that ship. What are the odds, Blandings?"

"I fear I could not at present calculate them, sir."

"That thing is leg lamp?" Tunna asked, pointing a tentacle toward their former hiding place.

Pelham said, "It is indeed."

"We keep is hear people say leg lamp, leg lamp. Everybody is argue about who is buy leg lamp. I is stay still. At last, we is know what is leg lamp."

A tiny squeak came from the youngling. "Leg lamp."

Keezo made the scratchy sound again. "Tunna, is that little's first word?"

Tunna's head bobbed with excitement. "First word. Say again, little. Leg lamp."

The youngling repeated it. "Leg lamp."

Keezo said, "That is little's name now. Leg Lamp."

"What?" asked Pelham. "You're going to name your youngling Leg Lamp? Are you sure about that, Keezo? I mean, dash it all, leg lamp? That's not really the done thing, eh? How about Archie or Reggie or something?"

"No. Little's name is always first word."

"Is it now? Astounding. One would think you would end up with bushels of younglings called Mama or Dada?"

Tunna shrugged. "A lot of littles is named Hungry. Our little is named Leg Lamp."

"Little Leg Lamp," Keezo said, caressing the youngling with a tentacle. "I is glad we find you."

Pelham said, "Well, Blandings, you have done it again."

"Thank you, sir. But in fairness, I can take credit only for the rescue of Keezo and the acquisition of the lamp. Tunna and little Leg Lamp appear to have located themselves."

"Don't forget your work on the mattress deal. I'm sure the Snoozer Mattress folks will be happy with their new vidcaster." Pelham clapped his hands. "Well, we can scratch Tucana Three from the itinerary. We're going home, Blandings. First, though, we have to take these three back to Danánn. I made a promise to Keezo, and it's the code of the Totleighs to always keep our promises."

"Indeed, sir."

How would you like to make my day?
Please review this book on Amazon and/or Goodreads.
Your honest words would mean the world to me.
Follow me on Instagram at garyrandolphstoryteller
and Facebook at GaryRandolphStoryteller.

Last Word and How to Get a Free Book

Thank you for reading *The Code of The Totleighs*. Every book has its challenges. The big challenges this time were working out Keezo-speak and figuring out how to write from Keezo's very limited perspective. Believe me, it took some head scratching. I hope you were pleased with the result.

Every book also has its joys. And it was a delight to get inside Pelham's head once more, especially as he deals with someone who has even less of a clue about what's going on than he does.

But enough about what I think. I would love to hear what you think about the book. If you could leave a quick review on Amazon and/or Goodreads — just a few words — I would really appreciate it. It genuinely helps move the book up the algorithm. I often see a bump in sales following each review.

I want to thank Kameron Robinson for another fantastic cover design. Also huge thanks to my proofreaders and all the readers who encourage me with suggestions, kind reviews, and simply buying and reading.

But I imagine the reason you stopped on this page is the free book offer. It's an ebook of short stories, *The Brief Detective Career of Reg Wilson and Other Stories*. Among its one dozen tales is Pelham's infamous incident of the drainpipe and the top hat. It also has two Galactic Detective Agency stories. one Molly Nolan Mystery story, plus tales of ghosts and Christmas and ancient Celtic warriors. There are even some short pieces about my life that I use in my storytelling performances.

All you have to do is go to my website at grstoryteller.com and subscribe to my mailing list. Now before you say no, realize I email subscribers only a few times a year. And I solemnly swear I will never sell your name to somebody else. I hate that sort of thing as much as you do.

240

Also by Gary Blaine Randolph

Pelham and Blandings

Pelham G. Totleigh is an unlikely hero. His species, Haplors, are smaller than most others in the galaxy. And as his Aunt Agutha constantly reminds him, he is hardly the smartest or most industrious of Haplors. He also has an unfortunate habit of stumbling his way into the most outrageous and hilarious predicaments. Fortunately, his faithful valet Blandings has enough brainpower for them both and is always there with a brilliant idea and an excellent cup of tea. This series is a loving tribute to and re-imagining of the Jeeves and Wooster stories of PG Wodehouse. Join Pelham and Blandings on their comic misadventures through space.

Book 1 – Viva Lost Vogus
Book 2 – The Importance of Being Pelham
Book 3 – The Code of the Totleighs

Alien World

If you were stranded, all alone on an alien world, if you were forced to hide your identity and try to blend in, how would you do it? What would it cost you? What would you long for most? *Alien World* is an exploration of what it would be like to be a stranger stranded on another planet and forced to live out decades there, trying to blend in while staying one step ahead of the authorities.

The Galactic Detective Agency

Gabriel Lake is just a regular computer guy from Indianapolis … until he is recruited into this series of lighthearted murder mysteries in space. Under the guidance of the brilliant Oren Vilkas, the Galactic Detective Agency hops from one weird world to another to take on quirky aliens and solve interstellar crime.

Book 1 – A Town Called Potato

Book 2 – The Maltese Salmon

Book 3 – Return of the Judy

Book 4 – The Big Sneep

Book 5 – Murder on the Girsu Express

Book 6 – The Cormabite Maneuver

Book 7 – Trouble in Paradox

Book 8 – The Wrath of Kah-Rehn

Book 9 – Double Indumbnity

Book 10 – Bumps in the Night (coming Summer 2026)

The Molly Nolan Mysteries

Molly Nolan had a plan all charted out for her twenties, and it had been going so well. College, check. Dream job teaching high school math, check. An apartment of her own, check. But then things began unwinding. The job went away, and a personal tragedy forced her to move back to the Indiana town of her childhood to live with her dad. And now, she keeps getting involved in murder mysteries. At least her logical mind and her enthusiasm for true crime podcasts give her an edge there. Follow Molly as she navigates getting her life back in gear, solving mysteries, and the problems of dating in a small town.

Book 1 – The Death Before Christmas

Book 2 – Molly Undercover

www.ingramcontent.com/pod-product-compliance
Lightning Source LLC
Chambersburg PA
CBHW060152180626
46813CB00007B/2718